The Milliner

by

Millie Curtis

1-17-13

Katherine,

This one was a long time
in coming. Thanks for your
help. Looking forward to your
novel with those risque gals
from 57. Always my best wishes!
Millie Curtis

Avid Readers Publishing Group
Lakewood, California

The Milliner

Avid Readers Publishing Group

http://www.avidreaderspg.com

ISBN-13: 978-1-61286-135-7

Printed in the United States

Acknowledgements

A novel is never the work of one person. I thank sincerely the following people who helped me on this journey:

Elizabeth Blye for the picture on the cover.
Anica Moran, my lovely model.
Katherine Cobb for cover design.
BJ Applegren, Catherine Owens, Elizabeth Blye and Jean Malucci for the laborious editing process.
My most helpful writing group: BJ Applegren, Tara Bell, Katherine Cobb, Karen Robbins.

Finally, I thank you readers. What purpose would be served by writing a book that no one read? Enjoy *The Milliner.*

This book is dedicated to the memory of my
beautiful sister-in-law,
Marilyn Cook Wilson

Chapter 1

Catherine Ramsburg wondered where she would be in five years. Until last year, when her best friend married and moved to Washington, D.C., she had been contented with her life. She didn't begrudge Carolyn's happiness, but it was the catalyst that forced her to take a good look at her own future. From where she stood it didn't look promising.

Catherine stepped out of her upstairs apartment onto the covered wooden porch that sheltered her millinery shop below. At twenty-five, she was considered a spinster, past her prime, as people liked to say. Most women her age were married with the responsibility of a family. Catherine had the hat shop.

The place had served as a bookkeeping office for her father. On his passing, it became the millinery shop for her mother. When she died four years ago, everything was bequeathed to Catherine. She appreciated the good fortune of owning property and having a means of support, but she longed for more than the small town, the apartment and the hat shop on Main Street.

Today was warm and sunny as early September mornings in Virginia tend to be. The milliner wore a long, beige, linen dress that covered black, ankle-high, laced shoes. They would eventually pinch her toes as the day wore on. Today was Saturday and she would close the hat shop at noon giving her less time in the sensible shoes of 1915.

As she sipped her tea from the flowered china cup she held, Catherine surveyed the main street of the quiet town of Berryville. In the next block up, Irene Butler was intent on cranking out a green canvas awning. Even from a distance, Catherine could see the familiar dour look on the face of the stout little seamstress. She shook her head at the thought that she might hold that same expression as the years passed. Close to marriage once, the engagement ended when Catherine's betrothed snuck away one night leaving her to face the humiliation of rejection. Oh, nothing was said to her face, but there were plenty of snide glances. With time she had overcome the hurt and embarrassment it caused, or so she tried to convince herself, but the whole sorry mess left a cloud of distrust toward men.

Across the street from Catherine sat the two-story, red brick bank with its large ornate clock jutting out from the corner of the building for all to see. It was as though the hands kept the town moving, ticking off hour-by-hour, life passing by. Catherine was beginning to see her life passing in much the same way.

Two doors east of the bank, innocent shadows darted around in the newspaper office. Jeremy Talley, editor of the weekly newspaper, the *Clarke Courier*, had reason to dance around the printing presses. Today was the wedding of two local prominent families. Social happenings were the life and breath of the small newspaper.

He and his wife, Lavinia, known as the town snoop, lived next to the *Courier* office giving her a perfect view of the comings and goings on Main Street. How convenient for her, thought Catherine.

Giving a wistful sigh, she sat the teacup back onto the matching saucer and tucked a stray strand of honey-colored hair back into the bun she wore. In her millinery shop below, there were three hats waiting to be finished. As was the trend of the well to do, they ordered at the last minute pushing the milliner into late nights and early mornings.

A long sigh escaped as she turned back into her apartment. Catherine placed the empty teacup in the sink, dabbed at her mouth with a tea towel, and sped down the rear set of stairs into the back room of the hat shop. She had twenty minutes to sweep the stoop and sidewalk before opening for the day.

After taking a broom from the corner of the room and walking through the long narrow shop, she unlocked the front door and stepped out onto the stoop. With a flourish, she swept the small platform, down the steps and was sweeping the sidewalk with gusto, when she was startled by a deep voice from behind her.

"Excuse me, ma'am. Are you the proprietor of this shop?"

Whipping the broom around, she found a slim, nattily dressed man twirling a woman's hat on his hand. He appeared to be near her age and wore his dark hair collar length, unusual for the style of the day.

"I'm the owner of the hat shop."

"I am sorry to bother you this early, but as you can see," placing the hat on his head in a playful style, "this hat has been damaged in packing and my mother must have it for a wedding this afternoon. Do you think you can repair it for her?"

He plucked the hat from his head. "You do see my dilemma?"

Catherine smiled at the comical display, but the thought was immediate that if Lavinia were watching …she was known to peek from behind her lace curtains…an innocent act, such as this, would get blown into embarrassing proportions.

The milliner felt an instant need to get the stranger off the street. "It is rather becoming. Come inside and I'll see what I can do."

With a dash of chivalry, he rushed up the stairs ahead of her and opened the door. "It will mean a great deal if it can be repaired," he said as he followed Catherine through the narrow wood door.

She rested the broom next to a brick fireplace and led the stranger to her work counter. The shop was dimly lit. Three individual bulbs, covered with translucent glass shades, hung suspended on long cords from the high tin ceiling. One was positioned over a three-way-mirror for ladies to have full view of hats they were considering.

Catherine took her seat behind the counter while the gentleman slid into a wooden chair facing her. He handed her the hat.

An unfamiliar fluster within caused her to hesitate before she spoke. It seemed important to have her voice sound in control. "I assume, if it is intended for today's big wedding, it must match your mother's outfit."

He answered, "You assume correctly."

He appeared satisfied to check over the handiwork of the hats strewn about her work area while Catherine examined the one that needed repair.

"I believe I can improve it," she announced. "But, it will take some time and I am quite busy this morning." Laying the hat on the worktable she met his gaze. "I can't promise you the finished product will be without blemish. I will do what I can to have it ready for you at noon."

He flashed a winning smile, "I couldn't ask for anything more. My name is Patrick Burke," he said as he offered his hand.

Her response was polite, "I'm pleased to meet you, Mr. Burke. I'm Catherine Ramsburg. Welcome to Berryville."

"It's my first trip here. Seems like a nice little town, Miss Ramsburg. It is Miss, isn't it?"

She felt her face turn pink and nodded in agreement.

"I must confess. When I inquired about getting the hat repaired one of the hired help at the hotel gave me your name. I asked if it was

Miss or Mrs. I believe his exact words were, 'She ain't married'." Patrick grinned and paused for Catherine's reaction.

Her response was to give him a peevish look before she whirled her chair around to search in a box of ribbon behind her.

He took the not so subtle hint. "I believe I should be on my way. We're just up at the hotel so I'll leave you to your work and be back at noon." He was out the door before she could respond.

Unbeknownst to Patrick Burke, the curious Catherine watched as he nimbly tripped down the short set of stairs and headed in the direction of the Berryville Hotel.

He was unlike any of the local men.

****

The morning passed quickly. A few customers interrupted the hatter's labor, but she was able to work around those distractions. The three hats that had to be finished for the wedding had been completed and picked up by those sent to retrieve them. She was left with one hour to work on Mrs. Burke's hat, which proved to be more difficult than she had thought. Patrick returned as she was trimming the fancy, expensive headpiece.

"You're prompt, Mr. Burke," she greeted him. "Would you mind turning the sign in the window to *CLOSED*? I'm almost through with the repair, and it is time to lock up."

He turned the sign, as she requested, before heading back to her work counter. "I made sure that I was here in time because I thought you might not let me in if I was late." He gave a teasing smile and slid his slim frame into the same seat he'd occupied earlier.

How Catherine wished she had finished before he returned. His presence gave her a flighty inner feeling. It had been a long time since she'd felt that way. "Do you, by any chance, know the kind of material in the dress your mother is wearing?"

Without hesitation, he replied, "A light green silk with an overlay of cream lace."

Both eyebrows rose at his unexpected reply. "Are you a fashion designer, Mr. Burke?"

"No," he chuckled. "My brother and I run a fabric import business so I have to know my materials."

Catherine smiled. "That's an ability few men possess."

"I'll accept that as a compliment."

"And well you should." She snipped a piece of thread and held the hat for him to view. "This is fine quality. I've woven the area back to suitable form except for this small spot."

Patrick took the hat from her for closer inspection.

Choosing a cream colored ribbon and a few feathers carrying a hint of green, she demonstrated her intent. "I believe these will cover the damaged area and be a perfect accent to bring the hat and dress together."

She looked up.

"They also accent the color of your eyes,"

Attempting to brush off his flirtation, she answered, "Perhaps." Inside she felt a rosy glow.

Patrick leaned back in his chair completely relaxed. She could feel his eyes watching her as she fastened the trim. She was flustered and pleased at the same time. The diligent Catherine kept her eyes on her work, although it was becoming more difficult to keep her mind and fingers working together.

"You would be a popular milliner in Washington," he observed.

Grateful the silence had been broken, she replied, "I get ladies into the shop from time to time from Washington. They stay over at the hotel or up at the Crow's Nest on their way to the mineral baths in West Virginia. Sometimes they order hats, pay for them, and never return to pick them up." She looked up at him and smiled. "I've never understood their reasoning. I place the hats back in the storage room and, if they aren't claimed, I redesign and sell them."

"Resourceful," he acknowledged.

The finishing touches had been applied. She held up his mother's hat for inspection. "Do you think she will be pleased?"

"I think she will be delighted," he answered with a smile that brightened his whole being. He rose from the chair.

Catherine stood and came around the work counter with the hat in hand. "I have a box in the storage room that will fit. It wouldn't do for you to carry your mother's hat out the way you carried it in."

He laughed. "No, I suppose it wouldn't. Especially coming from the milliner's shop. What would the townspeople think?"

Yes, a dapper gentleman descending the steps of her shop with a hat box, what would they think? She smiled to herself on her way to the back room.

When Catherine returned, Patrick was taking in the sights of Main Street from the front display window. "It looks like the town has come to life."

"Always on Saturday," she answered. "Most who come into town are coming for the general store. That's the reason I close the shop at noon. It gives me time to catch up on the bookwork that goes along with running a business."

He turned from the window. "I understand that. I spend far too much time in the confines of an office with bookkeeping."

Handing him the large round box containing his mother's hat, she said, "That will be two dollars. It would be less if I hadn't run into considerable difficulty."

He pulled a ten-dollar bill from a silver money clip.

"I'm sorry, Mr. Burke. I don't have change for that amount and the bank isn't open."

"I mean for you to have it. You don't realize how much this means to me."

"It's only a hat."

"Yes. But, if you knew my mother, you would understand."

Catherine was insistent. "No, it's far too much."

"Miss Ramsburg, please accept it with my thanks. It's the only way I can repay you."

` Obviously, they were at a standstill. She knew he wasn't going to leave the shop until she took the money. She had no intention of accepting pay for work she didn't do. An exasperated sigh escaped her lips. "I'll make a bargain with you. I'll accept your money on the condition that I make another hat for your mother at no cost."

He seemed to mull over the proposition before cocking his head to one side. "Will that satisfy your conscience?"

"Absolutely," came her reply.

He fiddled the bill through his fingers. "I'll place one more caveat, Miss Ramsburg. You agree to have brunch with Mother and me at the Virginia House tomorrow morning. You and she can discuss just exactly the type of hat she wants."

"That isn't necessary. She can send me a picture from a magazine."

"Mother has definite ideas about what she will wear. Besides, wouldn't it be nice to be treated to brunch?"

Catherine wasn't sure about the brunch, but she knew that it would be very nice to see Patrick Burke once more. She raised her hands in a gesture of defeat. "You win. I'll meet you and your mother tomorrow after church services. The Virginia House prides itself on their Eggs ala Berryville."

He laughed. "I shall have to try them. And, Miss Ramsburg, I believe we should be on a first name basis. Tomorrow, at the restaurant, it would be awkward to appear as complete strangers. I prefer to have you call me Patrick."

With a wink of his eye and a slight grin, "Catherine, if I recall."

She could only nod in agreement.

"Then I shall look forward to tomorrow morning, Catherine."

The sound of her name was like music coming from his deep voice.

Off he went in his jaunty and likeable manner leaving Catherine to will her heart back into a normal rhythm. She was giddy as a schoolgirl.

After he'd gone, Catherine swept and tidied up the shop before taking her week's receipts and a basket of lunch to the gazebo in her back yard; a restful haven from the cares of the day.

Working on the bookkeeping, it was around three o'clock when she heard a commotion behind the high board fence that separated her yard from the lane behind. The lane led to a large estate adjacent to the town where the wedding reception was to be held. She left the gazebo to peer through a knothole in the fence. That required climbing up onto a huge limestone rock. It was a precarious perch. A thick growth of honeysuckle hid her from view. With a crank of her head, she lined her up her eye with the knothole so she could see. This behavior was so unlike the mind-your-own-business Catherine, she felt like a common peeping tom. But, she paid no heed to the inner voice of her conscience.

There were townspeople on foot passing close enough that she could almost reach out and touch them. She could smell the sweat of the horses. There were carriages, buggies, and drays with everyone dressed for the occasion. Her heart gave a jump when she spied Patrick Burke riding in an open carriage with a lovely young lady on one side and his mother on the other. Catherine could tell by the hat. The sight gave her such a start that she lost her footing and slipped off the large rock. An immediate stabbing pain gripped her ankle. She clamped her hand over her mouth to stifle any sound. Collecting herself from a heap on the ground, she hobbled to the town run flowing through her yard, removed her shoe and stocking, and thrust her painful foot into the icy cold water. The cold helped to take some of the sting and burning away. She was crying, not only from the pain, but from her hapless condition. The thought of her friend, Carolyn, popped into her mind. She had been Dr. Hawthorne's nurse and she would know what to do.

A half-hour passed before Catherine could muster up the courage to bear the discomfort of the injured ankle and gather her things from the gazebo. With firm resolve, she retrieved the records and basket. She was exhausted. The pain was excruciating.

She climbed the back stairs to her apartment on hands and knees. Her mother's ornate cane still sat in the ceramic umbrella stand by the top step. With the help of the cane, she got to a standing position.

Hopping to the kitchen, she put the kettle on for tea before she rummaged through the cupboard to find the aspirin bottle. She threw two aspirins into her mouth and gulped them down with water.

Twenty minutes later the aspirin and tea helped to relieve some of the discomfort. She sat in the kitchen with her leg propped up on a chair. How she wished for someone to be there with her. Even little Mary Lee Thompson, who sometimes helped her in the shop, would be a welcome sight. But, there was no one, just the ticking of the clock and the throbbing of her ankle.

Self-pity can be so disheartening.

The bong of the clock announced seven o'clock. Catherine took two more aspirins before struggling into her light cotton gown. The bedroom furniture had been her mother's and the four-poster bed with pineapple finials required a stepstool to get onto it. She struggled up and fell into the feather mattress. After placing the cane at her side, she propped a pillow under her swollen foot and prayed for sleep.

****

The weather changed overnight to a light rain and she awoke to pain. Throwing the sheet back, Catherine gasped at the sight of the red, black and blue discoloration in her foot, which was swollen twice its size. It was so unsightly that she had a pang of nausea. As she became fully awake, it struck her that she wasn't going anywhere; not to church nor to brunch with the Burkes. Along with the throbbing of her ankle, she felt instant disappointment. There was no way she could get a message to them, which gave her another degree of discomfort. Perhaps it was Providence…more likely, it was just bad luck.

Attempting to get out of bed, the pain of putting weight on her foot was unbearable. She removed her nightdress, and threw on a slip and yesterday's linen dress just in case someone happened to stop by. Perhaps, if she wrapped her injured foot tightly, it would help to ease the incessant pulsating jabs. Why didn't she think of that last evening?

Grabbing her mother's cane, and with difficulty, she made her way to the kitchen where she kept old rags stuffed in a bottom drawer of the white kitchen cabinet. Finding one, cut from an old petticoat, she propped her leg up on a chair and proceeded to wrap the unsightly ankle in such a way that the ruffle circled her foot. Satisfied with result, she stretched a loose crocheted slipper over the wrap.

Somewhat relieved, Catherine hopped around the kitchen where she brewed a cup of tea and buttered a piece of bread. These she took, along with two aspirin tablets, into the living room where she planned to spend her day on the sofa.

It was eleven-thirty when the irritating clank of the front door knocker startled her. Calling down would be in vain because whoever was there would never hear her unless she went to the head of the stairs. She did not want to leave the couch. Perhaps they would just go away. But, by the third attempt of that annoying clanking sound, she decided the caller wasn't leaving. If it was that nosy Lavinia Talley coming to see why she wasn't at church, she was going to slam the door in her face. No, she wouldn't actually do that but she felt like it.

The clank of the door-knocker sounded once more when she reached the stair landing. "I'm coming," she called with irritation in her voice. With the help of the cane and the banister, she made it down the flight of stairs to the door. She opened it with a yank. There stood Patrick Burke.

"Good morning, Catherine." It was the same lovely baritone voice, but not as kindly. "I expected you to join us at The Virginia House."

Completely taken aback, it took her a moment to answer, "I am so sorry. I wasn't feeling well and I was unable to get a message to you. Please extend my apologies to your mother."

"May I come in?" he asked.

Her head was foggy. They stood facing each other in the doorway. She could think of no immediate reason for him not to be allowed to enter the foyer. It would get him off the stoop.

"Of course." Her awkward movements were noticeable as she backed out of the way.

His blue eyes opened wide. "I see you're struggling with a cane that you weren't using yesterday."

"I twisted my ankle in the back yard, but it will be fine in a couple of days. Your mother will just have to send me a picture of the hat she would like to have made."

He seemed more concerned about her injury than the hat. "I spent a couple of years in medical school so I know a bit about sprained ankles. It's important to wrap it properly."

"I understand that. I have it wrapped."

With gentleness in his voice, he said, "Why don't you sit back on the step and let me take a look at it? Another year and I would be called doctor. Would you allow a doctor to examine it? Of course you would." He smiled, and when he did, it melted her whole resolve.

All sense of reason disappeared as she sat back on the step, tightened her skirt around her calf and propped her foot on his bended knee. The knee of this man she had just met yesterday. He unwrapped the painful ankle, taking care not to cause her more discomfort in the process.

When he saw the swelling and discolored appearance, he let out a low whistle.

"You need to be off this foot as much as possible for at least a week. Keep it elevated. It would also help to put ice on it to reduce some of the swelling." He rewrapped the strip of petticoat. "That's the fanciest bandage I've ever seen." He gave a sly grin.

"You said I was resourceful," came her smug reply.

"Do you have someone who can help you with the hat shop?"

"Yes, I have a girl who can come in, but I can manage very well by myself."

Her heart was thumping at a record beat. She wasn't sure whether it was her ankle or her heart that thumped the hardest.

The injury was less painful with the way he wound the makeshift bandage.

"That does seem to be more comfortable. Is there a reason you left medical school? Did you change your mind?"

He gave her a half-smile as he helped her to her feet. "As I told you, my brother and I own a fabric import business. It was my father's until he died of a heart attack last year. Liam couldn't run the business by himself, so I had no choice."

"That seems a huge sacrifice. I am sorry to hear about your father. I've lost both of my parents. My father died when I was thirteen; he was a bookkeeper and made sure that I learned how to keep accounts. It has served me well, although I didn't like it at the time."

"And your mother?"

"She passed away four years ago leaving me this apartment and the hat shop."

"Are you happy with this arrangement?"

"I feel fortunate," came her reply.

Patrick handed her the cane. "Yes, but are you happy with it?"

She gave a wan smile. "As with your situation, we have to play with the hand we're dealt."

"I'll help you back up the stairs," he offered.

"That isn't necessary. I can make it back up myself."

"Catherine, has anyone told you that you are stubborn?"

"Not in those words. They have told me I'm too independent." She leaned on the cane and winced with the movement.

"Independent or not, I am determined to help you up that flight of stairs."

Catherine didn't protest. Her ankle burned like a hot poker. He held her arm as she hobbled up the stairs. The nearness of him gave her goose bumps.

"I am sorry I couldn't go to brunch and meet your mother. Please have her send me information about what kind of hat she would like. I will mail it to her when it's finished."

They reached the top landing of the wide staircase. "Why don't I come back and pick it up?" he asked.

"You aren't planning to return to Berryville, are you?"

"I hadn't until I met you."

She caught his second attempt at flirtation and pretended she hadn't heard those words. "Thank you for your help. You'll have to rush if you're going to take the car up to Bluemont for the train. Herbert doesn't wait for anyone."

He grinned, "If I didn't know better, I'd think you are trying to get rid of me. May I come back to see you?"

She surprised herself with, "I would be pleased to see you again."

"Good. Liam and I usually trade weekends to cover any problems with the warehouse. Which means, I hope to get back in a couple of weeks. How does that sound?"

"Perhaps you could send a note so I will not make any other plans." As if she had any other prospects.

"I will get it out as soon as I know for sure. Now, you need to get that foot up and I need to gather up my mother and sister-in-law, Sarah, to catch a train. I am so pleased they insisted on coming for the wedding. Lucky for me that they did."

Sister-in-law! What welcome news.

He was heading down the stairway when he turned, "By the way, Mother received compliments on her lovely hat. No one seemed the least surprised that you were the creator."

"I can't take credit for the creation, only the repair. I wish you a safe trip back. Do you mind locking the door on the way out? It's an old mortise lock with a button on the front. Just press it in."

Patrick Burke continued down the stairs. "I'll send a note as soon as I know my plan." He pressed the button locking the door behind him.

Catherine stood there mesmerized until her troubled ankle jolted her back into the present. A jab of pain sent her searching for the aspirin bottle once again. Yet, she could smile. How very interesting this weekend had turned out to be!

Chapter 2

The next day, Catherine worked her way down the back stairs to the millinery shop in a happy mood that continued until Lavinia Talley lumbered in. Catherine sat at her worktable and listened politely as Lavinia raved about the lavish wedding.

"Oh, Catherine, I wish you could have been there. The buffet was glorious: roast beef, leg of lamb, seafood fresh from the Eastern shore. Why, they even had a pig roasting on a spit. There were foods of every kind and a rainbow of vegetables… oh, I could go on and on."

Catherine hoped she wouldn't, but knowing Lavinia, she was not going to be that fortunate.

"And, the wedding cake." Lavinia cast her eyes toward heaven, placing her hand over her ample bosom. "The wedding cake was delicious… seven tiers high. I'd never seen anything so beautiful. It's just such as shame you weren't there to witness the affair."

Catherine busied herself gathering red silk material into a rose shape. "I wasn't on the guest list, Mrs. Talley, but many of my hats attended."

Lavinia twittered, "Catherine, you do have a different sense of humor." The woman continued, "By the way, who was that dashing young man I saw coming out of your shop Saturday morning? I noticed him at the reception. Unfortunately, we

21

weren't introduced because I was so busy pointing out notable people to Jeremy. It's very important to get the highlights in the paper." She never paused to take a breath. "To get back to the young man, I understand they are a well to do family in the Washington area." She hesitated to let the next words sink in. "Although, he is Irish. They're known for being brawlers."

"Yes, I suppose so, but we all come from somewhere, don't we?" Catherine picked up a hat and began trimming it with the rose she'd fashioned. She might as well give her nosy neighbor what she wanted to hear. "His mother's hat was damaged and needed repair as it matched the outfit she wore to the wedding."

"Wasn't that sweet of you to find time during your busy morning?"

By now, having sat in one position too long, the throbbing of her ankle let her know she needed to get it elevated. If she could bear the pain until Lavinia left, it would save her the explanation of how she had injured it. But, the inquisitive biddy hen wasn't ready to leave as she had more pecking to do.

"We missed you at church services, Catherine. It's not like you to miss. I could be mistaken, but I thought I saw the same young man on your stoop yesterday."

The pest didn't miss a thing. "Mrs. Talley, I wasn't at church services because I turned my ankle in the back yard. Yes, you did see Mr. Burke at my door. His mother has commissioned me to make another hat. Now, if you will excuse me, I have to put some ice on my ankle." The pain caused a testy edge in her voice…or was it Lavinia.

The woman hustled around the corner of the table to inspect Catherine's injury. "Oh dear, I'm sorry to hear that. Is there anything I can do? You know I would be more than happy to come over and help out. Your mother was my dear friend and she would want me to watch over you."

"You watch over me very well, Mrs. Talley," came Catherine's reply.

At that moment a customer came into the shop, a signal for Lavinia to leave. She called on her way out the door, "You take care of that ankle, Catherine dear, and don't hesitate to call on me, if need be."

"Thank you. I'll just take things at a slower pace," Catherine answered and turned her attention to the new arrival. The customer was another lady who was on her way to spend some days in Berkeley Springs. She had left her sun hat at home.

Catherine's movements were hampered with using the cane. Bearing the gnawing discomfort in her foot, she chose a smart-looking straw hat for the lady to try.

Seated at the three-way mirror, the customer turned her head this way and that. After a moment of close scrutiny she seemed satisfied. "I am so glad I forgot my hat. This one is much prettier. I need the wide brim to shade my eyes and, also, for sitting under the trees. I don't care to have any strange creatures falling into my hair."

Catherine smiled, "I'm sure this hat will work out well. It's very becoming on you."

"Yes, I believe it is," she said, and paid Catherine a handsome price.

Catherine's ankle was giving unspeakable pain. Once the generous woman was out the door, Catherine placed the closed sign in the window, and then made her way back up to her apartment. People may question her closing at noon on a Monday, but she didn't care. Resting her foot for the remainder of the day seemed to be the sensible thing to do.

****

Tuesday morning Catherine hobbled down to the shop to find Mary Lee Thompson waiting at the door.

Mary Lee became a widow at the age of eighteen. Two years ago she was the talk of the town after her no account husband got hit by a Norfolk and Western train on the Main Street crossing. At the time, Catherine thought it might have been the hand of Providence at work, but his demise left Mary Lee without any visible means of support. The townspeople thought she should have been compensated by the railroad. The company and their lawyers thought differently.

Catherine had taken Mary Lee under her wing to teach her all she knew about the millinery business. The income from the shop wasn't lucrative enough for Catherine to give her full time employment so Mary Lee cleaned houses and cared for the children of some of the town families to supplement her income.

24

"Good morning, Mary Lee. What brings you here?"

"I done heard you hurt your ankle and I came by to see if I could tend the shop for you?" The young widow looked more like a teenager than her age of twenty.

"You are a welcome sight. Come right in. I suppose Mrs. Talley has spread that news all over town."

"You know Miz' Talley, she cain't help tellin' everythin' she knows."

"Can't help telling." Catherine corrected her. Mary Lee was a local girl whose diction the well-intended milliner made attempts to improve.

"That's right, she cain't."

"I'll tell you what," Catherine said to her rescuer, "I'm going to let you brew both of us a cup of tea while I sit here and prop my foot up on that stool."

A dimpled smile spread across the face of the red-haired, blue-eyed Mary Lee who seemed pleased that she was of use to her injured benefactor. "You just sit right down there, Miz' Catherine and I'll go straight away to make us some tea."

"I'm going to do just that. I've never had anything hurt quite as bad as this ankle."

"I sure am sorry to have that happen. Did you just turn it while you wuz walkin'?"

"No, I was doing something foolish. I'll tell you about how it happened some other time."

When Mary Lee brought the tea, she took a seat at the work counter opposite Catherine. "I got lottsa' time this week. I been sittin' fer the Hawthornes fer a few days, but they're back now. Those twins are the best kids. They can pretty much take care of themselves. Doc Hawthorne pays me good and the money sure helps."

Catherine sipped her tea. "I'm sure it does. Do you think you could help me out by waiting on the customers? That would allow me to stay off my feet."

"How 'bout if I help you work on some hats? We could prob'ly make a few fer when it gets cold. Look at all them odds and ends you got around here. You know me, Miz' Catherine. I cain't sit idle."

That was true; Mary Lee was small but a bundle of energy. Whatever she did was done at a fast pace. She had already drained her cup of tea.

Catherine pointed to a shelf above her head. "Those big boxes up there have some suitable material in them. It's probably too high for you to reach so I'll get them down."

"Don't you move, Miz' Catherine. I'll get that stepstool out of the back room."

As the day wore on, Catherine realized this arrangement with Mary Lee would work out well. It was agreed that she would come in every day. The pay may have to come out of the milliner's savings, but it would be worth it.

By Saturday, Catherine's ankle was much better and the two young women had managed to make seven fashionable hats for the coming winter season.

Each day Catherine looked for a note or letter from Patrick. He had said that he would write. She was beginning to doubt that he was sincere, or maybe he came to his senses once he returned to Washington.

Mary Lee left the shop at eleven because Catherine insisted she was able to get around well enough to mind the shop by herself for one hour.

Lloyd Pierce, the tall angular postman who always had a ready grin, was later than usual delivering the mail.

He hurried into the shop after Mary Lee had gone. "Gosh, I'm sure late today. I got behind tryin' to help Irene Butler figure out some mail mix-up. Miz' Talley will have my hide if I don't get over there. Brought your McCall's and a fancy envelope from Washington, D.C."

Catherine's heart did a flip. "Probably from my friend, Carolyn."

"Nope that ain't Miz' Carolyn's writin'. I know that one by sight."

"Mailmen know too much," was her coy reply.

"Not as much as Miz' Talley. She's got the corner on the snoop market. I gotta' run. See you on Monday."

"I'll be here, Mr. Pierce. Have a nice weekend."

Catherine was dying to open the letter. With concentrated effort, she hung the closed sign in the window and locked the door before perching herself on the edge of a chair. She opened the linen weave envelope.

September 7, 1915

Dear Catherine,

I apologize for not sending this letter earlier. I had fully intended to write as soon as I returned on Sunday, but there were business matters to attend to. It took two days before I could find the time to write to you.

I trust that you have taken care of your injured ankle by staying off it as much as possible, but I suspect you continued to open your shop.

My mother is pleased you will be making her another hat. I told her that I would be returning to Berryville and she ordered me to pick it up on my next visit. She would like black for the winter months. I have already put the package of material in the mail. Do not feel pressured into making this hat, as I hope to make a few more visits before the colder weather sets in.

I will arrive in Berryville around six o'clock on Friday evening. I thought we could eat at the Virginia House after I arrive.

I look forward to seeing you again.

> *Sincerely,*
> *Patrick*

Catherine leaned back in the chair and closed her eyes. He had written and he was coming!

Chapter 3

The next week was a roller coaster of emotions for the milliner. She kept herself busy with any task at hand to keep her mind off the upcoming weekend.

A package containing black felt material with a picture of the type of hat Mrs. Burke wanted arrived on Tuesday. It was the perfect distraction to keep her occupied. She hoped it would be finished for Patrick to carry back.

It proved to be a frustration. Black felt collected every speck of dust and fiber that flew into the air. Plus, the thickness of the material was a challenge to sew. Catherine wasn't sure if it was the uncertainty of the upcoming weekend or the making of the hat that caused her to feel edgy and irritable. Relief came when Friday arrived.

Catherine waited in the foyer at the bottom of the stairs that led to her second floor apartment. A combination of the heat of the day and her apprehension caused the foyer to be too warm. She wore a blue-striped, cotton waist with lace around the v-neck and a royal blue broadcloth skirt that Irene Butler had fashioned. She stood to keep her skirt from wrinkling while fanning herself with a copy of last week's *Courier*.

The instant the doorknocker clanked, a pang of panic caused her heart to race.

29

She took a deep breath before opening the door. The hesitation was enough to give the impression of being the picture of composure when she greeted Patrick.

"Good evening. Please come in."

He removed his panama hat. "Catherine, it's so good to be here." With his other hand, he brought forth a bouquet of delicate pink rose buds. "I saw these on a cart when the train stopped in Leesburg and knew they were meant for you."

Taking the small bouquet, she sniffed the faint aroma and gave a sweet smile. "How thoughtful. They're lovely. I'll just be a minute while I get a vase from the shop."

"I'm in no hurry," he said.

Going down the short hall that connected to the back room of the hat shop, Catherine was thankful for a few moments to quell the fluttering of her stomach. It had been a long time since she had been courted.

Patrick wore a tasteful, summer-weight, sack suit and stood perusing the copy of the *Courier* that Catherine had used as a fan.

She returned feeling more in control and carrying the delicate rosebuds peeking out of a milk glass vase. "I'll put them here on the side table until we get back."

With a nod at the paper he held, she advised, "That's last week's paper, Patrick. I was using it as a fan."

"Ah, yes. I recall that you are the resourceful one. How is the ankle?"

"Almost back to normal."

He gave a questioning look. "Did you follow my advice?"

"As closely as I could," she answered, which wasn't a complete lie.

He took her arm as they reached the sidewalk. It was the gentlemanly thing to do, but it gave her a start. Had Patrick felt the same sensation? She glanced up and he responded with a relaxed smile, the picture of one who was used to taking a lady's arm.

The hotel, which was only a few doors from Catherine's shop, was busy with guests who had recently arrived. The dining room was adequate but not large and it appeared to be filled to capacity.

Catherine gave a quick glance around the room relieved that there was not a familiar face. Even the waiter was only a nodding acquaintance.

Dressed in a white shirt, black pants and black bow tie, the short, chunky waiter hurried over as the couple stood inside the door of the dining room. His greeting was cordial. "Miss Ramsburg, it's good to see you." And, before she could reply. "Mr. Burke, how good to have you back. I have saved a special table right over here."

They followed him to a corner that gave some privacy. "May I get something to refresh you?" he asked.

Catherine inclined her head toward the obliging man. "A glass of water will be fine."

"A cup of your finest coffee," answered Patrick.

When the waiter was out of hearing range, Catherine kept her voice low, "How did he know to save a table for you?"

"I phoned the hotel yesterday. I believe he remembers me from two weekends ago. It's never a bad idea to reward someone, especially if you will be needing a favor."

"You must have left a healthy piece of change. Otherwise, I doubt if he would have given you special treatment. You must remember, Patrick, you are not in Washington. There is no finest coffee, they have only one kind."

He grinned. "So, that would have to be the finest."

Catherine couldn't help but smile back at him. How easy he was to be with. The jitters had passed, and she found she did have an appetite. Her nourishment for the day had been toast for breakfast.

They picked up the menus the waiter had left on the table.

Patrick perused the bill of fare. "How are the steaks here?"

"I'm told they are very good. I will order the chicken and dumplings."

"I will try steak. I'm starved."

The waiter returned and took their orders.

"As I just told, Miss Ramsburg, I am famished. I see there is steak on the menu. Can you recommend it?"

"Mr. Burke, I will personally see that you get the best cut of meat in the kitchen."

Patrick responded with a satisfied nod. "Thank you, I look forward to it. Miss Ramsburg will have the chicken and dumpling dinner."

"Yes, sir," he replied as he set off with a determined look.

Catherine raised an eyebrow. "The finest cup of coffee and the best cut of steak? He'll be shining your shoes before we leave."

A hearty laugh escaped as Patrick looked across at her. "It never hurts to give people a purpose in life."

"Especially if they will be rewarded handsomely," she added.

"I've found that helps." He took a sip of coffee. "As for tomorrow, I'm sure I can find something to keep myself busy until you close the shop."

"Do you admire the world of horses? There is a horse show tomorrow."

He smiled back. "I have been known to bet on a race or two. That's the extent of what I know about horses, other than they can be smelly."

"And what animal isn't?"

"You have a point," he conceded. "Where will I find the show?"

They chatted a bit before the unctuous waiter, struggling under the weight of the tray he carried, served Catherine's dinner. Then, with a flourish, he placed a big sizzling slab of meat before Patrick.

"Best cut of steak in the kitchen as I promised."

"That you did, and I will savor every tasty morsel."

The burly little man clasped his hands together. "Will there be anything else, sir?"

Patrick turned his attention to Catherine. "Is there anything you would like?"

"I could use a cup of tea."

"Coming right up," responded the obliging waiter. He was off on another quest.

She eyed the offering set before Patrick. "I don't see how you can possibly eat that platter of meat."

"Don't let this slim frame fool you," came Patrick's casual reply. "People are always trying to fatten me up."

Catherine took a fork-full of dumpling. "Tomorrow, if you wait until I close the shop at noon, we can both go to the horse show."

"That sounds like a capital idea," he responded. "I can use some rest time in the morning."

The decision pleased her. It took the worry out of what would keep them occupied the next day. Now, all she had to worry about was the rest of the evening.

Patrick did indeed finish every bite of meat, along with the potatoes and creamed corn that accompanied it. Then he had a slice of apple pie.

For Catherine, she finished the chicken and dumplings and had no room for dessert.

She sat sipping her tea and peering at him over the rim of the teacup. "I never thought you would be able to put that mound of food away. I will not believe that you eat like that every day or you would be big as a mountain."

"I have been told that I must be a descendant of Jack Spratt."

Catherine chuckled. "Isn't he a fairy tale character?"

"Yes, but doesn't life sometimes feel like a fairy tale?"

"I can't recall any time I've had to pinch myself to see if I'm real."

"Haven't you wanted to be the queen or the princess who runs off with her Prince Charming?"

A wry smile appeared at the corner of her mouth, not since my Prince Charming ran off with another, she thought. "I don't think I ever believed in fairy tales. Besides, I was too afraid of *The Old Woman Who Lived in a Shoe.* Remember? *She whipped them all soundly and sent them to bed.* Fearsome words to a shy four-year-old.*"

That remark brought a wide smile. "And when did you overcome the shyness?"

"When I learned some of the lessons life teaches us along the way."

"Catherine, I believe we are going to have an enjoyable time, what little we will have. I leave on the early train on Sunday. I had planned on going later but a problem came up before I left. Do you mind?"

"Of course not," she answered, hiding her disappointment. "I'm pleased you came. I have your mother's hat finished so you can take it back with you."

"I trust you didn't burn out the lamp trying to finish. I told you there was no hurry."

"You did but I wanted to have it ready for you. Mary Lee stopped by and helped me in the shop, which freed up some time."

It was close to eight o'clock when they left the restaurant and reached Catherine's stoop. She turned the key in the lock and opened the door. Flipping a light switch caused a dim glow in the foyer. "Patrick, thank you for a lovely evening."

"The pleasure is all mine," he answered before bringing her fingertips to his lips. "I will be here tomorrow right after you hang that closed sign in the window. Shall I walk you up the stairs?"

"Kind of you to ask, but no. I will look for you tomorrow."

"I will be here," he said.

After Catherine stepped inside, Patrick turned in the direction of the hotel.

She locked the door, picked up the vase of rose buds and danced up the stairs.

****

The next morning, the contented Catherine hummed to herself as she went about opening the hat shop. It was going to be another pleasant day. The clouds in the sky were white and wispy. A gentle southwest breeze stirred the air.

The event of seeing Lavinia coming through the door didn't dampen Catherine's high-spirited mood. "Good morning, Mrs. Talley."

"Good morning, Catherine," she replied in a sing-song voice. "I came to inquire if you are up to church services in the morning or is your ankle still bothering you?"

"Thank you for your concern. It's almost back to normal."

"That is good news." Next came the truthful reason for her presence. "I understand you have a friend visiting."

How did this woman get her information? Catherine wondered. "A friend?" came her innocent response.

"The gentleman who was here two weeks ago for the wedding."

"Oh, you must mean Mr. Burke. He is in town and he invited me to have dinner at the hotel last evening. He came to get his mother's hat."

"He came all the way here to pick up a hat for his mother when you could have mailed the package?"

Catherine had taken her seat behind the work counter. She picked up a strand of braid smoothing it through her fingers, keeping Lavinia at the height of curiosity.

"Perhaps he didn't trust the mail." Then the teasing hat maker dropped the juiciest piece of gossip the prying woman could hope to hear. "He has invited me to go to the horse show this afternoon."

There was an audible gasp before Lavinia exclaimed, "How exciting for you!"

Catherine looked up from under her brow. "I have been to many horse shows, Mrs. Talley."

Lavinia waved her hand as if to sweep the notion away. "I didn't mean the horse show. I meant attending with a gentleman of his caliber."

A coy smile spread across the milliner's face. "I am looking forward to it."

That was enough said. "I'll be off now and let you get back to your work. I am so pleased to hear that your ankle has healed. I'll see you at services in the morning."

Catherine watched the woman edge out the door and knew the news was headed west. If it puffed up Lavinia's feeling of self-importance to be the first with news, perhaps that was all right. What is it Patrick had said? 'It doesn't hurt to give someone a sense of purpose.'

At noon, she closed the shop and ran up the back stairs to change her clothes before Patrick arrived.

When he did appear on her stoop, he was dressed in a casual shirt and slacks with colorful suspenders attached. He tipped his hat when she answered the blat of the doorknocker.

"Good afternoon, Catherine." His smile showed genuine pleasure.

"Hello, Patrick. I'm just about ready. Please come in."

He did as she asked, closing the door behind him.

"What do you say to passing up the horse show and going on a picnic instead?" he asked.

She gave a puzzled look at his unexpected suggestion. "Am I to assume the world of horses is not your bent?"

"Let's say that a picnic would be more enjoyable. I'm sure the hotel would be happy to pack a couple of boxed lunches. There must be a quiet spot where we could spend the afternoon."

She held a large-brimmed straw hat in her hand and delayed pinning it on. "It's going to get warm as the day goes on and I don't care to walk too far in the heat," was her response.

"I could rent a buggy from the livery stable," he offered in a cajoling manner.

She answered with a dubious smile. "If you are not familiar with horses, I doubt you know how to drive a buggy."

"I'm willing to learn."

"Perhaps, but not with me in it."

He laughed. "Do you have any suggestions?"

Catherine sighed and hesitated before answering. "This may prove to be against my better judgment, Patrick, but there is a quiet, restful spot right in my back yard. You will have to come in the back gate because I don't care to have you seen coming in my front door and not coming out for a few hours."

A sly grin creased his face. "A clandestine meeting?"

"Nothing so exciting. It's a way to avoid gossip. You don't care to go to the horse show and

I don't care to traipse about in the heat. I call it a good decision."

He gave an agreeable smile. "That sounds fair enough. How do I get in?"

"You go back to the hotel and give me a half-hour to pack a picnic basket. Go out the back door of the hotel and turn left down the lane behind. My gate is just before the fire station. I'll unlatch it so you can get in."

"A half-hour it is." He went out the door and tripped down the steps in his devil-may-care manner.

Catherine hurried up the staircase. What was she going to find to put in a picnic basket? The whole change of plans had left her mind a blur.

In the kitchen, she opened the icebox and hoped to find something suitable to make sandwiches. There was no ham, no roast beef, no chicken, but there were some boiled eggs and two olives left in a jar. Slicing a few pieces of bread from the loaf in the bread drawer she set about making egg and olive sandwiches. The thought struck her that Patrick may not like them. Well, he would have to make do. There was a hunk of cheese, which she cubed, and slices of dill pickle. Two molasses cookies were left in the cookie jar. She packed them into the hamper, along with two linen napkins and two drinking glasses. An earthen jar held tea. Satisfied with her makeshift picnic offering, she was prepared for the afternoon that lay ahead.

Patrick was at the back gate when Catherine lifted the heavy latch to let him enter.

In a low voice, she spoke through the crack between the fence and gate, "You'll have to push hard. The grass and dirt have grown up beneath it because I haven't opened this gate in a long time."

He pushed the gate open and, once inside, reset the latch. "I may not drive a buggy but I can latch a gate. We city boys are good for something." He stopped to survey the sizeable yard with the small footbridge over the town run, the white gazebo in the corner and the lovely oaks and bald cypress that allowed shade. "Do you have a caretaker?"

"A caretaker?"

He shrugged, "Yes, a man who takes care of your yard?"

She laughed. "No, I have a woman and her name is Catherine. I can get help if I need it."

It was his turn to smile. He fell in behind as she headed for the gazebo.

The picnic basket rested on a low wicker table separating two matching chairs. She apologized, "If I had known we were going to have a picnic, I would have been prepared. As it is, I packed what I had on hand."

"I could have had lunches packed at the hotel," he said.

"And why would you want to spend your money so foolishly?" She draped the table with a white tablecloth and began unloading the basket.

He sat relaxed with ankles crossed as he watched her prepare. "That's right, I forgot. You are the resourceful one."

"Keep that in mind as you unwrap your egg and olive sandwich."

Catherine took her seat opposite Patrick at the low table and waved away a pesky fly.

"I don't think you could have picked a more perfect spot," he said. "Do you get to spend much time out here?"

"Not as much as I'd like. It seems as though there is always something that gets in the way." She poured them both a glass of tea.

"I understand. I get caught up in mundane tasks."

"Do you like what you do, Patrick? I mean the fabric business."

"I do it out of a sense of duty. I still begrudge that I had to leave medical school."

She picked up the other half of her sandwich. "It seems to me, if that is your heart's desire, then you should go back and finish. You said it would only take a year as I recall."

"It isn't as easy as you make it sound. Liam couldn't run the business by himself. He's a salesman and keeps the customers satisfied. I do the rest. And, there's my mother to think about. She depends on me." Patrick bit into his sandwich. "This is one of my favorites. How did you know?"

She smiled. "It was the luck of the draw."

"Catherine, the reason I came to the wedding a couple of weeks ago was because Liam bribed me. According to him, we were both making a sacrifice. If I would take the ladies to the wedding, then he would stay and watch the business. It was supposed to be his weekend off."

"So you readily agreed."

"I would do almost anything to get away from there. Wasn't I the lucky one?"

Perhaps we both are, thought Catherine.

They finished their lunch and sat drinking tea.

"What about you? Your hat shop appears to be prosperous." He added, "You could earn much more in the city."

She paused before she answered. "Money isn't everything. I have no desire to live in the city. The hat shop is my security. I can support myself and I own property so I am fortunate."

"Fortunate?"

"I have accepted it."

"Yes, but are you happy?"

She sighed. "You asked me the same question once before. I have times when I would like to have my life going in a different direction, but don't we all?"

"I guess we both share something in common," he observed. "Maybe it's time we started new chapters in our lives."

She shrugged a shoulder and gave a half-hearted laugh. "I tried that once. It didn't work out."

He didn't ask for an explanation. "I'm glad we had this conversation. When I go back to Washington, Liam and I are going to have a talk. There are capable men to handle what I do and the company can afford to hire a couple of employees."

She continued folding the white tablecloth and repacked the remains of the picnic in the basket. "Good for you. How about a game of croquet?"

He jumped up from his chair. "Competition? I love it! But…there is one condition."

"And, what would that be?"

"I get the red ball."

Just as the game ended a storm began rumbling overhead. Catherine looked up at the sky. "Let's hurry and pick up the wickets before we get a cloudburst."

They ran around pulling up the wickets and posts and hurried to the shelter of her back porch. They had been caught in the sprinkles before reaching the shelter of the porch. They stood in silence listening and watching as the rain soaked the ground and chilled the air. Each seemed lost in thought until Catherine broke the quiet. "I have your mother's hat ready. Would you like to see it?"

"That I would." His clear blue eyes smiled down at her and she felt a flush of pleasure.

She led him into the back room of the hat shop. Catherine offered Patrick a chair at the narrow table and lit the kerosene stove before putting a kettle of water over to heat.

"I feel chilly from that damp air, Patrick. How about you? Care for a cup of hot tea?"

"I'm usually a coffee man but, right now, I can use a cup of tea. If I had a little more fat on me I could ward off the chill."

She laughed. "Do you realize how many women would love to have that problem? The magazines are touting all kinds of remedies for those who want to shed a few pounds."

"You don't seem to have that problem."

"I believe that's because I keep busy. My mother was rather heavy. She also liked to bake pies and cakes and all kinds of desserts. Unfortunately, she also liked to eat them. I'm more like my father. He was about your height and stronger than most."

Catherine put four scones on an amber glass plate and placed it on the table before she took a seat opposite Patrick.

"You use tea leaves instead of teabags," he observed.

"I believe they bring out the flavor of the tea. My friend, Carolyn, and I used to try to read the leaves. I'm told some people are very good at it but we weren't. According to my mother, you are supposed to drain what's left in the cup. The leaves that land around the inside of the cup tell your fortune."

He was eating a scone. "Let's try it when we're through. Maybe we can make something out of them."

She laughed. "I'm for it if you are."

They ate the scones and finished the tea before going to the sink to pour out what little liquid remained in their cups. Patrick watched as Catherine poured and with care set her cup back on the table. He mimicked her action and they both took their seats.

"Now before we begin," instructed Catherine. "We must intertwine our little fingers on our right hands. Next, we recite together, while our fingers are locked, ashes to ashes, smoke to smoke, may our good fortunes never be broke."

"Would you repeat that once more?" he asked, which she did.

They locked fingers and recited it together.

"Here's the final step. We count to three and break our hold quickly."

"And, why is that? I rather like our fingers entwined."

She gave a coy glance. "I do too but we must follow the steps."

He raised an eyebrow.

"Once we break apart we are ready to read the leaves."

"I'd like to see the way you decipher the remains in the cup," said Patrick.

"You'll have to come over here because I don't want to disturb the leaves."

Patrick came behind and leaned over her shoulder. "What do you see?" he asked.

"A glop of soggy black leaves."

"No look here." He leaned closer and pointed to a tiny straight piece that stuck halfway up the cup. "That's me. And, over here," he said, pointing to a small cluster of leaves, "that's you and maybe that pile of stuff is your hats."

"I'm trying hard to visualize what you're seeing but it isn't coming through. Besides, what kind of a fortune is that?"

He stood back and raised a finger. "Aha, we find the answer in my cup."

He took her hand in his as she rose from the chair and led her around the narrow table before resuming his seat.

Carefully picking up his cup. Patrick smiled as he inspected her handiwork. "And what is your take on this?" he asked.

Catherine stood watching over his shoulder as he pointed to a spot. "A pile of wet leaves?" she asked.

"My dear Catherine, you are missing the whole picture. Lean closer."

She did as he asked squinting as if to see the area more clearly. She shook her head. "Sorry, I don't see anything but ugly leaves."

"Follow my finger. You recall that in your cup there was me on one side and you on the other. Here we are together. Now, this string of soggy leaves is a path that we must both take."

She stood back and playfully tapped his shoulder. "You're making this up."

He turned to look up at her. "Yes, I am, but how does it sound to you?"

He had caught her off-guard. "Well…" She stalled for time and returned to her chair. "It has been my experience that paths sometimes go their separate ways."

"That's an observation not an answer."

A small sigh escaped as she replied, "Patrick, at this point in my life, I'm ready to follow wherever the path leads."

A wide grin spread across his engaging face as he took both her hands in his. "Perfect, just what I wanted to hear. Now, I believe you were going to show me my mother's hat."

She hopped up from her chair. "My goodness. It completely slipped my mind."

Off she went to the back room and returned with the hat. Patrick smiled as he inspected her handiwork.

"You do have a talent," he said, placing the hat back in its box.

"I did my best to copy the picture. Black felt was a trial to work." She wanted him to know it had not been an easy task.

"I suspected that would be the case, but it was my mother's choice. She is going to be pleased. Now, the rain has stopped and I need to get out of these damp clothes. I'll be back in an hour so we can catch that Charlie Chaplin picture at the cinema. Thank you, Catherine." He bent down and impulsively kissed her cheek before he hurried out the back door, crossed the soggy yard and exited the gate to return to the hotel.

Catherine stood there gaping out the window as she watched him go. Patrick was like a ray of sunshine. Was it possible a few murky leaves in a teacup were going to change her life? She shook her head, smiling to herself as she touched the cheek that had received the stolen kiss.

Chapter 4

The next week Mary Lee Thompson was in the millinery shop helping Catherine when a letter arrived from Patrick.

September 23, 1915

Dear Catherine,

I could not let more time pass before I thanked you for the past weekend that I spent with you. What a wonderful combination: a quiet gazebo, egg and olive sandwiches, a game of croquet, reading tea leaves, and, especially, you. Did you enjoy our time together as much as I did?

My mother is pleased with the hat that you fashioned. You should feel honored as she is particular about her attire. Your debt has been repaid.

There has been a change of plans for my arrival next week. I will be on the earliest Saturday morning train instead of coming Friday evening due to an important event I must attend. I am not pleased but it is better than having to cancel the trip.

I am earnestly looking forward to seeing you again.

My fondest regards,
Patrick

Disappointment was Catherine's first reaction until an idea popped into her head.

"Mary Lee, would you be willing to take care of the shop for me next Saturday?"

The young woman looked startled. "Miz' Catherine, I ain't fer sure that I can tend the shop without you bein' here. It ain't like I done it before."

"Isn't like you've done it, Mary Lee."

"Yeah, that's what I said."

The look of consternation on Mary Lee's face caused a pang of empathy from the milliner.

"It will only be for the morning. Mr. Burke was supposed to come on Friday evening but he can't get here until Saturday. I'd rather spend time with him instead of in this stuffy place."

Mary Lee was still undecided.

"How about if I stay upstairs? If you need me, I'll be close to come and help."

She could see her helper turning the prospect over in her mind.

"This Mr. Burke sounds like he's mighty important to you."

"Let's say that he is important enough that I would like to spend time with him." She cautioned, "Please don't tell anyone. Especially Mrs. Talley or who knows what kind of a story would be passed around."

"Miz' Catherine. You know you don't have to worry about that. That ol' busybody has her nose in everybody else's business and that ain't right."

"Isn't right. But, that's Mrs. Talley."

"She looks down her nose at me. Sometimes she's just plain aggravatin'."

"Is that nice to say, Mary Lee?"

"Maybe not, but it's true." She laughed causing creases in her dimpled cheeks. "I'll watch the shop fer you if you promise to be right handy."

Catherine gave her a bear hug. "You have made me very happy."

"Yep," Mary Lee grinned. "I'd say this Mr. Burke is mighty important."

****

Catherine watched out the hat shop window with the notion of catching Patrick when he got out of the twelve-passenger car. Herbert had left word that he would be back in town around ten o'clock. She wanted Patrick to know she was free for the morning.

Catherine finished a hat Ruth Caldwell ordered. She held it in her hand as she started for the storage area to find a suitable box. On her way to the back room, she said to Mary Lee, "Holler to me if you see Herbert's big car pull in."

Mary Lee sat at the work counter keeping busy. "I cain't rightly see from here," she answered.

"Never mind," Catherine called from the back room. "I'll only be a minute."

As she searched for the hatbox she heard the jingle of the shop door announcing a customer. Catherine peered out and saw Patrick coming in the narrow door.

51

She stopped what she was doing and hurried out to greet him.

Mary Lee kept up the pretense of working while keeping a watchful eye as Catherine rushed past her.

Anyone could see from the smiles on the faces of Catherine and Patrick that this was more than a simple friendship.

With suitcase in hand and a wide grin on his face, he said, "I decided to stop before I went on to the hotel."

Catherine was happy to see him. "I'm so glad you did. I wanted to tell you that I will be free of working in the shop this morning."

"That's welcome news. I'm sorry I couldn't get in last evening."

"Come and meet Mary Lee. She has graciously agreed to handle the shop this morning."

Patrick set his suitcase on the floor and they walked to the work counter. "Mary Lee, this is my friend, Patrick Burke. Patrick, Mary Lee Thompson."

He flashed a smile as he took Mary Lee's hand. "It's my pleasure. May I call you Mary Lee? Catherine has told me that you are her right hand when she needs help."

The young woman's face was crimson. "Yes, sir. I'd be pleased to have you call me by my given name."

Catherine gave a satisfied look. "Patrick, I promised that I would be close at hand if any problem crops up. Once you've registered at the hotel we can have coffee and cookies in my apartment."

"Nothing would please me more. It's good of you to hold down the fort, Mary Lee. I'll be back in a flash," he promised.

The young women watched him exit the shop.

"Oh, Miz' Catherine. He's right nice. He ain't like any men around here."

"He isn't like any men, Mary Lee."

"No ma'am, he sure ain't. I think he's right fond of you, too."

Catherine hoped Mary Lee was right. She was so excited she flew up the back stairs to prepare coffee and arrange the cookies she had baked to please him.

The thought of how they would fill their day had been put out of her mind: no worries, twitters, jitters or butterflies. She set out two mugs and a china plate full of peanut butter and oatmeal cookies.

The grinding sound of the doorknocker sent a tremor of anticipation as she ran down the flight of steps leading to the foyer.

She opened the heavy door. "Hello again." She smiled up at him. "Come in."

He removed his hat and stepped inside. "I've missed you," he said as he brought her hand to his lips and leveled his eyes on hers. "It's good to be back."

Did he notice the flash of pleasure he caused? "I'm pleased to see you. Come ahead upstairs. We can find something to keep us busy until it's time to close the shop."

Patrick took her arm as they went up the stairs. "Mary Lee seems like a sweet young woman. Can she handle the shop by herself?"

"Of course she can, but she doesn't think she can. Why do you ask?"

"It struck me that if you ever get a chance to go to Washington, perhaps she could take care of things while you were gone."

"I don't plan on going to Washington."

"Just a thought," he said.

They reached the top of the landing.

Catherine led him through the dining room, into the living room and offered him a seat.

He stood and looked around at the flowered chintz chair and sofa before he took a seat on the piano bench. "Do you play?" he asked.

"For my own enjoyment."

"Do you mind if I try it out?"

He plays the piano? "Please do."

Patrick lifted the lid and rolled it back to reveal the black and white ivory keys. He flexed his long fingers and began playing a mesmerizing Strauss waltz. Catherine came to stand behind him.

"Patrick, you are an accomplished pianist."

"Twelve years of lessons," he admitted. "I should have learned something." He pulled the cover back over the keys and went to take a seat on the sofa. "I'm not sure my father was for it until he came to one of my recitals."

He motioned Catherine to sit next to him, which she did. "My father was an Irishman from New York City. Quite rough and tumble up there, according to him. He worked on the boats that brought goods to Georgetown, liked the area and decided to settle there. He lived in a shanty while learning the ins and outs of the fabric trade."

She turned giving a knowing smile. "So, instead of getting a son who was into the fisticuffs, he got one with a more placid talent. What about your brother?"

"Liam?" He thought a minute. "A bit more Irish than I. He has talked himself into and out of plenty of altercations."

"What was your family like, Catherine? Any sisters or brothers?"

"No, unfortunately, just me. As I told you last time, I was only thirteen when my father passed away. He worked long hours but he refused to work on Sunday. 'Sunday is the Lord's day,' he'd say, 'and our time for family'."

"I think I would have liked your father," Patrick said.

Catherine smiled. "I have coffee and cookies We can sit in the dining room and talk."

"Coffee sounds good. Cookies, even better."

"Follow me," she said.

Passing through the hallway Patrick spied the cane Catherine used when she injured her foot.

"Did you say that was your mother's cane?" he asked as he lifted it out of the umbrella stand. "It is a handsome piece of work."

"Yes. She used it until she could no longer get out of bed."

He was empathetic. "That must have been a difficult time for you."

"My mother was a good person, enjoyed life. When she got sick she lost ground day by day until she was not the mother I remembered. Her illness made me a stronger person. Let's say I grew up in the process."

She poured the coffee and they took their seats at the table.

"What about your mother, Patrick?"

He picked up a cookie and took a drink of the hot coffee. "My mother is a bit more complicated." He sighed. "She lived in Alexandria and met my father at a band concert. According to my father, she was with her family and her father took an instant liking to him...my mother tells it differently... Either way, my father had to be established before they were allowed to marry, so my grandfather financed the warehouse. My father proved to be a successful businessman."

"Do you mind if I dip a cookie?"

Patrick chuckled. "I've heard of dunking doughnuts but not dipping cookies."

"Brings out the flavor," she said. "I only dip the peanut butter. It is a fine art that must be performed in a genteel manner: dip...nibble... dip...nibble."

He attempted to mimic her demonstration. "No good. I'll stick with dunking doughnuts, but I believe you have acquired a definite skill. You are proving to be a multi-talented woman: creating hats, dipping cookies, making egg and olive sandwiches. What other talents lie hidden?"

She smiled at him taking in his pleasant features. He was not the handsome, athletic type. It was the merriment in his eyes and his jaunty ease of manner that appealed to her. "You've always lived in Washington?" she asked.

"My father fixed up the shack in Georgetown and we lived there until I was seven years old."

"And?"

"My mother wanted a bigger house and respectability so we moved to the house on K Street. That's when she changed."

He gave a heavy sigh and took a drink from his mug.

"Changed?" asked Catherine.

"She hired servants, entertained with garden parties and became involved in all kinds of charitable groups. Instead of being the mother who played with us in the yard and cooked our meals, she was gone much of the time. Hired help took over those duties. Turned my world upside down."

"You seem to be close to her."

"I promised my father I would take care of her and I do." Patrick helped himself to another cookie.

"Patrick, I feel I should tell you this. I was engaged once."

He looked at her and placed his mug on the table ready to listen. "What happened?"

"He skipped out of town one night with someone else. Don't think that wasn't difficult to live down."

"I can imagine. Did you keep the ring?"

She held a puzzled look. "Why? Is that important?"

"If you kept the ring, it would mean that you still hold feelings for him."

"The ring." She smiled at the memory. "Right after it happened, I went to visit my aunt over in Pine Grove. I was still angry and ashamed. It was on the way back that I got this wonderful idea. I stopped the buggy in the middle of the bridge, walked over to the railing and threw that ring, as hard as I could, smack-dab into the Shenandoah River."

He laughed. "Smack-dab, huh?"

"It was like being baptized; washed all that guilt and pain away."

Patrick reached for her hand. "Well, lucky for me the cad didn't know what a prize he had. Enough of this reminiscing. How would you like to take the train over to Charles Town to see a performance?"

"Charles Town? That's in West Virginia."

"That it is, but its only fifteen miles away. I read in the *Washington Post* that there is a troupe from Washington who will be performing a *Salute to America Revue*. It should be a great way to spend the afternoon."

Catherine rose from her seat. "I'm not sure. I've lived here all my life and I've only been to Charles Town once. It was a memorable trip but not an enjoyable one. My mother read about John Brown and was fascinated by his story. My father hired a carriage to take us to Harpers Ferry. We had to pass through Charles Town. The roads were dusty and winding and it seemed we would never get to the firehouse where the troops trapped Brown and his men. We stayed overnight at an inn. I remember being up high and afraid I was going to fall down the hillside into the Potomac River rushing by below. On our way home, the next day, we stopped at the courthouse in Charles Town to see where the trial took place. We even had to go to the scaffold where he was hung. Of course the scaffold wasn't there. Can you picture that old madman swinging in the wind? I could and I was only eight years old."

She picked up the mugs and plate of cookies and headed for the kitchen with Patrick close behind.

"I've already bought the train tickets." He reached into his pocket and waved them before her. "Round trip."

She filled the teakettle with water while he took a seat at the table. "You're sure there's a train coming back?"

"Seven-fifteen, Norfolk and Western. We'll be back around eight."

She heard Mary Lee come running up the back stairs. "Miz' Catherine, there's a hired man down here sayin' he needs to pick up a hat for Miz' Ruth Caldwell and I cain't find it."

"Patrick will you listen for the whistle on the kettle and turn off the fire under it? I need to go down."

He nodded his head.

On their way down the stairs, Catherine said, "Mary Lee, it's a dark green velvet with a pheasant feather. I'm sure I labeled it and put it in the storage closet. Don't you recall? I was looking for a box for it before Patrick came."

Mary Lee was nervous as a cat. Her voice was at high pitch, "Well, maybe, but I cain't find it. I done looked all over."

When they reached the bottom of the stairs Catherine went into the shop and addressed the hired man, "I'm sorry to have you wait. It seems I've misplaced Miss Caldwell's hat."

"I don't mind waitin'. I'm likely to get a tongue-lashin' if'n I get back without it."

Catherine went back to the storeroom. There was Patrick at the foot of the stairs holding a dark green velvet hat. "Could this be what you're looking for?" he asked with a sly grin on his face.

The tension building within drained away as Catherine turned and saw what Patrick held in his hand. "That's it! Where did you find it?"

"On top of your icebox."

"Mary Lee, package this up. Miss Caldwell has paid for it."

"Yes, ma'am. I sure am glad you found it, sir. I was mighty worried."

She took the hat and addressed Catherine. "You know how nasty that Miz' Caldwell can be when she don't get her own way."

"I think we're safe. The hired man isn't going to tell her there was any problem."

Mary Lee went to get a hatbox. Patrick and Catherine went back upstairs.

Her mind was churning about how the hat landed on her icebox. Then she remembered. She had it in her hand when Patrick arrived in the shop. She must have been so absorbed with his presence she carried the hat upstairs. Worse yet, from the look on Patrick's face, she was sure he had guessed the reason for her absentmindedness. It was embarrassing.

When they returned to the kitchen, Catherine found the mugs and cookie plate in a dish of soapy water.

"This is a surprise," she said.

"You're not the only one who can be resourceful."

She set about washing the few soiled dishes. Apparently, he wasn't going to tease her about her faux pas regarding the hat for which she was grateful.

She placed the rinsed dishes on the drain board and wiped her wet hands. "I'll go down and lock up the shop; it's close to closing time. Let's use your tickets and go to Charles Town."

His answer was a satisfied smile.

Chapter 5

The train left the Berryville station on time. Forty minutes later they were in Charles Town where the stationmaster was tall, wiry and wore a handlebar mustache. Patrick asked how to get to the opera house.

"It's a mite over a mile," the man advised. "For a price, Garland, out there," pointing a long knotted finger, "will run you up."

Patrick thanked the man and came to where Catherine was standing. Taking her arm, he leaned in and, in a confidential voice, said, "I think we should let Garland, out there, give us a ride."

Catherine stifled a snicker as they went out the door of the station to where a horse and outdated carriage were waiting. The man, identified as Garland, sat in the driver's seat with a wad of tobacco pouching out his jaw. His long face showed disinterest or boredom, Catherine wasn't sure which. Two well-dressed passengers, a gentleman and a lady, sat facing each other on the seats of the open carriage.

"Good afternoon," Patrick greeted the skinny, long-legged driver. "Do you have room for two more? We are going to the opera house."

He spit tobacco juice out the side of his mouth before answering, "Climb in," and motioned them into the carriage with his thumb.

The gentleman moved across the carriage to sit next to the lady allowing room for Patrick and Catherine to sit side by side.

"Patrick Burke." Patrick offered his hand to the gentleman, "My friend Miss Ramsburg."

The man shook Patrick's hand. "Lucius and Nellie Parks."

The women nodded to each other.

The driver tapped the horse and they were on the way. He turned back to the first couple and announced, "I'll be droppin' the two of you off on Samuel Street before I go on to the opera house over on George."

"Home of the Washington families," said Lucius Parks with a proud smile.

"A notable family," agreed Patrick.

"We're pretty well-known in these parts. Nellie here is a direct descendent."

"My first visit to your town," said Patrick.

That seemed to open the floodgate of one-sided conversation dominated by Lucius. "All these streets are named after the Washingtons: George, Lawrence, Samuel, Charles, Mildred, and this here's Washington we're riding up. Yesiree, an important family." He nudged his wife. She answered with a disgusted look.

When they reached a stately home on Samuel Street, Patrick and Catherine were not sad to see the couple depart the carriage.

She whispered to Patrick. "Do you think his wife ever gets a chance to get a word in edgewise?"

He smiled and took her hand. "She struck me as the strong silent type."

"Silent for sure," observed Catherine.

The horse pulled the heavy transport up the quiet street of plush homes and neatly kept yards with tall trees beginning to show the colors of autumn. The ungainly carriage turned back onto the main street, another turn and the opera house came into view.

It was a huge red brick building. Wide steps led up to double doors that allowed entrance. Inside, lavish gold brocade drapes hung at the tall display windows contrasting with the green wool carpet that covered the lobby floor. The lobby held a set of steps, separated by brass rails, leading into the auditorium.

An usher escorted them to a row in the middle where they had a good view of the stage.

They were twenty minutes early and occupied their time with reading the program and watching the parade of people who were filling up the sizeable theatre. The sound of the orchestra tuning their instruments and the buzz of conversation around them gave Catherine a sense of anticipation. The Director of the Opera House came on stage in front of the curtains and introduced the extravaganza they were about to see. House lights were dimmed, the curtain rolled back, and the show began.

The *Salute to America Revue* was spectacular! Actors and actresses adorned in red, white and blue costumes shimmered with every move they made. The show opened with the playing of *The Star Spangled Banner,* followed by a chorus line of tap dancers, tapping to the tune of *You're a Grand Old Flag.*

The *Battle Hymn of the Republic, Dixie,* tunes of Stephen Foster, John Phillip Sousa, and Irving Berlin kept the show moving. The finale was the playing of *America the Beautiful* with the audience on their feet and joining in. The applause was deafening.

Catherine and Patrick remained in their places to avoid the rush of the crowd once the performance was over.

"Patrick, I've clapped so hard that even my arms are tired."

"Aren't you glad we came?"

Her green eyes sparkled. "Thank you for a grand afternoon. How sad that I live fifteen miles away and didn't know this place existed. But then, most likely I wouldn't have come anyway."

He took her hand and helped her up from her seat. "Plenty of good things to experience."

"No doubt," Catherine agreed. "I'd better slip on my shawl before we leave," she said while pinning on her hat, which she had removed before the show so that it wouldn't block the view of others.

Patrick unfolded the woolen shawl and, with a gentle touch of his hands, placed it over her shoulders.

"We aren't going to miss the train, are we?"

He pulled out his pocket watch. "We still have an hour and a half."

"Good. I can relax."

He smiled as he guided her out of the theatre. "Did you doubt?"

"Let's just say there was a speck of uncertainty."

"Just a speck?" he teased.

She slipped her arm through his. "It wasn't enough to keep me home."

Rain had fallen while they were in the theatre leaving puddles in the street and a chill in the air.

"I hope your wrap will be warm enough. We may have to walk that 'mite over a mile' because 'Garland, out there' isn't in sight."

She laughed at his comical interpretation of the stationmaster.

"I'll be fine. You're the one with a light jacket."

They walked a block and turned right onto Washington Street, the main street of Charles Town. The town was quiet. A large hotel, a block from the opera house, and a small shop down the street from it were the only signs of life.

"We'll pass up the hotel and try this little place," suggested Patrick as he opened the door to the shop.

The jovial man behind a half-partitioned area was placing a cap on a bottle of pills. "Come on in," he greeted them. "You've still got fifteen minutes before I close the shop."

"Good," answered Patrick. "We were over at the opera house and now we are on our way to catch a train. I thought we'd get a couple of candy bars."

"Got a few different ones. Getting kind of gray out there, isn't it?" He pointed toward the street.

"Kind of chilly also," replied Patrick.

"How would you two like a cup of coffee? I just bought a newfangled pot and I had Barbara Ann, that's my wife, put it on to see if the coffee tastes any different than in that old enamel pot we use."

"That's kind of you. We have a few minutes before we need to get the train, if it's on time."

"Runs pretty close to schedule they tell me. I'm not one to travel. Just have a seat and I'll get the coffee."

Patrick and Catherine sat on a wood bench and heard the man call into another room, "Barbara Ann bring out a couple of cups of coffee. We got a young couple out here with their teeth chatterin'."

"It's very nice of him to do this for us, Patrick."

"Yes, I'll see he gets rewarded."

She smiled at him. "You're liberal with this tendency to reward people."

"If someone goes out of their way to help me, there's no reason not to."

She placed her hand on his arm. "I like that."

67

The shopkeeper brought two cups of coffee on a tray with sugar and cream in small containers and set the tray on a low table in front of the bench. "She said she looked for a couple of cookies to go with it, but we're plumb out."

"Thank your wife for us," said Patrick. "We'll take two Hershey bars and a package of those sassafras drops."

The shopkeeper went to bag Patrick's request while they savored the warmth of the coffee.

Pointing to his cup, Patrick called to the man. "I believe you made a good investment in your new coffee pot."

"As soon as I close up this place I plan on tryin' it."

Dusk was settling in when they left the shop. It was a hike to the train station that sat on the west edge of town. The last block before the station was sparsely settled. Patrick took Catherine's arm as he guided her around puddles and muddy spots.

She pressed his arm. "Let's hurry. I don't feel comfortable here."

"You can see the station down there."

"I'd still feel better if we stepped it up."

No sooner were the words out of her mouth when a scruffy, shabbily dressed man seemed to appear from nowhere and approached them. His eyes were gaunt, his cheeks drawn.

"Got a nickel, mister?"

He was a big man and his appearance unsettled Catherine. She crowded close to Patrick.

If he was bothered, it didn't show. "Sorry to see you're down on your luck," he said to the beggar. Reaching into his pocket, Patrick pulled out a five-dollar bill. "This will buy you food and a room. I wish you luck."

The man's weary eyes opened wide as if he had just been handed a key to the city.

"Bless you, sir," was his grateful answer before walking away a head taller.

"Most likely, he's just going to spend it on booze," surmised Catherine.

"But, we don't know that," Patrick responded.

Catherine sighed. "No, we don't. A judgment call on my part?"

Patrick chuckled. "You're probably right, but I prefer to think it will get him back on the right track."

Patrick's kindness was a trait she admired. At that moment, she realized she was beginning to care too much for the man walking beside her.

****

Back in Berryville, the main street was deserted. Holding hands, they walked the two blocks up to Catherine's place where Patrick placed the key in the lock.

"Why don't you come up for a bite to eat and some hot tea?" she suggested.

"If you aren't concerned about the fallout it will cause, I'm all for it."

They entered the foyer and started up the stairs. "Patrick, I worried that you wouldn't come…

worried that you would come…worried about what people would say…and I'm tired of it."

"Come to your senses, huh?" He put his arm around her waist and gave a squeeze.

"Or lost them," she replied. "Let's go into the kitchen. I'll find something to eat and put the kettle over."

Although he had been there earlier, Patrick surveyed the kitchen. "Nice cozy place," he observed. "Look, I can touch the ceiling."

"I can remember my father having to stoop before coming through the door. It's my favorite room because it's always warm and comfortable. Have a seat, and I'll see what there is to eat."

She opened the icebox door. "How about scrambled eggs?"

"How about pancakes?" he countered. "I'm the best pancake maker this side of the Potomac."

"You?"

"I had a great nanny who said, 'Mistah' Patrick, you might jus' have to take care of yourself one day so you needs to know how to make easy food.' I loved the woman."

Catherine laughed as she threw him an apron. "Prove it."

"If you'll get the ingredients out, you'll be in for a treat."

She got out: flour, eggs, sugar, lard and milk, poured a cup of tea and took a seat at the small drop-leaf table. "Two performances in one evening? I'll get spoiled."

Patrick tied the apron around his waist. "To be dressed proper, I should have a chef's hat but we will forego that for tonight. Please note that I have a mixing bowl and a fork," which he showed to his audience of one. "We want the batter to be lumpy. Next, I take great care to measure the flour," he said as he dumped a heap into the bowl. "An expert flick of the wrist and the eggs are deposited into a separate bowl where I have placed a sizable dollop of lard. Slop these together really good, add them to the flour, and slowly stir in milk." His elaborate gestures and antics caused Catherine to laugh until tears came to her eyes.

He cooked up a big batch of pancakes, heated some maple syrup and they sat down to their breakfast/supper, including a cup of hot tea.

Catherine placed two pancakes on her plate, drizzled the syrup over them and took a bite. "Oh, Patrick, these are delicious."

"I am a man who is true to his word," he said before putting a stack on his plate.

I hope you are, thought Catherine.

They satisfied their hunger in silence, and sat drinking tea.

It was then he dropped the news, "I plan on going back to medical school at the first of the year."

She looked up in surprise. "Have you discussed this with your brother?"

"I haven't told anyone but you. What do you think about it?"

She shrugged her shoulder. "If it is what you really want, and you can afford to, then you would be a fool not to follow through."

He sat back in his chair. "It wouldn't bother you if we didn't see as much of each other?"

"I didn't say that," came her casual reply. She was fully aware of what would be sacrificed, but she kept her disappointment hidden. "It's not like we know each other that well. I mean, you have only been up a few times."

"Yes, but doesn't it seem as though we've known each other for years? I can hardly get through the days until I can get out here. The thought of not seeing you tears me apart," he confessed. "You're stuck up here in the hat shop and I'm seventy miles away."

Her smile was warm as well as the touch of her hand on his arm. "You said you would only have one year to complete medical school. That's not such a long time."

He gave a big sigh. "You do see the practical side of things. But, a lot can happen in a year."

"Where is that optimistic attitude that endears you to me?"

He looked up with a wide grin. "Does it?"

"Poor choice of words?" she asked.

"Not if you're truthful." He rushed from his seat and drew her up from her chair. Patrick was going to kiss her and she was not about to turn away.

His gentle, caring kiss was pure ecstasy to Catherine.

He reached up and twirled a strand of hair on her forehead. "You please me."

She cleared her throat. "You had better go before I lose my senses. I believe you have an early train to catch in the morning."

He playfully kissed her cheek. "I do, but I leave with a happy heart. I hate to think that it will be two weeks before I get back here."

" It will pass before we realize it," she said.

But, after he left, Catherine's cheerful façade fell apart. The announcement that he would return to school had fallen like a sledgehammer. He was right. A lot can happen in a year.

Chapter 6

In early October, Catherine was busy working on a hat when Lloyd Pierce, the postman, came by delivering the mail.

"Another one of them fancy letters from Washington," he announced, and waited to see Catherine's reaction. She offered a sweet smile. Lloyd held the letter a tad longer than necessary. She curbed the desire to snatch it out of his hand.

"Are you teasing me, Mr. Pierce?"

"Now, Miz' Catherine, you know me better'n that." His long face widened into a grin.

With a coy smile, she replied, "Oh, yes. I know you."

He laughed. "Wal' here's yer letter. I gotta' be on my way and get Miz' Talley all flustered. I keep her fidgeting while I fish around in my sack for her mail."

"It seems to me you could be gathering her mail while you're crossing the street."

"Now, that would take all the fun out of it, wouldn't it?"

"You'd better be careful. Mrs. Talley might retaliate."

"She ain't caught on yet, and knowin' Miz' Talley, she ain't likely to. Keeps my job from gettin' stale. See ya' tomorra'."

Touching Patrick's letter, a quick memory flashed through Catherine's mind. Over a week ago, the day after Patrick had left, Lavinia came marching into the hat shop. "Catherine, what do you mean by entertaining a man in your apartment without a chaperone? It will smear your good name."

"I assure you, Mrs. Talley, Patrick is nothing but a gentleman."

"Nevertheless, I thought it my duty to caution you." She huffed out of the shop.

And here Catherine held the news of when he would be returning. She cast Lavinia's warning aside. She would entertain Patrick in her apartment if she felt like it.

October 12, 1915

My dear Catherine,

I trust this letter finds you in good health. I had hoped to get this posted a couple of days ago, but I was unable to find the time. I ask you to forgive me for that.

I am finding this letter a bit awkward to write because I must ask an important question. Liam will be away on a buying venture, and he has decided that it would be a good time for him and Sarah to have a vacation. They will be in New York City for two weeks where there are endless cultural enticements.

I will be unable to leave the warehouse without an overseer, which brings me to pose this question. Would you consider coming to Washington for a weekend to visit Mother and me? I don't think I could bear not seeing you for a whole month.

I would be happy to purchase your train ticket and pay the fare for you to take the auto to the Bluemont station. Then, I will meet you at the train when it arrives in Alexandria.

Please give this careful thought before you decide against it. I realize this is a request purely out of my own want and selfishness. So if you find that it is an impossible proposition, I will understand.

There is much to see and do here in the city, and I'm sure you would enjoy the sights; perhaps visit with your friend, Carolyn. Please send me your thoughts as soon as you make a decision.

I often wish we were not so far apart. Every day I see something that reminds me of you, and it only serves to call attention to how much I miss not having you closer.

As always, I send caring thoughts until we are together again.

> *Affectionately,*
> *Patrick*

Catherine reread the letter. Her initial reaction was disappointment, followed by disbelief. She couldn't imagine that he would ask her to consider such an undertaking, wanting her to travel to Washington by herself to spend a weekend with him and his mother? The whole idea was unthinkable. Catherine stood up and jammed the letter into her apron pocket. She would start making plans for her trip right away.

Her first concern was the hat shop. Could she trust Mary Lee to run it or should she close it down for the weekend? Closing it for two days meant no money coming in, and it was the beginning of the busy fall season. She decided her best option was to ask Mary Lee when she arrived the next morning.

****

They were sitting at the work counter when Catherine posed the question.

"Oh, Miz' Catherine. There ain't no way I can take care of this place if you ain't around."

"Aren't around," Catherine corrected.

Mary Lee squirmed in her seat. "I mean to say that I'd jus' be a bundle of nerves."

"Do you know most of the customers?"

"Yes, ma'am."

"Do you know how to make change and take care of the receipts?"

"Yes, ma'am."

"Then that's all you would have to do besides locking and unlocking the door."

Mary Lee was quick to remind her, "You remember that hat business with Miz' Caldwell the last time? No, ma'am, there ain't no way I can do it."

"Isn't any way, Mary Lee," said the frustrated Catherine.

"Ain't that what I just said?"

Catherine gave a heavy sigh. "You couldn't possibly do anything that can't be undone. It means a lot to me to be able to go to Washington. It would only be a day and a half." She added an incentive. "I can pay you double."

Mary Lee's blue eyes opened wide. "I guess you really want to go."

"That I do."

The reluctant stand-in hesitated before she drawled, "Wal', I guess I can try it."

A satisfied smile crept across the milliner's face. "You can do it. I know you can."

****

The morning she was to leave, Catherine and Mary Lee went over all that was expected in her absence. They were both nervous. Catherine because of the unknown she was about to enter and Mary Lee because of the responsibility she was to assume.

Mary Lee tried to be helpful, "You jus' go on and have a good time. If I get beside myself over who-knows-what, I'm jus' gonna' close up the shop."

Catherine was about to get into the long twelve-passenger car that looked like a stretched out Model A Ford. "Do whatever you have to do, Mary Lee. I've got enough to worry about."

There were quite a few people on the street and Catherine wondered if it was because she was leaving town. That would be enough to get the curiosity seekers out early.

Herbert, the driver, had tucked her traveling bag into the back of the long car. There were nine other passengers causing Catherine to feel more comfortable that she was not the only one heading up the mountain for the train. After cranking the engine, Herbert took his place behind the wheel. "I 'spect this ol' gal can make it up the mountain one more time," he quipped, which did nothing to quell Catherine's apprehension. Then, when she glanced out the window and saw the forlorn look on Mary Lee's face, it was enough to make her change her mind...but not quite. She waved a weak hand as the gears grated and the car rattled away.

The auto seemed to labor onto the main pike and, even though the driver tried to maneuver around ruts in the road, the car hit plenty of holes that gave the passengers reason to hold onto their hats.

They crossed the bridge over the Shenandoah River into the small hamlet of Pine Grove where Herbert stopped to let a man get off. "Got to head over to see my brother," Catherine heard him say. "Pick me up on your way back."

No one was at the stop to get into the car so it moved on at a snail's pace as it started to climb the mountain on its way to Bluemont. There was a horseshoe curve in the road before a steeper climb. Fear gripped Catherine as she heard the car sputter and realized the tinny thing could roll back down the mountain and become a lethal missile slamming into the rocky hillside or catapulting into a ravine. She pictured herself flying through the air in the copper colored travel suit she had so carefully chosen. Herbert shifted the gears and the groaning auto chugged the rest of the way to the top.

To Catherine, the moment of fright had served as an awakening. What was there to be afraid of? If her life ended sprawled on the mountain, would that be so bad? Someone would see to the disposal of her hat shop, the contents of her apartment and give her a decent burial. There was a plot waiting for her next to her parents in Green Hill Cemetery.

Down the winding road into Bluemont they went. Herbert acted as a tour guide pointing out the places where people from Washington came to spend summers away from the heat and humidity of the District of Columbia.

The Bluemont station was small but attractive with its red roof and the waiting platform surrounding it. Catherine went into the cramped station and bought a round trip ticket from the burly man behind the counter. Patrick had advised that a round trip ticket was less expensive than one way and, since Catherine had insisted on paying her own way, she had listened and followed his advice.

The conductor helped her up onto the metal steps of the train car and offered to take her bag but she preferred to carry it herself. She found a seat next to a window. Watching the scenery along the way would take her mind off the trip, at least that was her intention.

The conductor came through taking tickets on his way to the back of the car. He came to Catherine's seat. "Looks like we're going to have a colorful trip down the mountain with all the fall colors on the trees. Your first trip ma'am?"

"Yes, sir."

"Well, if you have any questions or concerns, you let me know. I've been making this trip for over ten years."

Catherine gave a tentative smile. "I do appreciate that. Once we arrive at the Alexandria station, I'll be fine."

"A few stops along the way, but we should be about on time. The Leesburg stop is close to half way. That's a fifteen-minute wait but you can get out and stretch if you feel the need. They've got refreshments in the station."

With a jerk, the train lurched forward and a wave of panic swept through her. Had she lost all common sense? The long car was still parked at the station. She could catch Herbert and ride right back to Berryville...right back to what she wanted to get away from: the small town, the hat shop, the lonely apartment on Main Street. With all those flashes of thought came the vision of a welcoming Patrick waiting for her in Alexandria. The panic subsided as quickly as it had come. Catherine settled back into her seat.

The conductor was right. The autumn colors were at their peak and Catherine was lost in the wonder of nature. Surely the beauty of this landscape had to be the work of a higher power.

She had brought some crocheting in her large pocketbook and began to work on a doily she had started. Once it was finished, she would present it to Mrs. Burke as a thank you gift for her hospitality.

The train stopped in Round Hill, Purcellville, Hamilton, and Paeonion Springs before they reached Leesburg. Catherine rolled up the unfinished doily and carefully placed it back into her pocketbook. It had been over an hour of sitting so she decided to take a short walk. She picked her travel bag up from the floor and placed it in her seat as she did not want to return and find someone else sitting there.

Stepping off the train; she was thankful for the freedom of movement. There wasn't much to see except passengers arriving to meet their families and others bidding their loved ones goodbye. Some men, who had been on the train, took the fifteen minutes of holdover to sit on benches to smoke pipes and cigarettes. Catherine found the smoke offensive so she stayed upwind. She watched as a couple of the men took the idle time to blow smoke rings. Were they were having a contest as to who could blow the biggest?

The time passed quickly before the conductor called, "All aboard." She hurried into the train car and smiled when she saw her seat just as she had left it. The seat next to her had been empty since they left the Bluemont station but she wasn't so lucky at this stop. A bent old man with a long gray beard and clothes that smelled like they hadn't been washed for a good spell unsteadily eased himself into the seat. Now she was forced to hold her travel bag between her feet. Would he be getting off at the next stop? She hoped so.

He gave a long sigh as he placed his cane between his knees.

"Goin' into Alexandria?" he asked in a scratchy voice.

"Yes, sir, I am."

"Where you from, Miss?"

"Berryville."

"Went through there when we went to fight the Yankees up in Winchester. I was in Ol' Jube's outfit."

Catherine glanced over at his wrinkled face. "The Civil War?" she blurted out.

"Wasn't nothin' civil about it. I was a young lad."

"I'm honored to meet you," she said.

He then proceeded to tell her stories about his exploits in the War Between the States, as he called it, and he didn't stop until they pulled into the Alexandria station.

She watched his laborious effort to stand, but after he rose to as far as his stooped back allowed, he looked back at Catherine. "You're a right nice young lady to sit and listen to an old man's tales. That's about all I got left."

Her smile was sincere as she replied, "Sir, I hope all will be well with you. Do you have family waiting?"

"No ma'am. My family's pretty much gone. I got a train ticket and letter that says they got room for me at the Soldier's Home. They'll take care of me there so that's where I'm headed. Maybe find some other old coots I can swap stories with." He gave a lonesome smile revealing swollen red gums and a few missing teeth. "You're a right nice lookin' young lady. You got somebody waitin' for you?"

Catherine gave a wide smile, "A very nice gentleman," she answered and realized how fortunate she was.

"He nodded to her, "Wal', he's a lucky fellow."

"Thank you," she replied in a small voice.

Catherine sighed as she watched the old veteran totter away. Unknowingly, he had left her with a lesson in humility.

She remained in her seat to smooth her hair and adjust the tilt of her pancake hat that matched the copper travel suit she was wearing. From the train window all she could see were crates, trunks, and assorted luggage piled on the train platform. She picked up her tapestry travel bag and decided that if she didn't spy Patrick, she would sit in the station until he found her.

Catherine came down the short set of steps off the train and scanned the crowd that was milling around. She stepped forward onto the wooden platform, and saw Patrick hurrying toward her. Taking her bag, he sat it down and greeted her with a big hug right there in the middle of the crowd. "I am so happy to see you."

She blushed with his exuberant greeting. "This is a very busy place."

He held her hands in each of his as he stood back to admire her attire. "You look fetching."

"Patrick, people are going to notice."

"Let them notice." He picked up her bag. "I have a taxi waiting. Did you have a good trip?"

"Let's say that I have a true appreciation for the times you've come to Berryville."

The waiting taxi was a Model T Ford. The hackie wore a tweed jacket and newsboy cap with a visor in the brim and stood holding the back door of the car open. Catherine stepped up onto the running board and into the cab. Patrick took a seat next to her. The driver pitched her traveling bag on the seat next to him, opened the throttle and the car coughed to life.

Once they crossed the bridge over the Potomac into D.C. proper, Catherine was awed by the sight of huge, limestone buildings, many over four stories high. There seemed to be people everywhere. Men in suits and homburg hats hustled along the streets. She turned her head for a better view of a group of women dressed in Suffragette uniforms. The mixture of ooga-ooga from car horns and clanging of trolley bells made her head spin. What also struck her senses was the smell: damp, stale and unclean.

They sat holding hands. Any uneasiness Catherine had felt had disappeared with the contentment she felt just having him near. Patrick pointed out the government buildings as they passed. He seemed proud of his city that by definition belonged to everyone. Catherine understood why her friend, Carolyn, had found Washington so fascinating; Carolyn had the spirit of adventure and the city was alive and moving.

The jitney traveled into a quiet neighborhood of stately houses where the driver pulled up in front of a huge, white, stucco house sporting a portico supported by tall columns. It sat back from a wide expanse of lawn that stretched to the street. Catherine stood taking it in while Patrick paid the cab driver. The colors of autumn were just beginning and she wondered if these tall trees, bordering a stone walk up to the house, could rival the beauty of the ones she had just witnessed on the mountain.

Patrick came to her side. "Ready?" he asked.

"I'm not sure. I didn't envision such a grand place."

"It's only a house."

She tilted her head giving him a wry look. "Perhaps it is, but it's twice the size of any large house in Berryville."

He smiled down at her as he picked up her bag and guided her to the first set of limestone steps leading up to the pebbled path. Catherine lifted the hem of her skirt as they walked up the steps. They continued in silence until they reached the porch.

The tall door opened as if by an unseen signal.

"Good evening, Samuel."

"Evenin', Mister Patrick. I saw the car pull up."

"This is Miss Catherine. Please see that her bag gets to the guest room."

The colored man nodded to Catherine before answering Patrick, "Yes, sir, I'll see to it right away. Your mother is waiting for you in the parlor."

"Thank you."

Samuel left with Catherine's bag.

The entrance hall was high and wide and sound seemed to echo.

She whispered, "I'm nervous about meeting your mother, Patrick."

He kissed her cheek. "She's been wanting to meet you," he replied.

Catherine gave an inward groan and smoothed her dress as Patrick rapped on the parlor door to announce their arrival.

Chapter 7

Mrs. Burke was standing next to a white marble fireplace when they entered the elaborate parlor. She was an attractive woman of middle age, tall, statuesque and dressed in a flowing, rose-colored tea gown. Her coal black hair showed strands of gray.

She didn't move until Patrick guided Catherine toward her and then she came forward one step.

"Mother this is Catherine Ramsburg. Catherine, I'm happy to introduce you to my mother."

Catherine felt as though she should curtsy but that was out of the question. Extending her hand didn't seem appropriate so she gave an agreeable smile and said, "I am pleased to meet you, Mrs. Burke."

"Come and sit. I have ordered tea for us. Train rides can be so exhausting."

The room had a high ceiling with plush, light-blue, brocade drapes that hung at two floor-to-ceiling windows. Crewel patterned settees sat facing each other in front of the fireplace. Mrs. Burke chose neither. She led Catherine to an alcove containing a small marble-topped table with two blue velvet chairs. It was a cozy area in the large room.

"Will you join us Patrick?" asked his mother.

"No, I have to check in at the warehouse. I thought this a good time for you two to get acquainted."

Check the warehouse! What was Patrick thinking? Was she to be left alone with this woman to whom she had just been introduced? She'd told him she was nervous about meeting his mother. Nervous? She'd be lucky if she didn't spill her tea all over the velvet chair.

After they were seated, Patrick addressed Catherine. "I apologize for having to rush off. Polly will show you to your room when you and Mother are finished. You might want to rest a bit before we attend the program at Constitution Hall this evening."

He leaned down. She was afraid he was going to kiss her cheek so she daintily lifted a flowered handkerchief as if to stifle a sneeze.

Patrick patted her arm before he turned to leave. It may have been a reassuring touch but she could feel the burning gaze of his mother as he went out the door. Apparently, she did not approve of his small token of affection.

A melodious bell was rung by the woman of the house and a colored maid brought tea and flavored biscuits.

"I do enjoy my afternoon tea. Are you fond of tea, Catherine?"

"I am," Catherine agreed. "Sometimes a soothing cup of tea seems to solve the cares of the day."

"Tell me about your hat shop. You do have a definite talent when it comes to millinery. Do you find it difficult to be a woman on your own?" Mrs. Burke poured the tea.

"Women's independence is beginning to be a way of life," Catherine answered. "It's good to be able to support oneself for the very reason that one never knows when it might become a necessity."

Mrs. Burke took a sip of tea and offered Catherine a biscuit. "I suppose that might be the way it is for many, but, if one marries well, she need not have to work for a living. There are plenty of good works to be done. Sarah and I, that's Patrick's sister-in-law, find ourselves consumed with helping those less fortunate. I am surprised that you have not married. You are not a homely young woman. In fact, you are quite good looking in a comfortable sort of way."

Was that meant as a compliment?

Catherine was not about to tell Patrick's mother about her failed engagement. She answered, "I have never met the right person."

"I suppose that could be true in that small town you live in. Patrick has surprised me with his visits to that place."

The woman was becoming irritating. Catherine gave a syrupy smile, "I understand," she replied. "Perhaps he found it worth returning to

90

after he attended the wedding. I'm sure you recall that I repaired your hat."

Mrs. Burke sighed. "Ah, yes, the wedding. It would have been far better if his brother, Liam, had fulfilled that obligation. But, that wasn't the case. Perhaps Patrick has invited you to visit as a gesture of good will for the help you gave us. I trust you will enjoy the short time you spend with us here in the city."

Why doesn't she just come out and say I'm not welcome, thought Catherine. "Yes, short it will be. I thank you for the tea, Mrs. Burke. I believe I am ready to rest a bit."

"Of course," responded her haughty hostess. She jangled the bell once again and the maid appeared. "Polly, will you show Miss Ramsburg to her room? She desires some quiet time before dinner."

"Yes ma'am," Polly replied. Catherine followed the slender woman out of the room knowing full well she was leaving under the ever-scrutinizing eye of Patrick's mother.

Polly led her up a wide sweeping staircase to a short right turn at the top of the stairs. The large guest room faced the street where the view from the window was hampered by tall trees lining the pebbled walk.

"Miss Catherine, if there is anything you need press this button here by the bed. It buzzes in the kitchen and either me or Samuel will be right up."

"Thank you. Do I stay up here until someone comes for me?"

The maid smiled. "Oh no, ma'am. Mister Patrick said that you are to make yourself at home. He 'spects to be back around six o'clock. That's when he asked to have dinner served."

Catherine gave a weak smile. "I believe I will stay in my room until he returns."

"Yes, ma'am." answered the maid before closing the door.

Catherine's travel bag sat on a chest at the end of a four-poster canopied bed. With a heavy heart, she undid the latch on the bag. She had brought an evening dress, a day dress, a nightgown and toilet articles. The dresses she hung in a mahogany wardrobe and the rest was put into a dresser drawer.

Had Patrick told his mother that she was invited as repayment for mending the woman's hat? Mrs. Burke made it sound that way. Catherine felt deflated after meeting the uppity woman. It was obvious Patrick Burke's mother did not approve of women working. Or it could be that women who worked were below the Burkes' station in life?

Catherine wished she had followed her instincts and hopped into Herbert's car before she left Bluemont. She should have ridden right back to Berryville.

Washington, itself, with its big buildings, scurrying people and multitudinous modes of transportation had her mind swimming. But here she was, by herself, in the guest room of a great house; a guest room with a sitting area and its own toilet. She had been properly invited so she made up her mind to make the most of the time she was here. If Patrick had planned an evening at Constitution Hall, then a grand evening it would be.

Looking at her timepiece, she saw she had an hour and fifteen minutes before dinner. The day had been tiring. Catherine removed her jacket before turning down the lilac satin bedspread and lay down for a short rest.

She must have dozed off because she was awakened by a quiet tapping on the door. With a cloudy mind she left the bed and put her ear to the door. "Yes?" she asked.

In a voice above a whisper, she heard, "It's me, Patrick. May I come in?"

She opened the door a crack and whispered back, "I just woke up."

"Is that a problem?"

She rubbed her eyes and sighed. "I guess not. Come in."

Patrick closed the door with a quiet click. He smiled that broad adoring grin. "You look good with your hair mussed up."

She immediately raised her hand to refasten hairpins and while she was busy trying to tidy her errant strands, Patrick wound his arms around her and gave her a solid kiss. "I am so happy that you consented to come."

She stood back still fussing with her hair and with a sarcastic edge to her voice said, "Well, my goodness, how could I refuse such an extravagant repayment for mending your mother's hat?"

He looked puzzled. "What do you mean?"

"Never mind. I haven't recovered from a bad dream." She gave him a sweet smile. "Come and sit over here and tell me about this exciting evening you have planned."

He put his arm around her waist and kissed her forehead as they walked to the sitting area that held two comfortable stuffed chairs.

"Are you supposed to be in my room?" she asked.

"Ethically, we should be sitting with the door open, I suppose, but there's no one here but Mother and Polly. It's much more enjoyable with just the two of us."

He sat in his relaxed style with legs stretched and ankles crossed while Catherine sat forward on the edge of the seat.

"I know you enjoy concerts and we are in luck because the National symphony is at Constitution Hall. I have tickets for an evening of the three B's: Bach, Brahms and Beethoven. We'll have to get moving. Dinner will be ready at six and the taxi arrives around seven."

Her evening dress was a long, straight, teal crepe trimmed with white lace at the v-neck and three-quarter length sleeves. She rose from her chair and pulled it from the wardrobe. "Will this do?"

He took a moment to eye the dress. "You will be a hit. Do you have a warm wrap? It will be cool before we return."

"I am prepared." With a flourish, similar to a bullfighter enticing a bull, she unfolded a silk, burgundy, fringed shawl.

"Am I supposed to charge?" His wide grin showed his pleasure at her playfulness. "I believe we are going to have an evening to remember," he said as he rose from the chair. "I would much rather stay here but I have to get dressed."

Patrick was about to open the door when Catherine stayed his hand. "Tell me the truth. Is your mother in favor of me being here?"

"Why do you ask? When I told her that I had invited you for the weekend, she was looking forward to meeting you and thought it a good idea."

Catherine sighed. "I hope so. I believe your mother is much impressed by one's standing in society. I'm not sure I measure up to her standards."

"Whatever they are," he said and kissed her cheek. "You measure up to mine."

"Patrick, you do have a way of easing my worries. You will come by before dinner?"

He answered with a reassuring nod.

Once the door closed, she hurried to remove her skirt and blouse. The water left in a bowl on the dry sink was tepid so she freshened up, dabbed on some toilet water and struggled into the evening dress. Her long hair was brushed, combed and swept up on top of her head held in place with hairpins. A rhinestone necklace and earrings were put in place.

Catherine Ramsburg was ready for dinner and the evening ahead.

Patrick came to the door. He had changed into a black three-piece serge suit with a white high-collared shirt and black ascot tie. His blue eyes twinkled when he saw her. "Most appealing," he remarked.

"I could say the same," she said. "Aren't we the pair?"

"Would you care to take my arm, madam?"

With a tilt of her head and an enticing smile, she agreed, "I would be honored, sir."

Off they went in quest of the dining room.

****

Dinner was as Catherine had expected it would be: china, crystal, silver, linens and… stiff. When Mrs. Burke discovered the concert at Constitution Hall was going to be '*three of my favorite composers*', she fixed her eyes on her son. "Patrick, you should have informed me. Perhaps I could have found someone who would want to accompany me."

"I am sorry, Mother. It was an oversight on my part."

Catherine was going to suggest that she attend with them until she read Patrick's glance that said, *don't even ask.*

His mother's statement had left the visitor with an uncomfortable feeling. She did not want to be the third party that caused friction in the family. She decided to concentrate on the ham dinner Polly had prepared.

Patrick addressed his mother, "You could ask Mr. Scott. There may still be time to get tickets." His teasing eyes twinkled. "He does seem to take a fancy to you."

"Oh, Patrick, that old blowhard? I can't believe you would even propose that I appear in public with that bowl of jelly, much less do the asking. No, I'll find something here to keep my mind entertained."

"Good for you. That's the spirit I admire."

She shook her head. "Now, you sound like your father. Too much of the Irish in you."

Patrick looked over at Catherine and smiled. She averted his glance.

It was a relief when dinner ended and they left for the concert.

The taxi and its driver were the same that had brought them to the house earlier.

The hackie stood holding the door to the auto open. "Looks like a nice evening."

"That it does. Constitution Hall, please."

Catherine and Patrick climbed into the back seat once again. He held her hand as they sat close together. "I hope dinner wasn't too uncomfortable for you. My mother is good at making a person feel guilty."

"Shouldn't we have asked her to come along with us?"

"No. This is our time and I don't want to share it with anyone but you. Which brings to mind, did you tell your friend, Carolyn, you would be coming?"

"No. It all happened so fast I didn't have time. I could have telephoned from the hotel, I guess, but then the whole town would have known. I'll write her a letter of apology when I return."

"She won't be upset with you?"

"I don't think so and, if she is, it will pass. Good friends don't hold grudges."

He gave her hand a light squeeze. "I'd like to meet Carolyn."

"I would like nothing better. Perhaps one day."

Inside the large hall they were seated with a good view of the stage. Patrick was intent on reading the program while Catherine was fascinated with the dress of those attending.

He had said that she would be the hit of the night. From what she observed, she didn't rate a second glance. If Patrick was pleased, and he seemed to be, then what difference did mode of dress make?

When the crystal chandeliers dimmed, he reached for her hand. What a warm feeling she experienced with his hand holding hers and listening to the melodious sounds of classical music. People took this lavishness in stride, to Catherine, it was an evening only approached in a dream. Orchestral instruments were a distant cry from the monthly appearance of a brass band in Berryville.

The night was cool when they left the hall. Patrick laid the burgundy shawl around her shoulders as they waited for the taxi to pull up.

"What a grand performance," she said. "Its one of those happenings to store up in fond memories."

He smiled down at her. "I hope we have the opportunity to take in many more."

The closest they had to a taxi in Berryville was the long car that Herbert drove. Here there were hacks all over the city. Patrick signaled one for a ride back to the big house on K Street. "Did you know they've formed a union for taxi drivers in Chicago?"

"A union?"

"Banding together to make an impact on the owners. The rates will shoot up once it hits here in Washington."

"Is it for a good reason?" she asked.

"Everything starts for a good reason, then it gets out of hand," he answered.

When they reached his home, they made their way up the walk to the porch. A low light had been left on in the foyer and the front door was unlocked.

"May I take your shawl?"

"No, thank you. I'm comfortable with it on."

Patrick removed his outer coat and hung it on a hall tree. "How about something to eat? I'm sure Polly has left a pastry of some sort. I'm hungry. Can you use a cup of tea?"

"You seem to know me well."

"Not as well as I'd like to," he said as he brushed his finger down her cheek.

99

His suggestive answer caused her to give him a playful tap.

They started for the kitchen.

"Polly uses tea bags so we will have to forego the leaves reading ritual."

She offered a wry smile. "How unfortunate. No impromptu readings of the future? I rather liked the last one. I use tea leaves because they are less expensive than tea bags."

"The resourceful Catherine," he said.

"If I were truly resourceful, I would buy the tea bags and use them until they no longer colored the water."

"Ooh, how awful." Patrick scrunched up his nose as he placed the kettle full of water over the heat.

He lifted the handle on the icebox door and looked inside. "Apple pie. What do you say to us each having a piece?"

"If you cut the pie, I'll get the plates and forks. Just point in their direction."

The teakettle whistled and he was quick to remove it from the heat. "I don't want to wake the whole house."

They sat at a small table in the kitchen with cups of hot tea and slices of apple pie.

"I have to check in at the warehouse in the morning, but then we will have the whole day to ourselves. If you want to call your friend, perhaps we could meet up."

Catherine gave the suggestion some thought. "I don't think so Patrick. You have said that we should spend this time together and that's what I would like to do. This city has much to offer, as you've told me. I would like to see it."

"That's good news. I should return from the warehouse before noon. You can sleep in, if you'd like. Be sure and wear your walking shoes," he cautioned.

They finished the pie and drained the cups of tea.

"I'll leave these dishes in the sink for Polly to clean in the morning," he said.

"Patrick, I am not used to having a maid clean up after me and no one likes to wash dirty dishes that have been sitting around all night."

She laid her shawl on the back of the chair and shoved her sleeves above the elbows. "You wipe and I'll wash. We can use the hot water in the kettle."

"You win," he answered. He tied an apron around her waist. "You don't want to soil your lovely dress." But, when he finished tying the apron strings, he put his arms around her waist and began kissing her neck. She stood stock still until the unexpected tingling subsided.

"How am I supposed to keep my mind on washing dishes?"

He kept his arms around her and murmured in her ear, "What are we going to do about our situation?"

She didn't dare turn to face him. "Our situation? You mean about living seventy miles apart?"

"Exactly."

"Distance isn't the only bridge to be crossed. What does your mother think about you going back to medical school?"

He stepped back and picked up the drying towel. "I haven't told her."

Catherine put the plates into the dishwater. "Have you discussed this with your brother?"

"I plan on doing that when he gets back. I didn't want to spoil his trip nor did I want anything to get in the way of your visit."

"That was thoughtful."

She rinsed and placed the dishes on the drain board.

He stacked the ones he'd dried. "Doesn't it bother you that we can't spend more time together?"

She dried her hands and untied the apron. "We don't always get what we want in this life."

"What made you decide to come this weekend? I know you had to make some fast arrangements." He stood with his lower back resting against a counter in that easy manner of his with the dish towel draped over his shoulder.

"I assume you're looking for an honest answer."

"That's preferable."

She chose her words. "Two reasons: I wanted a change and I wanted to see you."

He raised his index finger. "Very good. Which one took precedence?"

Catherine picked up the silverware to put it in its rightful place. "Well…that's difficult to answer. What would you have me say?"

He laughed. "Catherine, are we playing a cat and mouse game?"

She offered a smug smile. "I don't know about you but I'm tired. If tomorrow is going to be another busy day, then I am all for retiring."

"Which means that you are ending this discussion," he said as he came to her side. "We might as well call it a night."

She looped her arm through his, "Let's call it the end of a perfect evening."

They went up the wide sweeping staircase. Patrick left Catherine at her door with an amorous kiss and a wish for a restful night's sleep before turning to go to his room.

She draped her clothes over chairs and changed into her nightgown. The evening had been more than she imagined. They had one more day to spend together and she would do her best to make it a happy one.

****

In the morning, Catherine was dressed and sitting in one of the comfortable chairs wondering if she should go downstairs. Polly wrapped on her door before bringing in a breakfast tray.

"Mister Patrick has gone to the warehouse. He asked that I bring your breakfast to your room. He will be back around eleven."

Catherine glanced at her clock. She had another two hours.

"Thank you for bringing up the food. I believe I'll go out for a walk after I eat."

"Yes, ma'am," Polly acknowledged and left the room.

Catherine found she didn't have an appetite. She ate the boiled egg and half a piece of toast and drank a cup of tea. She wasn't comfortable in this house without Patrick being here. It would be good to get some fresh air and walk the grounds.

She left the tray in her room and went down the front stairs. The day was cool so she set a fast pace to keep warm. The grounds were well landscaped. She wound her way through a boxwood garden, threw some pebbles into a small pond to watch the water ripple, and imagined the gardens alive with color during the warm months. But, this grand show was not for her. The backyard of her place in Berryville gave her all the comfort she needed. She pictured her gazebo in her mind and it brought an instant smile.

When she returned to the house, Polly was waiting in the foyer. "The Missus would like to speak with you, Miz' Catherine." It was the first time Polly had called her by name. If there was meaning to it, she wasn't sure why.

Mrs. Burke sat in on one of the crewel settees in the parlor. "Polly said that you were out for a walk. Did you enjoy the grounds?"

"Yes, they are lovely."

"Have a seat, Catherine. I have a question I would like to have answered."

Unsure and uncomfortable her knees shook. She was relieved to take a seat opposite Patrick's mother.

"It hasn't escaped me that Patrick has been making visits to your place because he is infatuated with something he finds there. What are your intentions toward him?"

Her words were like a dart between the eyes. Catherine squirmed in her seat and cleared her head before she spoke in a clipped, controlled tone, "Patrick and I enjoy each other's company. Mrs. Burke, if you think there is something objectionable going on when he comes to visit you may rest assured that he is a gentleman. I have a reputation to uphold."

The woman gave a wan smile. "That was not my concern. You must see that our lives here are very different from the way you live. We must maintain our stature in the community and I have hopes that Patrick will form a union with someone within our circle. You do understand what I'm saying."

Catherine did all she could to hold her tongue and sat silent until she felt in control. She rose from the settee in a dignified manner. "I don't know how you could make it any clearer. I am well aware of the different lives we lead. Patrick has promised me a day of seeing the sights of Washington and that's what I plan on doing. I will make it a pleasant day for both of us. You will not have to worry about me returning to Washington or this house once I leave on the train tomorrow."

The woman sagged in relief. "If we can keep this conversation between the two of us, I would be grateful."

"Of course you would. Mrs. Burke, you are a devious woman. To allay your fears, I will tell you that your words are safe with me because I do not wish to cause Patrick any distress. He has enough to contend with." Catherine turned on her heel and left the room.

****

Patrick returned at eleven as he had said. Catherine was in the guest room sitting in one of the easy chairs.

He knocked on the door. "It's Patrick."

"Come in."

He came in, pulled her to her feet and gave her a robust kiss. "I hope you've got your walking shoes on because we're going to the Smithsonian."

"I've already been out for a walk but I look forward to another foray into the chill."

"We can take a taxi," he offered.

"No. I am ready for a long walk."

They left the big house on foot. A few blocks away they began to pass the tall government buildings. One building was twelve stories high.

She remarked, "I can't imagine waking up in this city every day. Even though I don't like the smell of the city, I do enjoy seeing all the people bustling here and there. The trolleys take some getting used to. I feel like I'm taking my life in my hands trying to cross the rails."

"It's a good way to travel," said Patrick. "Once you get used to them you can cross the city for less than it costs for a taxi. When they form that union, I'll bet more people will opt for the trolleys."

They crossed a large grassy mall with the Smithsonian looming before them.

Catherine was in awe. "It looks like a castle."

"Wait until you see the treasures it holds," he said. "We can spend our whole day in here."

****

It was late afternoon when they left the Smithsonian. Patrick hailed a cab.

"We're going to a French restaurant for dinner and it's too far to walk."

"Good," she agreed. "My shoes are pinching." She leaned on his arm. "I guess it's out of the question for me to walk shoeless."

He laughed. "I'll rub your feet when we get in the taxi."

"How tempting. I shall have to pass."

It was a relief to sit in the back of the hack even though it was noisy and rattled down the street.

"Patrick, I think I could spend days inside the museum. What a wealth of information."

He took her hand. "Next time you come, we'll do it again."

She didn't reply.

The restaurant was cozy and romantic. Patrick ordered for her from the menu because she

107

couldn't pronounce the French words. Trying to read by candlelight was also a hindrance.

"Just order me something that tastes good."

The waiter brought a bottle of wine to the table allowing Patrick a taste before he gave permission to fill their glasses.

Catherine's meal was set before her by the formal waiter. "Patrick, it looks delicious. What is it?"

"I'll tell you after you've eaten."

She had drank a glass of wine on an empty stomach and felt giddy. "I'm so hungry for food, I think I can eat anyzing." She laughed, correcting her word. "Anything. I don't think it was wise to drink that wine before I ate."

"Dig in," Patrick advised.

His meal was different. "Would you like a taste of mine?" He asked.

"Sure," she answered. "Throw a spoonful on my plate."

He laughed." Methinks the wine has had an effect."

"She pointed her fork at him. "Methinks you are right. I'd like another glass."

"I'm not sure that would be prudent."

The confrontation with Patrick's mother popped into her mind. "Prudent can be tossed out the window. I think it is just what I need."

When they left the restaurant, Patrick flagged down a hack. He steadied her as she got up on the running board before flopping onto the back seat.

"Catherine, you're tipsy."

She snuggled close to him. "You never told me what we ate. Patrick. The small bite I had of yours was good and mine was delicious."

"Are you ready?" he asked.

She giggled. "I wouldn't ask if I wasn't."

"I had eel and you had snails."

"Egads!" she shrieked causing the driver to jump in his seat.

"No problem," assured Patrick. "I just suggested that we might take a swim in the Potomac."

The hackie shrugged his shoulders. "A mite cold for that this time of year."

Catherine put her gloved hand before her mouth to stifle her giggles. "Patrick, you were right," she whispered. "I shouldn't have had that second glass of wine."

The hackie received a handsome tip when the happy couple got out at the big house on K Street.

It was late and the house was quiet. Patrick kept his voice low, "I think it best if we go on upstairs. You have an early train. Do you feel all right?"

"Patrick, I feel so good. Come upstairs and let's sit in my room for a while."

"Are you sure?"

"This is our last night together and I want it to be as wonderful as you are."

"Don't make it sound so final," he replied.

****

Catherine had not slept well. She looked in the mirror and saw dark circles under her eyes. The two glasses of wine had been a poor choice. She held a cold washcloth to her forehead to relieve some of the hurt in her head. It helped a bit. She dressed and dabbed at her face with a powder puff.

The train to Berryville was scheduled to leave at ten o'clock.

Catherine checked to be sure she had packed everything she had brought. She pulled bedclothes up to make the room look presentable, although Polly would have to wash the sheets. It is a pleasant room, she thought as she took it in once more. The rest of the house was too big and uninviting, or was it just Patrick's mother who cast a cloud over the place?

The door to the room was open when Patrick came by. "Polly has breakfast ready for us. I'll have Samuel take your bag to the taxi when it arrives."

She looped her arm through his, enjoying the closeness. They headed for the stairs. "It has been a wonderful weekend, Patrick. I'm happy I came."

"I wish we'd had more time, but we will plan your next trip so it will not be so hurried."

She offered a weak smile. She didn't have the heart to tell him there would not be a next time.

Chapter 8

The train was on time. At the last minute, as Catherine mounted the iron steps, Patrick slipped something into her large pocketbook. "Don't open it until you get back home," he cautioned.

The seventy miles that separated Catherine Ramsburg from Washington, D.C. and Patrick Burke might as well have been the other side of the world. She waved to him. As the train pulled out of the Alexandria station she kept a stiff upper lip. His smiling face and the feel of his last kiss would stay with her forever.

Catherine paid no attention to the passengers in the train car or the scenery outside. Her mind was on the conversation she had had with Patrick's mother. It was cleat that Mrs. Burke did not hold her in high regard. This trip to Washington opened her eyes to the difference in the lives she and Patrick led.

Catherine had let her heart run away and now she would pay for it. How could she have allowed herself to get so carried away? She should have had the good sense to decline when he first asked to come to see her. But Patrick was so unlike anyone she had ever met: kind, witty, caring. She could go on and on in her mind. This wonderful weekend would remain as a gratifying memory and she would have to be content with that.

As the train chugged west, Catherine fumbled around in her purse for a handkerchief to wipe the tears she had fought so hard to keep from spilling over. In her unhappy state, the trip back seemed an eternity.

It was damp and cold when she departed the train at Bluemont. Inside the small station there was a wood-burning pot-bellied stove that warmed the interior. She was so dispirited she thought she would never feel warm again.

"Evenin' ma'am." said the station keeper. He was the same burly man she had met when she left on Friday. Was that only two days ago?

"Did you have a good trip to the city?"

She nodded. "I did."

"Herbert should be here soon. I'll bet you're tired. Got a message a car jumped the track and that's what put you way behind. She hadn't noticed.

Catherine took a seat near the stove. Fifteen minutes later the noisy, long car arrived. She picked up her travel bag and took it to the car.

"Hello, Miz' Catherine. Train's late. 'Spected it a few hours ago. People have been inquirin' as to if you're all right. Not used to not seein' you in the hat shop. There's only three of us goin' back to Berryville so you can put your bag on the seat next to you."

Catherine got into the long car and did as Herbert suggested. She was glad not to have to sit next to anyone as she didn't feel like talking.

The car with its dim headlights started the climb out of Bluemont to rattle back down the mountain. The late afternoon was cold and misty similar to her inner mood.

It was getting dark when they reached town. Herbert pulled over to the side of the street opposite the hotel. He helped Catherine from the car. "Watch your step goin' across the street. There's probably mud puddles. These gas lights ain't much for seein' to cross the street."

"Thank you," Catherine said. She picked up her bag and gathered the skirt of her copper travel suit in one hand before she ventured across to her place.

She pulled the key from her pocketbook only to discover that it was wound in the unfinished doily she had intended to give to Mrs. Burke. After meeting the woman and seeing the opulence of the K Street house, Catherine decided the doily was a trivial offering so it remained unfinished. Good manners dictated a note of thanks, which she would write. Thanks for what, she wondered. For the proud Mrs. Burke stating so bluntly that Catherine was no match for Patrick?

Irritating as it was, she managed to untwist the key from the tangled crochet thread and opened the door. She fumbled around to find the light switch in the foyer. Once she flipped it on it cast a grey ray of light matching her dismal mood.

Where was the joy of returning? This had been her home since she was born yet it seemed cold and unwelcoming. Catherine dragged herself up the staircase feeling the heaviness of her body as she went step by step. She would brew some tea and that would improve her mood…or would it?

Into her bedroom she took her travel bag and decided to change into her nightgown and robe. The apartment was cold but she was too tired to start a fire in the fireplace. If she had ever been so down in the mouth, she couldn't recall. She would have to be content with a cup of tea, and then, she would pour out her heart in a letter to her friend, Carolyn.

October 29, 1915

Dear Carolyn,

How I wish that you were sitting across from me at my kitchen table. I have just been through two of the happiest and saddest days of my life.

First, I must apologize to you for not letting you know that I was in Washington over the weekend. It was a quick decision on my part and I didn't have time to write. Yes, I could have telephoned, but you know how it is when conversations get carried over public lines. The town gets enough gossip without me feeding into it. Can you imagine what it would be if Lavinia were a telephone operator? The lines would probably burn up.

To get to the reason for this letter, you know how I have written so many letters about Patrick and how I was becoming concerned about my feelings for him. This weekend his brother was out of the city for an extended time for personal and business reasons and Patrick had to oversee the warehouse. He invited me to visit Washington. I made hasty arrangements leaving Mary Lee to tend the shop and followed my heart, not my head.

The time I spent with Patrick was pure rapture. He showed me as many sights as we could take in and I understand why you are so fond of the city. You are the adventurous one. It is not for me. I have the security of the hat shop and, although I say that I tire of this small town, I like the comfort of knowing what to expect. I cannot see myself living anywhere else.

Those words bring me to my decision. I will write to Patrick, thank him for the times we have had and break off any further contact so that I don't allow my feelings for him to overtake my good sense.

So, if I have made this decision, why am I writing to you? I guess that I seek your advice whether I am doing the right thing. Isn't that a turn-around? In all honesty, I have never felt so confused.

A conversation I had with his mother is too difficult to write in this letter. That's why I wish that you were here in person. It is so much easier to thrash concerns out face to face than to put them into a letter.

As you can tell, I am at low ebb. I can already read the puzzlement on your face. You will say this is not the sensible and confident Catherine you know so well. And, maybe in the morning I will change my mind and toss this letter into the *wastebasket. Who knows? Life will go on and so will I.*

I trust that all is going well with you. Give Asa my best regards.

Most sincerely,
Catherine

She folded the sheet of stationery, sealed the envelope, and pasted on the stamp. It would go out in the morning post.

After finishing the tea and tidying up the kitchen, Catherine snapped off the light. Her pocketbook was on the table in the hallway. Inside was the present Patrick had slipped into her purse with the instruction of not to open it until she got home. She picked up the pocketbook and carried it into the bedroom.

After stepping up onto the foot stool and climbing onto the bed, she pulled the present from her pocketbook. The package was wrapped in flowered paper and a bright blue ribbon. She undid the wrapping and opened the lid of the box. Inside was a lovely brooch. The brooch was silver with the silhouette of a lady wearing a fashionable hat. It brought tears to her eyes. Then she read the small note tucked under the pin:

My dear Catherine,

When I saw this pin in the jeweler's window, I knew it was meant for you. To have you here pleased me more than I can say.

All my love,
Patrick

And now she cried. Her body shook and tears blurred her vision so that she could not see to place the brooch back into its box so she set it on the little table next to her bed. The room felt as cold as her heart. She was worn out. Catherine lay in the dark of her bedroom allowing her unhappiness to drain out in big sobs until she drifted off to sleep.

****

The next morning her eyes were still puffy but she felt better. The apartment was colder than it had been the night before. Bundled in her chenille robe, she went down to the back porch and pulled some wood from the pile.

Back upstairs she lit the kindling and waited until it flamed enough to support a fat log.

After Catherine dressed, she made the bed and straightened up the room. She didn't want to look at the pin Patrick had given her, although it seemed to call to her from the bedside table where she had placed it. She picked it up and ran her fingers across the face visualizing his smile. How pleased he must have been when he bought what he considered the perfect gift. With a lump in her throat, she tenderly placed the brooch back into the fancy jeweler's box. Later in the day, she would wrap it and return it to Patrick with a letter of goodbye. Life had become so difficult!

Perhaps she could tackle that chore of writing the letter when Mary Lee arrived. The milliner knew Mary Lee would come because she would be overly concerned that all was well in the shop. That was just the way it was with Mary Lee.

After breakfast of tea and an apple, Catherine went down to the shop. It was orderly as she knew it would be. The cash box and receipts were stashed on the bottom shelf behind the work counter, hidden by two bolts of material. Catherine pulled the box out of its hiding place and opened the lid. Surprise. It appeared she wouldn't have to pull from her savings to pay Mary Lee after all. With the receipts of the sales of hats, gloves and scarves, she counted twenty-eight dollars and thirty-two cents. It had been a busy day and a half.

Mary Lee hurried into the shop at nine o'clock. "Miz' Catherine, am I glad to see you back! Maybe the colder weather brought people in, I don't know, but I was right busy. You know how I get flustered. Did I do everythin' right? Lord, I hope so."

Catherine smiled at the anxious young woman standing before her. "I knew you were busy because I counted the receipts in the cash box. Everything is in order and the shop is neater than when I left it. I thank you."

"How was your trip? Are you glad you went? Someday maybe I can go to Washington. I ain't never been to a big place."

Catherine offered, "Can you use a cup of tea while I tell you about it? Then you can fill me in on what went on in my absence."

"How about if I fix it? I cain't sit around." Before Catherine could answer, Mary Lee was on her way to the back room. The feeling in the shop had been elevated with the infusion of this kind girl's energy.

They had just settled down to drink their tea when the narrow door opened and Lavinia squeezed herself in.

"Catherine. The whole town was worried about you. It isn't like you to leave your shop. I do hope it wasn't bad news that drew you away." This meant that Lavinia was fishing for the reason for Catherine's absence.

"No, Mrs. Talley, it was a pleasure trip after a quick decision to visit friends."

"Friends?" The nosy neighbor gave a wry look. "I trust that if you met up with Mr. Burke you were properly chaperoned. You know how stories get around."

"Ah yes. I am well aware of that." Catherine bent the truth to her liking. "Mrs. Burke invited me to their lovely home. I assume it was repayment for assisting when she came for the wedding."

Lavinia cast a wary eye. "It had nothing to do with her son's visits out here?"

"Of course I saw Patrick and he showed me the sights of the city."

"That sounds harmless enough. I found it hard to believe that you would just take off on a whim. And, you left poor little Mary Lee, here, to take care of the hat shop. I did question your good sense, Catherine."

Poor little Mary Lee's face turned beet red and Catherine was afraid she was going to let her temper rule her mouth, so she said, "Mrs. Talley, Mary Lee is quite capable of taking care of this shop. You may alleviate everyone's concern that I was properly chaperoned."

Lavinia's eyes lit up in her round chubby face. She had the news straight from the horse's mouth. The tone of her voice changed. "Of course, Catherine, you must understand that I was worried about you. You will have to tell me about your trip. Perhaps Jeremy could put an item in the *Courier*. But for now I must be off and let you girls get back to your tasks."

As soon as she edged out the door, Mary Lee exploded. "That ol' busybody! Why'd you have to tell her why you went away? You know that she's just goin' to blab to everyone she sees. I was so mad at her…look what she made me do." A wrinkled and frayed piece of expensive silk dropped from her hand. "I was goin' to make this into a fancy rose."

Catherine laughed. "Its fancy all right. If it was a chicken, you would have wrung its neck."

"I'm sorry. I'll pay for the piece I ruined."

"No. It was an accident and you have no idea how I needed a good laugh. Let's brew another cup of tea and forget the hat business while I tell you about the wonders I saw in the city."

****

It was around noon when Catherine asked Mary Lee if she would watch the shop as she had a chore to finish. Mary Lee agreed. Catherine went up to her apartment to compose the dreaded letter.

October 30, 1915

Dear Patrick,

I wanted you to know that I am back in Berryville without incident. It pleases me to report that Mary Lee did a fine job of running the place in my absence. I will not say it was a joyous return after the grand time we spent together but this is my home.

I am finding this letter so difficult to write that I have decided I must state my reason for writing as quickly as I can.

Patrick, I did much soul searching while I was on the train. The visit to Washington served to solidify my fears that we live two very different lives. So different that, although I care deeply for you, I cannot see a future together. Rather than keep hoping that circumstances can change, it is obvious they cannot.

Once you are out of medical school, you will have a full life ahead of you and, perhaps, find someone who fits into the more sophisticated ways of the city.

I am returning the beautiful brooch you so thoughtfully gave to me. If I kept it, it would only serve to remind me of you and my heart would break each time I touched it.

Millie Curtis

Thank you for bringing a ray of sunshine to my life. I wish you much happiness in the future.

Sincerely,
Catherine

She folded the letter with care and placed it in an envelope. In a larger box, she put both the letter and the brooch and sealed it. Catherine threw on a shawl before carrying the package to the post office. When the clerk took the package from her hand it felt like a curtain closing the final act of a play. With a heavy heart, the milliner returned to her lonely hat shop on the main street of Berryville.

Chapter 9

In the warehouse in Georgetown, Patrick's disillusionment, when he received the pin Catherine had returned, made him irritable. His unpleasantness spilled out onto his co-workers, and it was his brother, Liam, who had to confront him. He stepped into Patrick's office unannounced. Patrick hesitated before he looked up from his ledger.

"What do you need, Liam?"

"Patrick, I know you're the senior partner, but we need to have a brotherly chat. I just saw Jonas down in shipping. He said that you nearly tore his head off because an order had gone awry. He's not the only one who has approached me. Your secretary, Miss McKay, is jumpy as a cat."

"You know I don't tolerate sloppy work, Liam."

"Mistakes happen, Patrick, especially when we're pushed for the holidays. That's not the root of the problem. Mother says you've been a bear at home. I suspect it's whatever happened while I was away. She told me your friend, Catherine, had visited. There's something eating at you and you'd better get it straightened out. We can't afford to lose good workers." Liam started for the door.

Patrick was irritated by the abruptness of his brother's accusation, but he also knew he was right. They needed to talk. "Wait, Liam. Come back and have a seat. It's true. I haven't been myself, and I guess I've hit a low in the tolerance department. Perhaps I have been taking it out on the help."

Liam settled his athletic frame. Leaning back in the chair and crossing his long legs, he said, "I'm listening."

"I gave Catherine a gift the morning she left. She sent it back in the mail over a week ago. She's written me off, Liam. I received the pin with a note of a kindly thank-you, I had a wonderful time, good-bye."

"Not the usual way ladies respond to you, is it?" Liam's face held a half-smile.

"Don't let that smile widen any farther, Liam. I feel like punching something."

"I can't help it. Could it be that Patrick Burke has been hooked? Not that you've ever been a ladies' man. There are plenty who consider you a good catch." Liam's smile spread into a wide grin. "What are you going to do about it?"

"I mailed the pin back to her. If that's the way she feels, there's not much else I can do to change her mind." Patrick got up from his desk chair and went to look out the grimy window overlooking the Potomac River. "She says our worlds are too far apart. What she means by that, I'm not quite sure. She didn't elaborate."

"She must have passed mother's inspection. I didn't hear anything derogatory, which is a feather in her cap or should I say hat?" He chuckled at his own play on words.

Patrick turned his head and glowered at Liam over his shoulder, "That's not funny."

Liam ignored the scowl. "You probably overwhelmed her. I'm sure Washington is a far cry from what she is used to in that little town she comes from. Most likely it was a difficult weekend for her. I doubt she would have come if she didn't have some kind of feelings for you. Mother did say she wishes she was more like Sarah."

Patrick turned from the window and perched on the edge of the desk. "That's what I find refreshing. She isn't like the finishing school type. She's her own woman. If the fireplace went cold, she wouldn't go looking for a servant to start it. So what's your advice, little brother, now that you're a man of the world?"

Liam uncrossed his legs and rose from the chair. "If you feel about Catherine as I feel about Sarah, I wouldn't let her get away."

Patrick rose and extended his hand. Liam grasped it with both of his, "Don't make a big mistake."

Patrick returned to his seat as the door closed behind his brother. He pulled the weighty ledger in front of him and attempted to settle his mind back into the day's business.

****

On the first day of December, Lloyd Pierce, the postman, pulled a small package from his bag as he entered the millinery shop. "Came in from Washington this morning. Must be someone's thinking of you at Christmas," he grinned.

"Probably my friend, Carolyn. She wouldn't let me down at Christmas."

"Maybe that fella' who was out here courtin'."

His wink caused a nonchalant raise of Catherine's eyebrow. "Do mailmen always think they know what's going on?" she asked.

"Now, Miz' Catherine, you know the return address is in plain sight." He was slightly apologetic. "Anyway, I hope it is cause you and him made a nice lookin' couple."

"Appearance isn't everything," she answered, as she accepted the proffered package.

No sooner had Lloyd Pierce left the shop than Lavinia Talley waddled in. They must have crossed in the street. It wasn't like Lavinia to be absent when the daily mail arrived. Catherine hid the package under a large scrap of material.

"My goodness, Catherine. I've been so busy decorating for Christmas I haven't had a chance to stop by."

"It's nice to see you, Mrs. Talley," came her tongue-in-cheek greeting.

Lavinia was known to prattle on incessantly. "Catherine, you must come over and see the tree. I'll have it up by the end of the week and it will look so impressive with the new glass bulbs I ordered through the catalog. Lloyd delivered them over a week ago and not a one was broken. They came all the way from Germany."

"I'm sure they are beautiful. Thank you for asking. I'd like to come by. Your house always looks so festive." If there was anything Lavinia liked, it was praise.

She twittered as she fingered some material on the counter, "I haven't seen your young man in a few weeks. In fact, not since you returned from the city."

"He is not my young man. He is a friend." Catherine continued to work on a hat she was trimming, avoiding Lavinia's nosiness.

"Yes, well he seemed to be quite taken with you. Catherine. It isn't everyday that a dashing young man comes into our town. Everyone assumed he must be a romantic interest."

"Never assume, Mrs. Talley."

Lavinia hesitated for a moment. Catherine glanced up from her work with a look seeming to dare the woman to ask another question regarding Patrick.

Lavinia changed her mode of questioning. "Can we plan on you coming over on Christmas Eve after church services? We'll have a nice cup of warm nog."

"I would enjoy that." Catherine gave Lavinia a slight smile, which served to smooth out some of the tension she felt building within.

"Oh good, Jeremy and I will look forward to your coming. I thought I would also invite Reverend Smythe and his wife."

"It sounds like a lovely evening," said Catherine.

Lavinia left and Catherine pulled the package from its hiding place. It was, indeed, from

Patrick. She was a bundle of nerves as she opened it. Inside was the box containing the brooch she had returned, along with a note, *"This was meant for you, Patrick.*

The terseness of the message gave her a start, followed by the realization as to how deeply she had wounded him by returning the pin. It stabbed her with a fresh jolt of guilt.

Now she had the tangible and the intangible as reminders of what might have been. The beautiful pin and the wonderful memories would be enough to give her solace, but not until she'd had a good cry!

Chapter 10

Christmas Day arrived with a slight trace of snow and flakes still falling. Catherine had done her duty by having a cup of nog with Jeremy and Lavinia Talley after church services the night before.

Jeremy had said that he wanted to put a short article in the newspaper about her trip to Washington, but Catherine declined.

"We like to put the social news in the *Courier*." At least he hadn't begged.

Lavinia, on the other hand, had drawled her very best whine, "Catherine, are you sure? It is exciting news. You never go away. It will explain your absence."

Catherine hadn't backed down.

"It's been a few weeks, Mr. Talley; hardly current news," she had said with finality.

This afternoon Catherine had promised to have an early Christmas dinner with the Barber sisters. They were sweet, elderly spinsters from her church. It was kind of them to ask her, whether out of pity or not, and she did enjoy their company. A twenty-five-year-old spending the holiday with spinsters was not the Christmas of her dreams. To top that, she'd spent Christmas Eve with the Talleys, and the minister and his wife. Catherine cringed at the thought of the stagnant life she saw looming before her. If that was the way it was going to be, she might as well get used to it. She'd had her fling and it hadn't worked out.

Dinner at the Barber house was scheduled for three. Leaving her apartment at two o'clock meant she could walk the few blocks to their home, chat a bit before dinner, and still get home by four-thirty. At this time of year it was getting dark around five o'clock. It always gave her an eerie feeling if she got caught out in the dark, besides the fact that proper ladies did not walk the street in the evenings.

Promptly at two o'clock, she pulled on her galoshes, and checked once more to be sure she had her door key before she pressed the button on the old mortise lock on her front door.

The air was cool, but it had a dry, crisp feel despite the smattering of snowflakes that continued. Bundled into her black wool coat with the fur collar, she pushed both hands into a fur muff and headed for the Barber house. On her arm she carried a canvas bag that held two small gifts of dusting powder for the ladies: violet scented for Jane and rose scented for Betty.

She climbed the steep steps leading up to the front porch of their house. Before she could lift the large, pineapple-shaped doorknocker, the door opened.

"Catherine, we've been watching for you, Merry Christmas." Betty was the more talkative of the two quiet southern ladies.

Catherine greeted them warmly with an affectionate hug after she stepped inside.

"We were afraid that you might not come because of the snow. Rebecca has left such a lovely dinner of turkey and dressing. She cooked it up yesterday before she left and said we need only to heat it up."

Catherine unbuckled her overshoes and hung her coat on the coat tree.

The little ladies looked at each other. Jane nodded to Betty and she again spoke for them both, "We thought you might help us with that chore. We're not familiar with running the stove."

"I'll be happy to help," replied Catherine, which brought a look of relief to their pinched faces.

Catherine removed her outerwear before firing up the oven. Rebecca, their weekly housekeeper, had left the carved turkey meat, mashed potatoes, gravy, dressing and glazed carrots in individual dishes so that Catherine had only to pop them into the oven for warming.

"It will take a few minutes for them to heat up." She smiled at Betty and Jane as she closed the oven door.

Catherine expected they might clap their hands; they were so delighted.

"Let's go into the parlor and sit for a spell," said Jane. "We do have a lovely, toasty fire going."

Catherine followed them in toting the canvas bag. After taking a comfortable chair by the warm fire, she offered the gifts she had brought each of them. Their faces lit up when they saw the festive packages wrapped in gold satin material and tied with red velvet ribbon.

"Oh, my goodness, Catherine, they are too pretty to open," murmured Jane in her soft, dignified voice. She turned to Betty, "Sister, will you be so kind as to get the gift we have for Catherine and we will all open our presents together."

Betty hobbled out of the room and returned with a large box. Catherine felt a bit sheepish when she saw the the size of the present. It dwarfed the small packages she had given.

"We shall open them all at once." Betty was like a child with her enthusiasm.

The ladies neatly unwrapped their dusting powders exclaiming at the flowered boxes that held the talcum powder and how the scents were their favorites. Catherine was astounded as she pulled a beautiful, royal blue, knitted cape with tasseled trim out of the box.

"Try it on, Catherine, we knitted it ourselves, just for you." And, this time they did clap their hands in sheer joy as Catherine modeled their creation.

She kissed the cheeks of each. "It is the most beautiful piece of clothing I have ever owned. It must have taken you a year to knit it."

"Not quite a year, was it Jane?"

Jane smiled. "Eleven months, two weeks and two days. We were worried that we wouldn't finish it in time for Christmas."

"This calls for dancing," said Catherine. They held hands as they circled around the parlor.

Dinner was delicious and Catherine was a few minutes late in leaving after she helped the ladies clean up. If she hurried, she would make it to her door a bit after five. The Barber sisters had insisted that she take some of the coconut cake Rebecca had made for their dessert. It was a three layer cake, light and fluffy, decorated with red and green icing to look like holly. At their insistence, Catherine accepted it. The sisters found a box that they thought would be 'just the thing' to carry it in. Catherine had her misgivings as to whether it would survive the walk home, but she placed the boxed piece of cake in the canvas bag she carried. She gave them each a hug before she left and started on her way with a Christmas feeling in her heart.

Galumph, galumph went her galoshes as she walked along. The snow had turned to sleet. In the quietness of the evening, the only sounds were the plodding of her galoshes and the scrunch of the snow beneath her feet.

When she rounded the corner at Church and Main Streets, she fumbled in her handbag to pull out her door key. Looking up, she stopped at the sight of someone standing on her stoop. Her heart started to race. There were rough characters that came into town on the weekends to frequent the taverns. But, it was Christmas Day and none of the taverns were open.

A light from the inside of the Berryville Hotel cast a dim glow. She could duck in and ask the desk clerk to accompany her to her door. That wasn't necessary because as she stepped closer she knew from the stance and dress of the shadowed figure who he was. Her heart pounded with a fury that frightened her.

He waited until she came to the steps, "Hello, Catherine."

Choked with emotion she could hardly say his name. The duskiness of the evening became her friend so he couldn't see the upset she knew was written on her face. Her hands shook as she fumbled with the key.

"May I help you with that?" he asked. Without waiting for an answer, he took the key from her hand and turned it in the lock.

The tenseness of the moment had given her time to regain her poise. She stepped into the foyer and turned to face him as he waited to be asked to enter. "I think it goes without saying you more than surprised me, Patrick."

"May I come in?" he asked.

"Of course you may come in."

He placed his hat on the stand, hung his overcoat on the hall tree, and removed his overshoes, just as though he did it every day.

"I'm sure you have a warm cup of tea, I could use some. It got a bit chilly waiting on your stoop. You've told me that you are never away overnight and you like to be home before dark. So, I took the chance on your return."

There didn't seem to be anger under his easy manner. Why had he come? Thoughts ran through her mind with lightning speed. She hurried up the stairs ahead of him and said, over her shoulder, "It will only take a few minutes to make some tea. I'll join you in the living room. You can stoke up the fire and warm yourself. It may need another log."

Patrick went into the living room as Catherine went to the kitchen. Her mind churned. How had he gotten here? Perhaps the trains were running, but she knew Herbert was not going to take the passenger car over the mountain. He'd said so himself. Her Christmas had crumbled in the matter of a few minutes.

As she busied herself with making the tea, she heard Patrick come to the kitchen doorway and felt his eyes follow her as she moved about the stove.

"Aren't you interested in why I'm here?" he asked, in that deep baritone voice she loved so well.

Catherine kept her back to him, "I couldn't very well say I'm not curious, now, could I?"

He came and turned her to meet his eyes. "I want you to tell me face to face, not in some cutting letter you've written, that you never want to see me again. And, if you do, I promise that I will walk right out of your life."

Did he not understand? "Don't you know how difficult it was for me to write that letter? No, I can't tell you to get out of my life, as much as I want to, because it wouldn't be the truth. Furthermore, you have so upended my life that you will always be a part of it, whether I choose it that way or not!"

He stiffened at her response and hesitated before his face relaxed. "I'm glad we got that over with." He smiled. "We have much to talk about." He didn't touch her, although she wanted him to. He turned and went back to the living room.

Catherine stood there trying to collect her senses. How could he be so calm? It took her a few seconds before she recalled what she was doing. Tea…tea. What could she serve with it? She flitted about like a butterfly. Then she remembered the coconut cake. She had been in such a dither with Patrick showing up, she had tossed the canvas bag on the kitchen table. Almost afraid to open the box that held the cake, she peeked in and found just what she had suspected. The cake was a mess! Beautiful coconut frosting was mashed to the sides of the box the red and green holly decorations looking like a squashed rainbow. It didn't look fit to serve but there was nothing else. Catherine scraped the frosting from the inside of the box and spread it over the cake the best she could. Irritation was building and she wasn't sure if it was with herself or Patrick. He had no right to come and upset her life, especially on Christmas day. The more she thought about it the more irritated she became. She piled the lumpy cake onto two dessert plates, placed two forks on the tray, and headed for the dining room. Laying the tea on the table, she announced that tea was being served.

Patrick entered the room. If he was surprised when his eyes caught the jumble of cake, he gave no expression.

"You will have to excuse the appearance of the dessert. It rather matches the way my day has turned out."

He let out a belly laugh. "If I'm that much of an influence, I'm delighted," he said.

He held her chair while she took her place. He sat opposite and watched as she poured the tea using both hands to steady the handle of the teapot.

"I suspect you're a bit upset with me." He placed a linen napkin across his lap.

Catherine took a sip from her teacup and looked across the table at him. Her tone was caustic. "Why Patrick, should I be? I have almost been contented to settle back into my daily routine, and here you are to roughen the edges once again. It seems natural that I might be upset."

"Let's talk about that letter. Perhaps I'm the one who should be disgruntled." He was serious. "What exactly did you mean our worlds are so far apart we have no future?"

Catherine took sip of tea before she responded, "I would have thought it was perfectly obvious when I visited. A voluminous house on K Street is a bit more opulent than this upstairs apartment above my hat shop."

"If where you live had been a problem for me, I wouldn't have returned."

"I wasn't prepared for such a contrast. Although we had a perfectly wonderful weekend in the city, I returned feeling that I am no match for the Washington scene."

"What do you mean by that? I have never measured you up to anyone."

"No, Patrick, you haven't. But, I do." She leaned forward and looked at him in earnest, "Your mother talks of hosting teas, garden parties, charity balls. I work for a living. My charity work consists of taking a meal to a shut-in or serving at a church dinner. I would never feel comfortable in those settings she described." She locked her eyes with his, "What you take for granted are luxuries to me. I would always be out of place and feel like I didn't belong."

She poured more tea, picked up a fork and jabbed it into the glop of cake.

"Tell me how you got here, Patrick. I know Herbert wasn't going to take the coach over the mountain today." She poured some hot tea into his cup.

Between bites of cake he explained that he had taken the transit line to Purcellville where he found a man to drive him to Berryville. "If you pay enough, you can always find someone willing, even on Christmas."

She gave a heavy sigh as she spoke with honesty. "I must admit that I am pleased to see you."

"You had me worried. You're not unhappy that I came?"

"I was at first. And I will be tomorrow after you're gone."

She left her chair and moved about the table to pile the dishes onto the tray. He stood and moved behind her. When she leaned to pick up the tray, he put his arms around her and held her close. "Dear God, how I have missed you," he murmured into her ear.

Catherine felt the strength of his arms and his warm breath on her neck, "Why does it have to be impossible?" she whispered before slipping from his arms.

He strode away. "I'll be in the living room when you feel like talking," he said.

Catherine carried the tray to the kitchen. She wiped some tears from her eyes and blew her nose. She was not going to cry in front of him. If he wanted to talk then she would listen and keep her feelings in check.

He sat calm and quiet thumbing through a magazine. They sat on the flowered sofa in the living room, he on one end and she on the other.

Patrick was the first to speak. "I want to know what happened after you returned from that weekend in Washington. We had a marvelous time. When I received the brooch, I was crushed. Something caused your change of heart because I know you care for me. Did my mother say something to offend you? She can be tactless."

Catherine had promised his mother that she would keep their last meeting confidential. "I am not sure that my lifestyle is up to her expectations."

"You have to realize that she is always trying to push away the fact we lived in the unsavory Georgetown area of Washington. It's been my observation that those who come from money are comfortable with themselves; while those who have had to work for it are always trying to make themselves look good."

"I have never been to Georgetown so I wouldn't know."

"It's improving. I still own the house we lived in. When we moved to that big house, I lost my home, my security, my best friend." He said no more.

She played with a lose thread on the cuff of her sleeve. "Is there supposed to be a lesson in this somewhere?" she asked.

"I'll let you think about it," he said. He raised his arms behind his head and leaned back on the sofa.

Catherine moved to the chintz chair. She reached down and pulled out the checker game from under a side table. "Do you want to play a game of checkers?" she asked.

"No," he replied, without moving. "I want you to think about what I just said. I came with a purpose."

She slid the game back under the table with her foot. "I know what you're saying. You think I'm afraid to leave this place because it is my security. And, maybe you're right. But it's not that I haven't thought about it. Sometimes I get so squeezed here, I could scream."

He rose up and looked at her. "I hope it registers that our worlds aren't as far apart as you think they are." Patrick was off the sofa and down on one knee beside her.

"Catherine, will you marry me?"

She was speechless.

He stood and pulled her to her feet. "I know this is sudden, but I've had plenty of time to think about it. Sending that goodbye letter drove me to come. I don't care to live my life without you being a part of it."

Her voice sounded tight and pinched, "I couldn't possibly give you an answer. As much as I've wanted to hear those words, please understand that I just can't give you an answer right now."

His face fell. "I had visions that you would jump into my arms in some kind of wild ecstasy. I love you, Catherine." He traced his finger down the side of her cheek until his head bent to let his lips meet hers in a tender kiss.

His touch thrilled her from her head to her toes. He held her close as she rested her head on his shoulder. "How am I going to work this out?"

"I know you well enough that I didn't expect an immediate answer. I will give you one week and not one day more."

She stood back. "That's more than fair."

He looked squarely into her eyes. "I'm not going to get a letter that says thanks and goodbye, am I?"

"Not this time. I promise an answer when you return."

He gave her an impassioned kiss. "Are you sure you can't give me an answer tonight?"

"You do make it difficult for me. Patrick, think about what we have to settle: the hat shop, medical school, your business, my property, this apartment…need I say more?"

"Why do you have to be so practical? You brought me back to earth. Now, I had better be going. I asked the fellow who drove me up to wait because I have to get right back to Washington. It's dark enough that your Mrs. Talley may not spy me leaving."

"No, but I'll bet she had her nose to the window watching you on the stoop."

They both laughed.

He kissed her once more before he lightly tripped down the stairs. There was a graceful movement in his tall, slim body that gave her pleasure. He pressed the button to lock the door and blew her a kiss on his way out. He had thrown her into a tailspin. How could she make a decision? There was so much to think about.

Sleep was out of the question. Catherine stayed up until two o'clock in the morning cleaning her apartment. She had washed and dried the dishes, swept the floors and dusted the furniture. Wasn't marriage exactly what she had hoped for? Yes, but without so many complications.

Chapter 11

By Friday, it had been a long week. Patrick was to arrive that evening and Catherine was to give her answer. Why did he have to live seventy miles away? Why couldn't he be someone who worked in the bank or at the hotel or owned a farm outside of town? Well, he wasn't. Marrying him would mean leaving all that she knew. She wanted her life to change, but did she want it to change that much?

There had been few customers in the shop all morning. That was usually the way it was during the week after Christmas. Catherine put up her new calendar for 1916, and the thought struck her that she would be turning twenty-six within the year. How many women of that age would have the prospect of marriage with someone they loved as she loved Patrick?

Lloyd Pierce came by around eleven, his usual time for delivering the mail. "It's cold out there this mornin'."

"Yes, I've got the fireplace roaring. I worry about that sometimes, whether or not it might cause a fire. My father was always cautious about the fireplace."

"You keep your chimneys cleaned out and it shouldn't be a problem." With a wink and a sly smile, he handed her the mail. "No mail from Washington today."

Her smile matched his. She replied, "Oh, how very sad. Perhaps there will be news that doesn't come in letter form."

"Oh?" He gave a questioning look before moving to the fireplace to warm his hands, "I gotta' be on my way. Miz' Talley will be lookin' for her mail. She always checks on how much time I spend in here."

"Now, how do you know that?"

He turned toward Catherine, "Wal' ya' know Miz' Talley. She gives herself away cuz' she cain't help from askin' questions. See ya' tomorra'."

"Not tomorrow. Mary Lee Thompson will be tending the shop."

"Goin' out of town, agin'?" he asked.

"I swear, Mr. Pierce. I believe Mrs. Talley's ways are rubbing off on you."

"Aw, now, Miz' Catherine, you know I was only teasin' you."

"I know…and, no, I'm not going out of town, but I just might stir up some gossip." She gave him a sideways glance.

"That's what keeps us goin'. Next week I'll tell you how the story gets twisted." His smile was genuine. "For a quiet young woman, there's a lot goin' on there underneath."

If he only knew, thought Catherine.

"Wal', I gotta go face Miz' Talley. Got any news she may want to hear?"

Catherine smiled and shook her head.

"I thought not," he said, and left to continue his route.

By closing time Catherine was ready for Patrick's arrival. She had made a pot roast with carrots, potatoes and onions. It had been in a slow oven most of the afternoon and should be just right whenever he came. She had baked bread the day before and had prepared custard pie for dessert. The custard pie had been a recipe from her friend, Carolyn. Not only would she greet Patrick with a delicious meal, she was ready to give her answer. Much thought had been given to what she was willing to give up for marriage. If she said yes, it would mean giving up her shop, her familiar way of life in the town, and, most of all, her independence. On the other hand, she would be creating a new life, where Patrick would be hers, and they could share the intimacies of marriage she could only imagine. It was both wonderful and unnerving to contemplate.

Catherine put the closed sign in the window, locked the door and turned out the lights before she went upstairs. The smell of the pot roast dinner filled the apartment with its stimulating aroma making her realize that she was hungry. She had eaten like a sparrow the whole week, agonizing over what her decision would be.

In her bedroom, she brushed her hair and piled it atop her head, holding it in place with large hairpins. She rubbed some rouge on her high pretty cheekbones, patted her face with a powder puff, and shook on some LaFrance Rose talcum. Her cream-colored crepe blouse was bordered with Empire green chenille, and matched the eight gored, crepe

145

skirt Irene Butler had fashioned. The outfit had cost more than she wanted to pay, but this would be a special evening.

At six-thirty, Catherine heard the front doorknocker, and her heart did a flip. The time had arrived! She took a quick look in the hallway mirror before she sped down the front stairs to meet him.

There was Patrick with a wide smile and his blue eyes dancing with merriment. Wrapped in a black wool coat, he held a package in his arms.

Stepping inside, he carefully unwrapped the package revealing a dozen beautiful red silk roses. "All the way from Washington, my good woman." He smiled and kissed her on the cheek. "Sorry they are not real, but roses in January would never have made the trip even if I could have found them."

"Oh, Patrick, they're beautiful." His kindness and thoughtfulness sometimes overwhelmed her. She held them to one side and gave him a welcoming kiss. "I'm so happy to see you. Let's hurry on up. I have dinner ready. I hope you're hungry," she said.

"I'm famished," he replied.

"Good. The table is set and all I have to do is pull dinner from the oven. I have a bottle of wine chilling. If you don't mind, you can open it while I'm putting the food on the table."

Catherine went into the kitchen and Patrick went into the dining room. "By the way, I didn't tell you how lovely you look tonight," he called as he uncorked the wine.

She entered, carrying the platter of roast and vegetables. Patrick had poured a glass of wine for each of them. Catherine placed the food on the table before he pulled her chair to be seated. He took the seat to her left.

"To an evening of wine, roses, and a beautiful lady to share them," he raised his glass in a toast.

"I'll drink to that," she responded. They linked elbows and sipped their wine peering into each other's eyes. How could they be so calm? He had come for an answer and she was ready.

The conversation throughout the dinner was kept to their week of work. Patrick said that he talked with Liam and his mother about leaving the warehouse and going back to medical school.

"How did they take it?" she asked.

"The way I expected. They weren't pleased. Liam didn't cuff me upside the head so I assumed he wasn't too upset."

Catherine laughed. "Is he prone to lash out?"

"He used to be, but he's mellowed. We do leave our childish ways. At least most of us do."

"What about your mother?"

He cleared his throat. "She was a different story. I heard about a fifteen-minute lecture before she said she wasn't at all pleased with decisions I've made as of late. Then she added, 'You might as well do what you want because you will do it anyway'."

"You didn't tell her you had proposed to me, I hope."

"That didn't seem the time."

"She might think that going back to school is unfair to Liam or that she'll lose you. She probably likes having you around."

"To do her bidding?" he asked.

"Perhaps. I'm sure having you in the house is company for her, especially when Liam and Sarah are not home."

She rose from her chair. "Let me clear this table and we can take our dessert into the living room."

"You get the dessert ready. I'll clear away this table."

"You don't mind?"

"It will give us more time together."

They cleaned up what was left of dinner. Catherine put two pieces of custard pie on plates. She fixed a pot of tea and covered it with a tea cozy. Patrick carried the tray into the living room where he set it on the low table in front of the flowered chintz sofa.

They sat side-by-side savoring the pie and seemingly lost in their own thoughts until Catherine said, "Patrick, I've thought long and hard about what marriage means and what I am willing to give up. I would look at my work and my independence as sacrifices."

He sat bolt upright and almost choked on the pie. His face held a strained look, but he said nothing.

She chose her words carefully, "I believe that I have looked at this proposal as deeply as I'm able. I've come to the conclusion that I would not be happy without you. So your answer is…yes, Patrick, yes, I will marry you."

Without a word, he stood up and pulled her into his arms. He held her so tightly she could hardly breathe.

"I have been so worried. I was afraid you would refuse."

To discover him so deeply moved, gave yet another facet of him to appreciate.

From his pocket, he pulled a jeweler's box. She watched as he popped up the lid to reveal a sparkling diamond ring. There was silence as he lifted it from its resting place and placed it on her finger.

"Oh, Patrick, it's gorgeous!" She threw her arms around his neck and kissed him with guileless fervor. When Patrick caught his breath, he held her close. "I believe I am the one who is supposed to sweep you off your feet."

She answered with a satisfied smile. Cradled in Patrick's arms, Catherine knew she had made the right choice.

****

The next morning, Mary Lee Thompson was at the hat shop door at eight o'clock sharp. She was dressed in a warm coat and bonnet revealing her pretty round face delicately sprinkled with freckles. Her eyes widened and her warm smile greeted Catherine when she opened the shop door.

"Good Morning, Mary Lee, you look ready to greet the day."

"I just love to watch your hat shop, Miz' Catherine. I hope you've left me somethin' to work on. You look mighty nice yourself. I'll bet Mr. Burke is in town, cuz' you always have that special glow when he's around."

"You'll make me blush. But…you are right. Mr. Burke is over at the hotel. He'll be here soon. We will both be upstairs, if you have questions."

Mary Lee's blue eyes widened even further. "You'd better not let Miz' Talley know that. She's big on that chaperonin' business. It does give me comfort to know you'll be close if I need anythin'. I like to watch the shop but I'm not right fond of bein' here myself."

"I don't know why. You did a fine job when I had to be out of town. There is plenty of change in the drawer. If you need more, I have some in my apartment."

"I wouldn't want to bother you and Mr. Burke."

"He and I have much to discuss. I assure you we won't look on you as an interference."

Catherine glanced out the window and spied Lavinia Talley waddling across the street.

"I'll be on my way upstairs," she said. "I see your first customer coming."

Mary Lee looked out the window and groaned, "Oh, no, not Miz' Talley. You know she ain't gonna' buy nothin', Miz' Catherine. She'll just nose around."

"She isn't going to buy anything, Mary Lee."

"Yeah, that's for sure."

"Be discreet, Mary Lee, be discreet." Catherine smiled as she headed for the back stairs and left the young girl looking chagrined.

Upstairs in her apartment, Catherine pulled out the paper where she had written every concern she wanted to discuss with Patrick when he came. Perhaps he would think it silly of her, but she was of the opinion that if two lives were going to merge they should merge in the same direction. Her friend, Carolyn, had implied, in a few of her letters, that there were some areas she and Asa should have talked about more in depth prior to marriage.

Patrick had spent the night at the hotel and arrived at Catherine's apartment around nine o'clock.

She was ready with the list of concerns safely tucked in her apron pocket.

They sat at the kitchen table where she poured coffee before handing Patrick the list. There wasn't a relaxed bone in her body as she watched him read it. She restrained herself from chewing her nails, but the knuckles of her left hand, pressed against her lips, were white. For the first time, she worried about how he would accept it. She scrutinized every blink of his eye, twitch of his mouth and shake of his head trying to interpret his reaction.

Finally, he raised his eyes to her with a solemn look, "You're sure you've covered everything?"

"Well, I think so," she replied, yanking the paper out of his hands and scanning the list.

"I'm glad," he said, "because I want to get on with the day of just you and me together."

"But, what about this?" She pointed to the paper. "We have to talk about it."

"All right, Miss Ramsburg, let's go into the living room and I'll answer every one of your concerns."

"How can you be so easy about it, Patrick? This is serious business."

"Indeed it is, my love." He swooped her up into his arms and carried her off to the living room.

Catherine found herself giggling like a schoolgirl and threw her arms around his neck as he ventured down the hall.

He sat her down on the sofa and took a seat next to her, easing into the corner. "Now, tuck your feet up, lean back on me and we'll examine this literary work together."

She snuggled into his arms, feeling goose bumps at the gentle touch of his lips on her neck. "I have to agree with you, Patrick. This is much better than sitting at the table."

He kissed her again, and held the paper so they could both read. "You have some valuable points here, Catherine. I'm glad you let me know your doubts about…"

She interrupted, "Patrick, I have no doubt I want to marry you but, I will feel so much better once we talk about this. At least, I think I will."

"Then we shall answer them one by one."
He gave her a squeeze.

Catherine sat up. "Do you think I'm a
ninny? It seems as though the women I know who
have become betrothed are in such a delirious state
of mind their only worry is what they're going to
wear on their wedding day."

"That's just the practical side of you showing. Or your maturity, most of those women are in
their teens." he teased.

She gave him a playful pat.

Just then, there was a knocking on her back
door. Catherine answered and found Mary Lee
Thompson with an anxious look on her face.

In a hushed voice, she said, "Oh, Miz'
Catherine, I hate to bother you, but it's that Miz'
Caldwell again. She's upset about a hat she said
she ordered for today and I cain't find it." Her soft
voice was beginning to squeak.

"Ruth Caldwell, again?" Catherine gritted
her teeth. "How is that possible?"

"This time it's her, it ain't her hired man,"
answered Mary Lee.

"I'll be right down."

Ruth Caldwell was known to have a temper.
The wrong choice of words would cause the gentle
Mary Lee to dissolve in tears.

Catherine hurried back to the living room
to tell Patrick she had to attend to something in the
shop. Ruth Caldwell was one of her best customers
and she couldn't afford to have her unhappy. He
nodded.

She rushed down the back stairs and into the shop where she greeted her customer. "Good morning, Miss Caldwell. It seems there is a problem with a hat you were to pick up today."

"Miss Ramsburg, I specifically had our driver bring in a note when he was in town last week. I had cut a picture out of a McCall's magazine and asked to have one just like it in black velvet."

"I am sorry. Perhaps I misplaced the note."

"There is no excuse! I must have that hat today!" Her face was becoming as red as her hair.

"Come and have a seat. I'll see if I have one that will suit your needs."

Ruth Caldwell flounced to the counter and took a seat in front of the three-way mirror. Catherine went to the storeroom and pulled every velvet black hat she could find that she and Mary Lee fancied up in their spare time. The most expensive one was brought out last. She had added a white ermine band and attached a curled ostrich feather to the back.

"It's absolutely beautiful." The young Miss Caldwell was delighted and her spiteful mood had passed.

Once she left the shop, Mary Lee marveled at how Catherine had defused the situation. "She was hoppin' mad when she came in. I didn't know what to do. How did you know she would like that one?"

"First of all, it was the most modern. Second, I knew what she was wearing because Irene Butler had bragged about the outfit she had made for Miss Caldwell for some big party this weekend. In a bad situation, if you can turn it around and not lose your temper in the process, it will usually work out."

"When she came stormin' in here and bawled me out, I'd like to have cried."

"Miss Caldwell was just upset that she had an important engagement and she wants to look her best. I wouldn't want to be the driver who didn't deliver the note. On the other hand, if she's happy enough, maybe he'll get off with a simple reprimand."

"I wouldn't want to work for her. I think our two red heads would clash."

"Then it's good you don't have to work for her."

Mary Lee smiled her cute sideways grin. "I 'spect you're right."

Catherine suggested, "It's almost noon. Why don't you go ahead and close up now? I don't expect anyone else to come by in the next fifteen minutes."

"Yes, ma'am. I'm sorry you had to come down here. You better get back upstairs. Miz' Catherine, do you mind if I ask you a question?"

"Of course I don't mind."

"Well, I couldn't help but notice that beautiful ring on your finger. Does that mean you're gonna' marry Mr. Burke?"

Catherine held out her hand for Mary Lee to admire the diamond engagement ring. "It does, indeed. Can you keep this a secret until I feel the time is right?"

"I won't tell a soul. And. Miz' Catherine, I am happy for you. I think Mr. Burke is a nice man."

"And so do I." Catherine smiled and hugged her friend.

Mary Lee turned bashful, "I guess you can say that we have a secret."

"We surely do," Catherine answered. "Now, you go ahead and close up and I'll be on my way upstairs."

" 'deed I will."

Catherine hurried upstairs and found Patrick playing the cherry spinet piano. She loved to hear him play, whether it was classical or ragtime. His strong fingers skimmed over the keys.

She sat beside him on the piano bench. "You play so beautifully."

He hit a key, stopped, and turned to look at her. "There's something very important I haven't told you."

Catherine rolled her eyes.

"I've already talked to the faculty at Georgetown and they've accepted me back into the program."

She let out a sigh of relief. "That's no surprise. I think it's wonderful. You said you had told your family."

"But, I didn't tell them when. I should have told you before you gave me your answer."

"I don't understand. Why would that make a difference? If it is only one year before you finish, that would be perfect. That's an accepted time for an engagement."

He got up from the piano bench and ran his hand across the back of his neck.

"I don't want to wait a year to get married. I want to get married as soon as we can."

She turned sideways on the bench to look at him. "When did that notion pop into your head?"

"When you said 'yes'."

She shook her head as she chuckled. "It's not possible."

"And, why not?"

With a shrug of her shoulders, she answered. "Because it just isn't."

He didn't move.

"Patrick…you're serious aren't you."

He pulled her up from the bench. "Let's do it. I start school the middle of the month. That would give us two weeks."

A gasp escaped before her concerns tumbled out one on top of the other. "We just went over that list of mine. Did it mean nothing to you? Besides, you'll be up to your nose in studies and what would I be doing, trying to learn the art of raising money for charities? And, where would we live? Not with your mother on K street. I told her she wouldn't see me back there. No, Patrick, it is not possible."

His eyes widened. "Now the truth comes out. So, you and she did have words. I suspected that might have been the case. When I received the brooch, I felt there was more written between the lines of that letter you sent with it."

157

He led her back to the sofa. "I've given this hours of thought."

"You said this idea just popped into your mind."

"Well, it kind of did." He smiled and took her hand. "Remember me telling you about the house my father bought in Georgetown?"

"You said it was a shack. Do you expect us to live there?"

"It was a shack when he bought it but he had to improve it. It is a nice little cottage with a kitchen, living room and two bedrooms. I didn't have the heart to tear it down even though I had a larger house built behind it. How would you like to have it for a millinery shop?"

With a quick jerk of her head, she turned to face him quickly dismissing the idea. "I can't just close up and leave town."

"Perhaps you can get Mary Lee to manage the shop while you make a decision about what you want to do with it."

"And then what? I lock up the apartment and steal away?"

"I wouldn't put it in those words, but, why not? You could rent it out. You do realize we have crossed off two of your big stumbling blocks on that list of yours."

"There is the third big one. But...I guess I gave up my independence once I accepted the ring."

"I don't care to have you talk like that," he admonished her. "I look at marriage as a partnership.

Give and take. You will be giving up Berryville to come live with me in Georgetown. I will be giving the little house to you as a wedding present."

He took her chin in his hand. "You will not be giving up your independence. The hat shop, its proceeds and management is yours. I want nothing to do with it."

She reached up and patted his cheek. "I guess we have that settled."

He sat back and laughed. "Catherine, I don't want to wait a year. Neither one of us are teenagers. The quicker we get on with our lives, the better."

"I know you're right, Patrick. When you return to Washington tomorrow, you will have to tell your family. Once you're done that, I will do my best to make arrangements here. Agreed?"

He rose from the sofa and pulled her up to face him. "I do love you, Catherine."

He kissed her soundly.

"Patrick…you complicate my life."

"I could say the same. I'm hungry. Do you have anything for a starving man?"

She had to smile. "I made some chicken soup and baked a loaf of bread. Will that take the edge off your hunger?"

"For food." He gave her a playful poke. "Let's indulge in your savory soup." The words oozed from his lips before he whisked her away to the kitchen.

Chapter 12

Patrick returned to Washington with a light heart. He had been flippant with Catherine about how she should be able to tie up her affairs easily when he knew he still had much to do to settle his own. He decided to walk home after he left Union Station. Walking was his way to let his mind unwind. He wasn't sure how he was going to spring the news of his engagement on his mother.

Last Friday he had told Liam of his plans to go back to school, live in Georgetown and ask Catherine to marry him. Patrick recalled the unpleasant meeting.

"What are you thinking of? You're just going to leave us in the lurch while you go off on some crazy notion? Mother isn't going to relish the news."

"I don't understand what you're so upset about, Liam." Patrick said. "And, as far as the business is concerned, there are plenty of savvy men around who would jump at the chance to have a share in running it."

"I don't see the reasoning in why you want to go back to medical school and take a step back living in Georgetown. We're financially sound. This house is big enough for all of us. And…if you plan on asking Catherine to marry you, I'm sure she isn't going to want to be a physician's widow."

"What does that mean?"

"Just what it implies. You'll be gone all the time and she'll be alone."

"I'm sure she's considered what it involves," answered Patrick. "She's the one who encouraged me to go ahead. She's a smart young woman. I don't think it was an idle suggestion on her part."

Patrick was at the door to leave.

"Besides," Liam used an entreating tone, "You're the senior partner. I'm not sure I can run the place by myself."

Patrick slammed the door shut and turned to face his brother. "After all the grown-up advice you gave me? Don't try to play me for a fool. You're afraid you'll have to take more responsibility, both at home and at work, and you won't be able to have as much freedom. You've been able to get away with it because I've allowed it. Now it's my turn!" He stormed out of the house.

That was how he and his brother had parted two days ago. Now Patrick was back with the news that he and Catherine were engaged. He wanted it to be a joyful occasion.

It was around seven when he walked through the door. The huge house was quiet; unusually quiet. Polly and Samuel, the household help, had Sunday afternoons to themselves. But, where were Liam, Sarah and his mother? It wasn't like his mother to be out after dark unless they were together. No lamps were lit; no fires in the fireplaces.

By seven-thirty, when no one had returned, Patrick began to get concerned. If they were all going to be gone into the evening they should have left a note. That was only common courtesy. As the minutes ticked away, Patrick's concern turned to annoyance. He was in the kitchen making a sandwich when he heard the heavy front door opening. He slapped the top piece of bread over the cold chicken and went to hear what explanation they would give. He walked down the hall to the foyer.

Sarah was hanging up her coat. Her eyes were red-rimmed and swollen. When she spied Patrick she rushed to him and fell into his arms, his sandwich toppled to the floor. It was all he could do to hold her upright. "My God, Sarah, what's happened?"

"Patrick, I'm so glad you're here." She burst into tears and he led her into the parlor until she could compose herself.

It was unlike the ebullient Sarah. She spoke in a level tone," Oh, Patrick, it was terrible! We were on our way to an early afternoon brunch when a car ran into the side of our taxi. Liam is in the hospital with a broken leg and hip. Mother Burke was in the back seat when the impact forced the door open and she was thrown to the ground. The doctor said they will have to wait to see how seriously she is injured. She's been in and out of consciousness all afternoon."

"What about you Sarah? Are you all right?"

"Yes," she sniffed. "The driver and I were unhurt. Mother Burke and Liam were on the side that was hit."

Patrick sat holding Sarah, his mind suspended, as though the room was closing in around him. Fleeting thoughts penetrated like arrows: mental images of Liam and his mother, the house in Georgetown, medical school, the promise of marriage to his lovely Catherine. How quickly his wonderful day had turned into devastation. What would he do now? Medical school would slip away once more. And what about Catherine? Would she slip away just as easily?

Once Sarah had recovered from relating her tale, they went to the kitchen where Patrick brewed tea. The maid always left something easy to nibble on for Sunday evening. Patrick heated up vegetable soup for Sarah and made another chicken sandwich. He would clean up the one on the foyer floor before he left for the hospital. Sarah had assured him that Liam was expected to recover. His mother was wait and see. Once Sarah was settled in for the night, Patrick would be off to the hospital.

****

Catherine was up early on Monday morning. She had an unsettled feeling that kept her from sleep most of the night. It was a dull gnawing and nagging sensation in the pit of her stomach. She couldn't shake it off. When she heard the crank of her doorknocker before eight o'clock, she knew something was wrong.

The boy from the hotel was at her door. "There's a person to person call for you, Miz' Catherine. Long distance!"

Catherine threw her coat on and hurried behind him into the hotel. She picked up the ear piece of the telephone and held it to her ear before raising the speaker to her mouth. "Hello."

"I have a person to person call for Miss Catherine Ramsburg from Mr. Patrick Burke," came the operator's voice.

"This is Catherine Ramsburg," she replied, trying to keep her voice from shaking.

"One moment, please."

Catherine heard voices in the background and then, "Go ahead, Mr. Burke."

A shudder went through her as she heard Patrick's voice on the other end of the line. "Catherine, this is Patrick. I didn't want to upset you so early in the morning but I had to tell you what has happened to…"

She interrupted, "I knew something was wrong. Are you all right?"

"Yes, I'm fine. It's Liam and my mother. They had an accident yesterday and are in the hospital. Liam is in a cast from his ankle to his waist. He'll be laid up for quite some time. Mother has a head injury. She is now conscious most of the time but has difficulty with memory. She knows me so that is good."

Catherine took a deep breath. "Thank God it wasn't worse than that."

Sadness crept into his voice. "Do you realize what this means to both of us?"

Of course she knew the minute he told her. Any plans they made would hinge on the recovery of his mother and brother. She swallowed hard, "What it means, Patrick, is that I will come to Washington as quickly as I can. If Mary Lee can't watch the shop, I'll close it up until this is all settled."

"I don't want you to do anything that would cause a hardship for you."

"Would you rather I didn't come?"

"No...no, I would like nothing better, but..."

"Then I will be there. We had better get used to going through difficult times together."

"I love you, Catherine."

She heard the click of the disconnection before she hung the receiver back on its hook. That conversation was going to raise eyebrows!

****

Two days later she was on the train headed for Alexandria where Patrick would meet her. Was it more bravado than courage to tell him she would come? She didn't feel courageous.

Mary Lee Thompson was watching the hat shop. Mary Lee readily agreed and Catherine was comfortable leaving it in her hands.

"You take as much time as you need, Miz' Catherine. It's mighty important for you to go," she had said.

The window of the train was hazy causing the countryside to look the same. Nothing is pretty in a January landscape. The train snaked its way down the mountain and made stops in the same small hamlets: Round Hill, Purcellville, Hamilton, Paeonian Springs, Leesburg...each stop meant more people boarding. By the time they reached Alexandria, the car was packed. Two plump elderly ladies had squeezed into Catherine's seat until her hip was mashed against the side of the train car. It was with relief when the train stopped. She stood and rubbed her hip before picking up her valise. The conductor assisted her off the train. Patrick said he would meet her inside the station, but instead, he came rushing to where she stood on the platform. He took her valise from her hand, let it drop and pulled her into his arms. She held onto her hat with one hand.

"Patrick, we're in the middle of a crowd of people," she whispered in his ear.

"I don't care. I'm just so glad you're here."

"And so am I."

He led her to a taxi and gave the driver instructions. Patrick opened the door of the cab and they climbed into the back seat.

"How are Liam and your mother?"

"It's been a few rough days. I guess they are both as well as can be expected. Liam will be in the hospital for a month or more. Mother's condition has stabilized so the doctor says she will, most likely, be in the hospital another week."

"Patrick, I am so sorry for all of this. But, we can be thankful that they will recover."

"Yes, that's true, but it has ruined all plans. It isn't fair, Catherine."

She reached over and took his hand. "Would putting off medical school for six months be so difficult?"

"It's not just that, Catherine. We were to be married, if you recall."

"Yes. I also recall that we had not settled as to when. This accident may be the hand of Providence keeping us from making hasty decisions."

"That isn't the way I see it," he grumbled.

The cab pulled up to the curb. Patrick paid the fare and helped Catherine out of the back seat. The huge white house on K Street looked inviting on this cold January day. The sun was shining and sparkled on the large bay windows behind the portico. Patrick took her valise in one hand and placed his other at the small of her back as they made their way up the walk.

Sarah greeted them when they entered. Before Patrick could make the introductions, she said, "Catherine, do come in. I'm Sarah, Patrick's sister-in-law. I am pleased you're here. It has been a dreadful few days."

She looked tired and drawn, but pretty women seem to keep their beauty through any unrest. Sarah was no exception.

"Thank you. Patrick has told me that Liam and Mrs. Burke are both improving. I realize it has been difficult for all of you."

Catherine took off her gloves and was reaching to remove her hatpins when Sarah exclaimed, "Catherine, is that an engagement ring?"

Her face flushed as she gave a guilty look to Patrick. "You haven't told them?" she asked.

He put a protective arm around her. "I'm sorry. I haven't had time. I was bubbling over with happiness when I planned on giving the news only to find the world turned topsy-turvy. Yes, Sarah, Catherine and I are to be married."

"I am delighted. Oh, I am so excited and Mother Burke will have us hosting a grand affair." She took Catherine's hands in hers. "This house is big enough for all of us."

Patrick piped in, "Everything is up in the air at this point. But, when we are married we will be living in the house in Georgetown."

Sarah scowled. "Georgetown? Is that wise?"

Catherine threw an uncertain look at Patrick.

"The area's improving," he said. "I didn't have that house built over there to stand idle."

"I suppose not," Sarah answered. "We all wondered about why you built a new house over there. Mother Burke said she didn't understand why you didn't tear down the little house. She views that place as an eyesore."

Catherine's eyes widened at that statement.

"Mother has no appreciation for nostalgia. All this talk is premature, why don't you see if Polly can feed us some sandwiches. I'm starved. Catherine has had a long ride in on the train."

This flustered Sarah. She threw both hands into the air. "Oh, goodness. How inconsiderate of me. Of course she has food ready. I'll see to it right away." And, off to the kitchen she flew.

Patrick led Catherine into the dining room. "Sarah's a bit high-strung. This accident with Liam has really thrown her off base."

They sat next to each other waiting for their lunch.

"I am embarrassed, Patrick. You told her I was coming but you didn't say that we were engaged? She must think I'm a loose woman running after you."

"She could have thought that before, but now she knows that we're engaged there's a reason for you to be here."

Catherine wagged her head. "It's still embarrassing. Patrick Burke, sometimes I don't think you quite understand."

Sarah jounced in and joined them at the table. "Polly will be right in. Well, I do have to say that I am not only surprised but overjoyed to hear that you and Patrick are engaged. Have you set a date to be married?"

Catherine groaned inwardly before she answered, "We haven't set a date. Patrick has the business to run. I have to resolve what to do with my hat shop. I came to see if I could be of any help until this crisis passes."

That's when Sarah's façade fell apart. "Oh, it is so awful. Liam will be laid up for months and Mother Burke will require care. I just don't know how I'm going to handle it."

Catherine reached over and touched the anxious Sarah's arm. "We will all get through this together and we'll be stronger for it. Although I'm

169

not a member of the family yet, I soon will be, and there is strength in family." Catherine glanced over at Patrick.

He winked.

Polly set a large tray of sandwiches on the table and poured tea.

****

Soon after lunch, Patrick and Sarah were off to the hospital. Catherine had been invited but she declined. She wanted Patrick to tell the news of their engagement to his mother and brother before she made an appearance. She held some reservation that Sarah might blurt out the story and cautioned Patrick of that possibility before he left.

Catherine's travel bag was settled into the room she had occupied on her last visit. Hadn't she told Patrick's mother that she wouldn't be back? Circumstances change. That visit had been such a whirlwind she could not get in touch with her good friend, Carolyn. The Burkes' had a telephone; why not do it now?

Catherine rifled through her pocketbook to find Carolyn's phone number: 1472-W2. The last digit meant the number of rings. For Carolyn, the operator would ring twice in succession, which would be the signal for her to pick up the phone. Those on party lines waited for their appointed number of rings before answering. It wasn't polite for others to listen in on someone else's conversation, but not everyone could resist the temptation.

"Hello."

"Carolyn? Is that you? This is Catherine."

170

"Catherine! Oh my goodness! What's wrong?"

"Nothing's wrong, well, almost nothing. I'm in Washington. I hoped that we might get to see each other."

"You're in Washington? I don't believe it! How long will you be here?"

"I'm not sure. I have much to discuss with you. I thought we might meet for lunch."

"Catherine, are you sure there is nothing wrong? Your letters have not been upbeat. They don't convey the well-grounded Catherine I know."

She cleared her throat. "I'd rather not talk about it over the telephone. Patrick will be busy tomorrow, I'm sure. Would one o'clock suit you? It will be my treat."

"It will be my tlreat just to sit and talk with you in person," Carolyn said. "Let's eat at the Willard. Will you be able to get there without any problem?"

"Patrick has said he will see that I get where I have to go. I have so much to tell you."

"I can hardly wait. I'll meet you at the Willard at one o'clock." There was exhilaration in Carolyn's voice as she continued, "Wait until I tell Asa that you're in town. I still can't believe it. I also have some news. Some of it is as gossipy as what Lavinia Talley peddles."

"I thought I left her in Berryville," Catherine laughed.

"Well, I wouldn't like to be compared to Lavinia. I'll keep this under my bonnet until tomorrow. One o'clock," Carolyn repeated.

"Patrick isn't here right now, but I'll tell him as soon as he returns. If anything changes, I'll call you this evening. Thank you, Carolyn."

"Goodbye, Catherine."

Chapter 13

The next day, Carolyn was waiting at the Willard Hotel when Catherine arrived with Patrick accompanying her. He had wanted to meet Carolyn and this would be his chance.

"Patrick, you do understand that Carolyn and I would like to have a private conversation?"

"I promise once I've met your friend, I will leave you two to enjoy your time by yourselves."

With that understanding, Catherine had agreed. Then, upon entering the dining room, she saw Carolyn sitting with Asa and her heart sank.

What was with these men spoiling all plans for a 'just for girls' chat?

Asa rose when Catherine and Patrick entered. It was a table for two.

Carolyn hurried to Catherine and they wrapped their arms around each other.

"I have your seat, Catherine," Asa said, holding the chair for her to be seated. His deep authoritative voice had not changed. "I assume that formal introductions are in order."

"Carolyn and Asa this is Patrick Burke. Patrick, my friends, Carolyn and Asa Thomas."

Asa turned to Patrick, "I thought we might share a cigar and drink in the tavern."

Patrick shook his hand. "My thoughts exactly. Good to see you again, how have you been Asa?"

The two women were momentarily speechless. "You know each other?" they asked in unison.

"Aha, we got you. We've known each other for quite some time," said Patrick. "We supply the cloth for the Army uniforms and, as the procurement officer, Asa has to sign off on all purchases. It was always strictly business until I let it slip last week that I had to make a trip to Berryville. He said his wife was from that area and we started comparing notes."

"How astute," Catherine said, as she looked over at Carolyn, who was obviously enjoying the ruse. "Did you know about this?"

Placing her hand over her heart, Carolyn replied,"On my honor I did not but I think it's grand."

Patrick confessed, "I called Asa after you told me of your lunch plans. We thought it would be great fun to see the startled looks on your faces. You didn't disappoint us."

Catherine smiled across the table at Carolyn. "Trickery, that's what it is, sheer trickery." She looked up at the men still visibly enjoying their prank. "You had both better be getting to the denizen of sin because Carolyn and I have much to discuss." It was the first lighthearted moment she had had since she arrived.

"We'll be back in one hour," said Patrick. The men went off in the direction of the tavern.

The waiter approached with a pot of hot tea. "Would you ladies care for tea?"

They nodded. He poured the brew into their cups as they pored over the menu.

"I will have your special lunch of the day," said Carolyn as she folded the menu.

"I'll have the same," chimed in Catherine.

With the waiter out of earshot Carolyn leaned over toward Catherine. In a soft voice she advised, "It's been my experience if one orders the special lunch of the day it is delivered faster than an order from the menu. If we get the waiter out of the way, we can get on with our conversation."

"That's one quality I admire, Carolyn, there is no subtlety about you."

"Is that a compliment?" she asked, with a raised brow.

"Of the highest order," laughed Catherine. "Although I'm not sure what we've ordered because you didn't give him a chance to tell what the special of the day is. And it doesn't matter. I only ordered it because you did. It's wonderful just to be sitting here and chatting face to face. Letters keep us going, but it's not the same."

"I understand that. You don't know how many times I have wanted to sit as we are doing now." She must have spotted a glitter from Catherine's engagement ring. "Good heavens! Is that a ring on your finger?"

175

Catherine reached her hand out and Carolyn grabbed it to admire the ring. "Aren't you the sly one. It is a beautiful ring and I am most happy for you. I am not completely surprised because I could tell from the tone of your letters that Patrick is special. What does surprise me is that you have only known him for four months and you're ready to say, I do."

Catherine chuckled. "I have surprised myself."

"Have you picked a date?"

"I believe Patrick would be married tomorrow if I agreed. There are too many obstacles in the way."

"Why the sadness in your voice when you called? Don't deny it, Catherine, I know you too well."

"It was last weekend when I accepted. We were both elated until he returned to Washington to find both his mother and brother had been in an automobile accident. They are in the hospital."

"Oh, Catherine, how dreadful! So that's the reason you're here. How are they doing?"

"Patrick assures me they're doing fine. But recuperation is a matter of months. It has just about ruined all of our plans."

"Do they know about your engagement?" Carolyn asked.

They were interrupted as the waiter brought their lunches."The tomato bisque is delicious today and I've heard remarks that the chicken salad is some of the best we've served," he interjected. "Would you care to have your tea refreshed?"

"Please," they answered.

With polish, he poured the tea and left the area.

Carolyn prodded Catherine once more, "Well, do they?"

"Do they what?" Catherine answered, absentmindedly.

"Does the Burke family know of your engagement?"

"Patrick hasn't had the proper time to tell his mother or brother."

"What, pray tell, would be the proper time?"

Catherine folded a linen napkin over her lap. "I think he plans on telling them this evening. I have to decide about getting back to Berryville. Mary Lee can't watch the shop indefinitely."

"Mary Lee Thompson? She's a sweet little thing." Carolyn held a spoonful of tomato bisque to allow it to cool before putting it into her mouth. "I think you should be married as soon as possible. It would be best for both of you. You can solve the difficulties together."

"That's easy to say, Carolyn. I'm nervous enough at the thought of marriage. Now there are all of these problems going on at this moment. " She took a bite of her chicken salad. "The waiter is right, this is most tasty."

Carolyn looked dreamy. "Don't create obstacles. It used to make my stomach churn thinking about marriage before I took the big step. Now I'm married, it's churning for another reason." Carolyn gave a sly glance toward Catherine to see if she caught the meaning of her words.

Catherine contemplated her friend, who was grinning from ear to ear.

"You're going to have a baby!" The tenor of her voice disturbed the couple at the next table and they glanced over at the two young women. Catherine acknowledged them with a smile as though it was perfectly within the bounds of good taste to exclaim aloud.

"Yes, and we are so happy about it."

"I thought I saw a special glow about you."

They raised their teacups and clinked them together in a salute.

"When will this wonderful event occur?" asked Catherine.

"The end of May. I was just bursting to tell someone."

"I am going back to Berryville and tell Lavinia that you're expecting. You know she will be chagrined that she wasn't the first to hear."

"Oh, please do," Carolyn consented. "I can hardly wait to hear how the story turns out. I am sure that Berryville hasn't changed in that respect. And, Catherine, while you're talking to Lavinia, pry out of her what she knows about James Anderson's predicament."

"James?"

"Yes, you know. The good-looking driver at the Caldwells' when I took care of Elizabeth

Caldwell. I understand that old Mr. Ramseur left quite a few debts and James will have to clear them or lose the estate."

"Didn't he marry Amanda Ramseur just to inherit that place?"

"Exactly. I told him it was foolhardy to marry that insufferable woman regardless of the material rewards. It sounds as though he is getting his just due."

"Carolyn, you are being cynical. Where did you get this information?"

"From Andrew…Andrew Caldwell. You do remember that he and Asa are like brothers?"

Catherine peered over her cup at her friend. "Why are we discussing this anyway, unless you've still got a yen for James."

Carolyn was indignant, "I just told you this so that if Amanda comes into your shop and orders all kinds of hats, you might not get paid."

"Of course, you did," Catherine gave a knowing smile. "I promise that I'll hang Lavinia from the rafters until she tells me what she knows… or thinks she knows."

"Gosh, Catherine. I do miss our chats."

There were a few moments of silence as they delved into their food in earnest.

Carolyn asked, "What about your hat shop? Are you going to rent it after you're married?"

"I'm still up in the air about it. Mary Lee will do fine until I get back. Patrick will have to break the news to his mother and brother, although his sister-in-law is aware. She might blurt it out without thinking. She's a pretty girl with refinement."

The waiter returned with a slice of white cake with vanilla frosting for each of them.

"We didn't order this." Carolyn was to the point.

"Compliments of two men in the tavern. They have also paid your bill."

"I wonder who they can be?" mused Catherine. "Carolyn, do you think we have admirers?"

The waiter stood with hands folded as though waiting for a message for him to deliver.

"Ooh, how exciting," gushed Carolyn. She turned to the waiter. "You may tell those gentlemen, whoever they are, that we would be delighted to meet them...once we finish this luscious looking dessert."

The man turned beet red and replied, "Yes, ma'am."

When he left, the two friends looked at each other and giggled into their napkins.

"That wasn't very nice of us, Carolyn. The waiter was put on the spot."

"I'll be sure that Asa rewards him well."

Carolyn dug her fork into the cake. "Catherine, Patrick seems to be a good person, even though I've just met him. I could tell from your letters that he is someone you shouldn't let get away. You do love him?" Carolyn asked.

"So much I can't think straight," Catherine admitted.

"I believe you should give serious thought to what I advised about getting married."

The men returned.

Patrick was his jovial self. "The waiter said there were two attractive young ladies who wanted to meet us."

Catherine looked around. "I wonder where they could be?"

The two women went back to smothering their laughs into their napkins.

Asa, his military bearing pulled up to full height, signaled an end to their merriment with the words," I believe we should be on our way before you create a spectacle."

Carolyn touched her husband's hand. "You must see that the waiter is compensated. I'm sure we embarrassed him."

"We've taken care of it," replied Patrick.

Asa held the chair for his wife. His tenderness was evident as he gently helped her rise. Did Catherine catch a subtle glow of pride?

How lucky we are, she thought. Right at that moment her decision was made.

Outside the hotel, Catherine and Carolyn embraced each other before they got into their respective waiting cabs.

"Did you enjoy seeing your friend?" asked Patrick.

"It was so good to see her. I can say that it was a boost to my morale."

He patted her arm. "Good. I like her. I wonder what the odds are on Asa and I knowing each other?"

Catherine looked at him. "How could you keep that a secret?"

"I'll be in training as a physician and testing out confidentiality."

She smiled and shook her head.

They rode in silence past the tall, square, stone government buildings lining the streets of Washington. Catherine's mind was elsewhere. With a bold gesture she reached over and took his hand. "Patrick, what would you say if I suggested that we get married while I'm here."

She felt his body stiffen. Had she said the wrong thing?

He inclined his head toward her. "Did I hear you right?"

"You did. I have been thinking. What if something else unforeseen happens and we can never get married?"

He hugged her to him until she thought she would have to fight for air. "I'll make the arrangements right away before you have a chance to change your mind. If we do this we won't be having a traditional wedding, you realize."

"Of course I do," she said. "We will have no church, no flowers, no well-wishers, no showering of presents, no fancy reception. Is that right?"

"I think you've covered it," he replied. "You will be happy to know that I have informed both Mother and Liam of our engagement."

"When?"

"This morning. Liam and Sarah are so wrapped up in his trouble I'm not sure it hit home with him, but my mother was vocal." He squeezed her shoulders as reassurance.

"I know she wasn't pleased. Perhaps we should wait until everything has settled down."

He tilted her chin to look at him. "No changing your mind. Leave it to me, Catherine. I promise a wedding to remember." And, he kissed her full force right there in the back seat of the Model T taxi.

Chapter 14

There was a three-day wait for a marriage license, which gave them time to make arrangements with a magistrate. Carolyn and Asa had agreed to be their attendants. The vows were to be taken on Saturday. Marriage on a Saturday might be the only traditional happening in this wedding, thought Catherine.

The young women met on Thursday to pick out a dress. As early January was so close after the holiday season, the pick of dresses was slight. They had been into three dress shops before stopping to admire a fancy, cream-colored lace dress in a window of a small shop. The fitted bodice was beaded with rhinestones. The long sleeves came to a point at the wrist with delicate lace trim.

"Oh Catherine, isn't that exquisite?"

"It is that. I'm sure the price is exquisite also."

The dressmaker motioned then in. "It's too chilly a day to be standing looking in the window. Come in and warm yourselves. I have some cider on the stove."

The friendly woman seemed relieved to have company. "Business is a bit slow after the holidays."

"Ah yes, I understand that. I'm a milliner," said Catherine. "I enjoy the lull after the busy season."

"If you're a milliner, then you understand fashion. I saw the both of you admiring the dress in the window."

"It is lovely, but above my means." Catherine was straightforward.

The woman stepped into the display area. "With your lovely coloring it would be most stylish on you. And look here." She removed the dress from the dress form. "Just look at this fitted bodice with these delicate rhinestones." She moved the dress close to the dull light of the shop so that the stones sparkled. "Even in this poor light they dance."

Catherine fingered the soft flowing lace. "I'm afraid to ask the price."

"Do you have a special occasion in mind?"

"My wedding," Catherine murmured.

"Oh, glory, glory, how wonderful! Let me put you in on a little secret. The lady who ordered this dress to be made gave me a comfortable deposit and never returned. I could let you have it for half the price it cost. Thirty-five dollars," the little lady whispered.

It was so tempting.

"Catherine, you must buy it. Patrick would be so pleased. I can lend you some of the money." Carolyn was enthusiastic.

"I don't know." Catherine dallied still fingering the lace. "Patrick would appreciate it." She hesitated. "I'll have to be very careful of anything else I purchase."

Turning to Carolyn she said, "You mustn't talk me into anything else because I don't have much money with me. I hadn't planned on getting married before I left Berryville." It was a friendly admonishment.

"Do try it on." Now the dressmaker was enthused. "I can make it fit like a glove. A bride must look like a picture on her wedding day."

In the fitting room the seamstress put a pin here, a tuck there, until Catherine's pleasing shape was evident.

"You're going to have your young man doing summersaults," the dressmaker cooed as she stepped back to admire her handiwork. "I can have it ready before noon tomorrow."

"That's more than I could have asked for," said the pleased Catherine. The seamstress wanted no payment until it was tailored.

The two friends left the shop and walked a few doors to a small eatery for a late lunch.

"I'm paying for lunch because I'm famished," said Carolyn. "It seems as though I can't get enough to eat these days now that I'm over that awful morning sickness. Do you think I'm going to turn into one of those pudgy girls once the baby arrives? Remember last year how Leanne turned pudgy after her baby was born? I hardly recognized her."

Catherine didn't mince words. "Leanne was pudgy before the baby was born, now she's just plain fat."

"Well, maybe she wasn't a good example," Carolyn replied. "I am concerned about it though. Some men don't find their wives as attractive once they've had a child."

"I don't think you have to worry about Asa. I catch him eyeing you with adoration."

"Yes, but what if I turn out looking like a chunk of cheese?"

"Carolyn, you have too much energy to end up looking like a chunk of cheese."

They stopped to read the bill of fare that was posted on a window.

Catherine snickered. "Do you see the lunch special for today? It's a cheese sandwich."

"Just my style," came Carolyn's sarcastic reply. "Let's go in."

Chapter 15

Catherine awoke early on Saturday morning because she had tossed and turned all night. The wedding was scheduled for two in the afternoon. January 17th didn't sound like a romantic day for a wedding. In her teens she had visualized her wedding day as a beautiful, sunny, warm June day. Her dress would be of spotless white lace with gobs of ribbons and bows. Her long hair would be trimmed with garlands of roses and ivy that her mother would pick from her garden. Now, a cool January day had replaced the warmth of June, the pristine white lace was a winter cream with rhinestones, and, as her mother was gone, the garland of flowers was replaced by a headpiece that matched her dress.

The expensive dress was carefully laid out on the bed in the guest room. A pair of cream patent leather shoes rested on the floor. A pair of shoes that took her last penny but her only other pair was black. She had little choice.

Before finding the shoe store, Catherine had passed a jeweler's. In the window was a gold tie bar sporting a caduceus symbol. She had debated whether to purchase it as she was uncertain that it was an appropriate wedding gift, but she knew in her heart that one day Patrick would be a physician. She had it engraved: *Patrick Burke, M.D.* When the jeweler handed the box to his assistant he said,

"This is to be a wedding gift. Wrap it with great care."

Catherine sat quietly and admired the packaged tie bar as she placed it in her carry bag with a note that read: *"A gift on our wedding day and for the future. May we always be as happy as we are today. With love from your wife, Catherine."* The word wife made her realize that was just what she would be. She liked the sound of it as she repeated it aloud.

There was a knock on her bedroom door.

"Who is it?"

"It's Polly, Miz' Catherine. Mister Patrick said I was to bring you some breakfast."

Catherine opened the door. "Come in, Polly. This is a surprise. Has Patrick left the house?"

"No, ma'am. He sez' it's suppose to be bad luck for the groom to see the bride before the wedding and he's had enough bad luck and he's not tempting fate. Whatever that means."

"I suspect it means he is as nervous as I am." She took the tray from the helpful maid. "I do thank you very much."

"Yes'm. You'd best get at it 'afore it gets cold."

The maid closed the door as she left.

The plate under the warm metal cover held scrambled eggs, two pieces of bacon, fried potatoes and buttered toast. Catherine's stomach was so uneasy that she knew it wouldn't be wise to eat much, yet she also knew that she should eat something so she decided on the toast.

Millie Curtis

She carried the toast and a steaming cup of coffee to the dressing table where she sat and studied her image in the mirror. Her mind turned to Patrick. He had broken the news of the engagement to his family, but he did not want Catherine to visit Liam and his mother until after the wedding. She didn't ask for an explanation accepting that Patrick knew best.

Once the hasty decision to be married was made, he had spent hours at the warehouse. 'No interruptions,' he'd said. 'Just you and me for this weekend. I'll unplug the phone and lock the bedroom door.'

Catherine smiled at the thought.

Later, when Polly came to get the tray, she handed Catherine a note.

My darling Catherine,

I am sending a car for you at one o'clock to bring you to the magistrate. I am so excited I feel like a child waiting for Christmas to come.

I send my love,
Patrick

Catherine kissed the note as she placed it into her bag and felt tears sting her eyes. She gave a silent prayer that all would go well.

As the clock in the foyer struck one, a gleaming, black, touring car pulled in front of the house on K Street. Asa Thomas got out in his impeccable uniform, his military bearing apparent in every stride he took as he made his way up the walk.

190

Catherine was in the foyer where she had donned her long, navy wool cape and was picking up her muff when the doorknocker sounded. Without hesitation she opened the door.

"Asa! This is a surprise. Patrick said he was sending a car."

"He did. It just happens that Carolyn and I are in it." He smiled as he tipped his cap.

"Well, I am delighted. I can use some friendly company."

Asa took her arm as they walked to the car to join Carolyn.

All three squeezed together in the back seat. Asa told the driver to go ahead.

"Catherine, you look lovely." Carolyn greeted her. "Where did you find those shoes? And your headpiece…it's just perfect. I can hardly wait to see your dress."

"Let Catherine catch her breath, dear. It's the bride who's supposed to be all in a fluster," Asa said as he patted his wife's hand.

Catherine linked her arm through Carolyn's. "I am so happy to see you. It's been a trying morning. Polly had to help me button all of the buttons lining the sleeves. If that wasn't enough, this dress is so fitted, I could hardly bend over to put on my shoes." That brought a chuckle from both of the riders.

"To answer your question…the headpiece was tucked in with the dress. I think it looks like a saucer with lace fringing, but it matches. I pray my hair looks all right. The hairpins kept slipping out so it took some fancy winding to keep them in place. And, where is this magistrate's office anyway?"

"My goodness, Catherine, you are jittery aren't you?" Carolyn observed in a good-natured way.

"We're almost there," chimed in Asa.

Catherine looked out the window of the car. "I don't recognize this area."

"This is Georgetown," he informed her.

From the looks of the houses and yards, it looked like the unsavory part of town.

The big car turned a corner and stopped in front of a small red brick church.

"This isn't a magistrate's office, it's a church," Catherine exclaimed.

"True," agreed Asa. "But, I was told this is the place."

He led the way. The young ladies linked their arms and dutifully followed. They entered through heavy, wood, double doors into a cozy vestibule.

Once inside, a middle-aged lady appeared. She asked for their wraps so they could be stored in an adjacent room. Catherine removed her cape. Asa, Carolyn and the lady caught their breath. She was stunning!

Carolyn kissed her cheek. "Oh, Catherine, you are pretty as a picture."

"Indeed you are." Asa was not one to hand out frivolous compliments.

The lady stored the outer wraps. It was when she returned that she introduced herself as the minister's wife. "Captain Thomas, you are to follow me." Asa obeyed and winked at the two young women standing there with gaping mouths.

"I don't understand any of this," Catherine whispered to Carolyn.

"I believe Patrick will have some explaining to do," she whispered back.

The minister's wife reappeared. She pinned a corsage on Carolyn and placed her in the aisle at the entrance of the sanctuary. Then she put a bouquet of white roses in Catherine's hand and placed her three steps behind Carolyn.

After whispering into Carolyn's ear, she disappeared once again.

The bride and her attendant stood like marble pillars, afraid to move from the spot where they had been placed with quiet authority.

All of a sudden the stillness of the small church was filled with organ music.

Carolyn turned back and mouthed, "Follow me."

The organist, who was also the minister's wife, didn't play a hymn or traditional wedding music, she played a Broadway tune: *You Made Me Love You.*

Catherine gave a wide smile. That had to be a request from Patrick. It was her big moment. She started down the aisle of the small church, past the empty wooden pews. The afternoon light danced through the stained glass windows and caused a pleasant glimmer of color as it caught the rhinestones sewed into the bodice of her dress. She looked up and saw Patrick, beaming with anticipation. As she approached, the music stopped. He reached forth and took her hand. The warmth of his hand and the strength she felt standing beside him was joy beyond words.

Here was the man who had turned her orderly life upside down. In the quietness of this quaint church, where Patrick had seen that it would be a memorable occasion, they took their vows: *I now pronounce you man and wife.*

****

After the ceremony, and the kissing and handshakes ended, both couples squeezed into the back seat of the grand car that had brought them.

"Asa, I've instructed the driver to drop Catherine and me off at the hospital. We'll get a taxi and meet you at the Willard."

"We'll see you there," Asa answered.

Moments later the newlyweds were at the Georgetown Hospital. Once inside they removed their wraps and Patrick hung them in a coat room.

Catherine whispered to him, "We're overdressed. People are either staring or stealing a second glance as we pass by."

"And well they should." He grinned at her and kissed her cheek, "I want Mother, Liam and Sarah to see us on our wedding day. We owe them that much," he said as they started down a hall. "They are going to be surprised."

She stopped. "You haven't told them?"

"I did tell them we were engaged." He was lighthearted. "How could I keep my planning a secret if I told them?"

194

"Patrick, I'd like to die right here on this spot."

"Now that would cause people to gape, wouldn't it?" He laughed as he took her arm. "Come on, it's not going to be so bad. Mother will be happy to get me settled down."

Catherine knew Mrs. Burke was not going to be pleased about any part of this surprise. Patrick was still unaware of the stinging conversation between his mother and Catherine.

They continued down the corridor with Catherine nervously trying to smooth her dress. "Am I a mess of wrinkles in the back?"

"My dear, you look delectable."

They reached his mother's room. Catherine thought the best that could happen would be for Mrs. Burke's head injury to have erased the memory of their last meeting. The woman lay languidly in the bed. Patrick kissed his mother on the cheek, "Mother, I brought Catherine with me."

"How nice to see you, Catherine." She held up a limp hand.

Catherine moved nearer the bed, unsure if the lady was seeing her clearly.

"I am so sorry for your misfortune, Mrs. Burke. Patrick assures me you are convalescing to the doctor's satisfaction."

"So the doctor says. Where have you been for the past couple of days, Patrick? Sarah has dropped by. She reports that Liam is as ill-tempered as a grizzly bear, and she hasn't seen you except in passing." Her weakness seemed to pass as she voiced her displeasure with Patrick.

"I have been quite busy," he answered without excuse. "Mother, Catherine and I came by to give you the news that we were just married."

She gave an audible gasp."Married! Patrick, how could you!"

"It wasn't difficult. We stood before the preacher and repeated what he said." Patrick put his arm around Catherine's waist and pulled her to him.

"You have always been so difficult to reprimand. I would have liked to have had a grand gathering. You do enjoy going against convention."

Catherine spoke up, "I'm afraid that Patrick and I both have a tendency in that direction."

Mrs. Burke turned her attention to Catherine. "That does not come as a surprise. I am still having some difficulty with fuzzy vision, but I can see how lovely you look. Are you happy?"

"I am very happy," Catherine replied.

"I'm sure you are," said the new mother-in-law in a disinterested tone. "What will we do with three Mrs. Burkes in the house?"

"We'll talk about that later. We have to go break the news to Liam and Sarah and then we are going to the Willard for our dinner."

"Yes, well…I do hope this isn't one of those necessary weddings. I'm not sure I could live that down."

Catherine reddened but held her tongue.

"Mother, how about wishing us well?" suggested Patrick.

"I wish you well," replied his mother in a flat voice. "You had better get on to break this wonderful news to Liam."

Patrick guided Catherine from the room.

"It's easy to see Mother is overjoyed. Let's see how Liam takes it."

The door to Liam's room was closed. Patrick knocked and Sarah came to the door and stood there.

"May we come in?" asked Patrick.

"Please do. I think Liam can use some company besides me." Her eyes were red as though she had been crying. When she saw Catherine her face brightened. "How good of you to come. You look absolutely beautiful. You two must be off to some memorable event."

"We have already been to a memorable event and that's the reason we came by," informed Patrick.

"Oh, my goodness. Here I am standing in the doorway." But, before she opened the door completely, she said to Liam, whose bed was behind the door, "It's Patrick and Catherine."

"Well, tell them to come in." It was easy to tell he was not in a good mood.

Patrick walked right over to his bed and shook his hand. "Not the best day for you?" he asked.

"I am tired of laying in this bed and not able to do one thing for myself."

"And, taking it out on Sarah, it appears. It isn't easy for her, either, you know."

Patrick changed the subject before Liam could protest. "Catherine and I came with good news. Would you like to hear it?" He motioned her to come and stand next to him.

"I apologize for being in a rotten mood." Liam addressed Catherine. "My brother has lapses of memory. He has forgotten that we haven't met."

Patrick was quick to remedy the awkward situation. "I am sorry. Catherine, my brother, Liam. Liam, meet my wife, Catherine."

It took a couple of beats before the announcement sunk in. Sarah came rushing over and hugged each of them. "I am so happy for you."

"Do I get to kiss the bride?" asked Liam, sporting a sly grin.

Catherine stepped forward expecting a kiss on the hand. Instead, he pulled her forward and gave her a smacking kiss.

She refused to show any fluster because of this rude behavior. Wasn't that what he was hoping for? When she stepped back, she met him eye to eye. "It seems your earlier complaint about being helpless was pure self-pity."

Sarah took a deep breath.

Liam seemed to be taken aback but only for an instant. "Patrick, I believe your wife is one who can stand up for herself. Catherine, I salute you," he said with a mock lift of his hand. "My brother needs someone to rein him in. Have you told Mother?"

Patrick's arm circled Catherine's waist. "Liam takes some getting used to."

He turned to the patient. "As for Mother, we stopped by her room first. I think she will have to ruminate on it for a while."

Liam scowled. "That would be Mother. Is she ever satisfied?"

Catherine felt hemmed in. The hospital room was small and warm without air circulating. Suddenly, she felt faint. She had to get out of there.

Perhaps it was a sixth sense perception or maybe her face paled for Patrick said, "We have to be on our way. We have friends waiting at the Willard Hotel for dinner."

"Aren't you the lucky ones?" came Liam's snide reply. "I wish we could join you, but as you can see I'm a bit incapacitated."

Patrick ushered Catherine to the door. "Time for us to go. Would you care to join us, Sarah?"

"No, thank you. It's kind of you to ask. Have a wonderful evening."

They closed the door behind them. Catherine stood and breathed deeply.

"Are you feeling all right? I'll apologize for him. Sometimes he's too full of himself. I give him quarter because of his condition," Patrick said.

"The room was closing in on me," she replied and took another deep breath.

Patrick took a serious look at her. "The room was getting stuffy for me, also."

Catherine patted her face. "I can understand your brother's disheartened mood but it is no excuse for his brash behavior."

"I agree. Let's get out of this cheerless place and get on with our wedding day."

****

It was after five o'clock when they reached the Willard Hotel. They were escorted to the table where Asa and Carolyn were seated in a private corner. Asa was enjoying a glass of red wine. Carolyn was sipping a cup of hot tea.

A low round centerpiece on a silver tray featured a dozen dried white roses interspersed with sprigs of green holly. Colored ribbons tied into delicate bows surrounded a white pillar candle. The sight brought life to the linen tablecloth underneath it and warmed Catherine's heart.

Asa stood and waited for them to be seated.

"I hope we haven't kept you waiting too long," Patrick greeted them.

"We've been enjoying a quiet chat. How did the news go over with your family?"

"About as I expected," Patrick replied.

"They will all be much happier once they get back home," Catherine added.

"That's understandable," Carolyn said. "Hospitals can be depressing places."

"Enough of this talk," said Patrick. He motioned to the waiter.

"Yes, sir?"

"I would like your best bottle of champagne."

"Of course, Mr. Burke. And, may I offer my congratulations?"

"We accept them, heartily."

The waiter left with a spirit in his step.

"Would you gentlemen excuse us?" Catherine asked.

The men stood as their wives rose and went to the ladies room.

"I have to frequent these nauseating places too often," Carolyn said as they entered the room. "They seem to throw a lot of lavender around to mask the odor, but I don't care to be in here any longer than necessary. It causes my stomach to churn."

She entered a stall and called to Catherine, "Tell me, honestly, Catherine, how did it go at the hospital?"

"Considering the fact that I don't know them very well, and that Patrick hadn't told them in advance, it was accepted." Catherine pulled a powder puff from her handbag and dabbed at her face.

"Perhaps Patrick thought the news would be too much for them earlier."

"You are too kind, Carolyn. I was not pleased."

"Tell me what they said," Carolyn persisted.

"His mother was unhappy we went about it the way we did. She says Patrick can be quite unconventional. One day I'll let you in on a conversation she and I had the last time I came to Washington."

"Ooh, it sounds like we need to have a gab session." Carolyn came out of the stall smoothing the long skirt of her fancy dress. "Is that a surprise to you that Patrick is unconventional?"

"No, that's one of the things I love about him."

Carolyn checked her image in the long, gilded mirror. "Look at this, Catherine. These new, tighter fashions are just not fitting for a woman carrying a child."

Catherine was empathetic toward her friend. "It looks becoming today. Next week I believe you will be tucking that lovely dress away in your trunk for another year."

Carolyn sighed. "And hope I can squeeze back into it then."

They stood together looking into the mirror. Carolyn, the shorter of the two with olive complexion, dark eyes and shining black hair was in contrast to Catherine's light coloring and hazel eyes.

Carolyn turned to the side to survey her profile. "I know I'm going to be round as a balloon."

Catherine was resetting the hairpins into her long hair under her headpiece. She smoothed the cream lace wedding dress. "You worry too much about how this baby is going to alter your appearance. I'm getting jittery about what my wedding night holds in store."

Carolyn gave her friend a hug. "It'll be exciting! Remember when the minister said, 'from this day forth you will both be as one'? Believe me, you will be."

Catherine gave a nervous chuckle. "That's what gives me the jitters. I wonder what the year will bring us?" she mused aloud.

Carolyn patted the small lump beginning to show in her tummy. "All kinds of surprises," she answered. "I would never have believed you and I would be in Washington, but here we are."

"Yes, here we are. Me, twenty-five years old acting like an impulsive teenager. Everything I know and own lies seventy miles away in Clarke County. I haven't the least inkling of how I am going to solve that dilemma. Come on, Carolyn. Let's get out of here before I start thinking too much."

****

Dinner had been a five-course feast. Patrick had seen to it that they had a wedding cake and everyone in the hotel dining room was treated with a piece of the four tier delicately iced cake.

Catherine was overjoyed with all of the planning Patrick had put into the day to make it a memorable a one. It only served to heighten her feelings for him.

It was past eight o'clock when the newlyweds parted company with their good friends and found their touring car and its driver still waiting to carry them home.

Catherine was light-headed from the two glasses of champagne, but she noticed the car wasn't headed for the house on K Street. It was going in the direction where they were married. Back in Georgetown, the car pulled in front of a two-story, colonial style, brick house like so many houses in Virginia.

Patrick got out and turned back to offer his hand to Catherine.

"Patrick, it's getting late. I thought we were going home."

"We are home," he beamed.

She was awestruck as she stepped from the car and stood looking at the house, while Patrick settled up with the driver.

"Thank you kindly, Mr. Burke." He tipped his cap toward Catherine, "I wish you much happiness."

She acknowledged the driver with a nod.

Patrick led her up the short path. Four white columns held up a covered porch that spanned the front of the house. It wasn't like the one on K Street, but it was inviting. Candles had been lit and gave a welcome glow from the two front windows.

"Don't you remember that I said I had built a house in Georgetown?" He smiled at her, waiting for her answer.

"I didn't pay much attention."

"I was given the deed to this property, if you'll recall. This house has been in the process of building for five years. It's not a grand house, Catherine, but it's ours." He swooped her up in his arms, nudged the unlatched door open with his foot and carried her across the threshold. "Welcome to Just in Time, Mrs. Burke!"

"Just in Time?" she laughed.

"Yes. They finished painting yesterday. It's just in time for us to have our wedding night in our home in our own bedroom."

"Oh, Patrick." She buried her face in his neck. "You have given me more today than I ever dreamed possible."

He held her tighter, nuzzled her hair and neither of them said a word...until the thought struck Catherine that her only belongings besides the ones she wore were back at the house on K Street.

She squirmed out of his arms. "Patrick, I haven't any nightclothes!"

"Are they necessary?" He grinned that sly grin of his.

She felt heat rise in her face.

"I'm sorry, Catherine. I had your friend, Carolyn, pick out suitable nightclothes and a day outfit. I was sure you didn't want to climb back into your wedding dress tomorrow. We'll pick up the rest of your belongings later."

Catherine was relieved but held a few reservations about what Carolyn might pick out for a nightgown. Carolyn had a penchant for the unorthodox side of fashion, especially if she wasn't going to be the one to wear it.

"I will pay you back, Patrick, as soon as I settle my affairs in Berryville."

"You are my wife and this is my gift to you," he said with an edge to his voice. "You may have to get used to that."

"I'm sorry. That wasn't kind of me. You have given me the best wedding day I could have hoped for. It will take some time for me to realize that I don't have to take care of everything by myself."

He kissed her with a pent up desire that kept her spellbound; his strong hands caressing her as he had never done before. "We have much to learn about each other," he whispered. "It's time we got at it."

****

They spent the next two days without leaving the confines of the house. Patrick did not mention the warehouse or the hospital. Catherine was in a state of bliss. She was happy just to be with him. The house he had built was pleasing: three bedrooms upstairs, a parlor, dining room, kitchen and sitting room down. Catherine Ramsburg Burke was exactly where she wanted to be. She would settle her affairs in Berryville as quickly as she could.

Chapter 16

Tuesday morning Patrick and Catherine stood on the platform of the Alexandria station waiting for the nine o'clock train. The morning was damp and cold with a blustery wind that made it seem even colder. Catherine wore a fur stole Patrick had received as payment for a debt. He said he had no use for it but it helped the man save face so he accepted the stole. Catherine was pleased because it was warm and fitted over her navy cape that the Barber sisters had knitted for her.

"I wish you could wait to return to Berryville until I can come with you," Patrick said. "I'm uneasy about you traveling alone."

"I have traveled alone before."

"Yes, but now you're my wife."

She was nonchalant, "I fail to see why that makes a difference."

Patrick hesitated as though digesting what Catherine had said. Then he laughed. "I guess it doesn't. What I mean is that I hate to see you go. We have had such a wonderful few days I don't want to break the spell."

She looked up at him. "It has been wonderful hasn't it?" Catherine leaned her head on his shoulder. "I don't want to leave you, and I don't want to face the task ahead of me but I have to."

He made one more plea, "We could both leave on Saturday. Mary Lee would most likely be willing to watch the shop for another week."

She took his hand in hers. "No, Patrick. You have much to do with your family and the warehouse. I need to get my affairs in order. The sooner we have those problems behind us, the sooner we can get on with our lives."

With the sound of the train nearing the platform, the waiting passengers seemed to come to life.

"All aboard for Fairfax, Leesburg and points west," called the conductor as he jumped from the slowing train onto the platform.

Catherine was in no hurry. She lingered with Patrick until she was the last to board.

He kissed her soundly. "Until I see you on Saturday," he said.

The conductor was helpful. "Let me take your bag, ma'am. A lady such as yourself, shouldn't carry her own bag."

Catherine looked at Patrick and gave an amused smile. She went up the two metal steps of the train car, blew him a kiss and mouthed the words, "I love you" before she entered and took her seat next to a window. She could barely see him through the smoke filmed window as he stood on the platform and watched the train chug out of sight.

She had so much on her mind that the trip to Bluemont didn't seem as tedious as her previous trip. When the train pulled into the station, there was a heavy fog, which wasn't unusual on the mountain. She hoped that once they started the descent down the other side toward Berryville that the fog would clear. Weather on the mountain seemed to live by another set of rules.

Harvey Marks was waiting with the twelve-passenger car when the train arrived. It was unusual for Harvey to be on time. Ten passengers were going to take the car, which gave him great pleasure. A full car meant a generous gratuity at the end of the ride.

It was afternoon when they got into the town of Berryville. Catherine decided to go into the hat shop rather than up to her apartment. The bell tinkled when the door opened and Mary Lee Thompson came from the back room.

"Miz' Catherine! I am so happy to see you. I wasn't sure when you would git' back."

"And, I am happy to be here. I thought of calling over at the hotel yesterday and asking for someone to fetch you to the phone, but I didn't want the whole town to know my business."

"We was all worried because you left so fast. Is everythin' all right down there?"

"Yes, at this point it is. Mr. Burke's mother and brother are recovering from the automobile accident." Catherine removed her hat as she looked around the shop. Everything was in order and more orderly than when she had left in such a hurry.

"The shop looks very nice. I knew you would take good care of it."

"Miz' Talley has asked me every day if I heard from you. I was glad you didn't call 'cause I prob'ly would have told her even if I didn't want to. You know how she can twist her words so you end up sayin' somethin' you don't mean to say."

"I know exactly what you mean. Let's put the kettle on and have a cup of tea. I have many things I would like to discuss with you." Catherine glanced out the front window. "Oh no, Mary Lee, look who's waddling across the street."

"Miz' Talley. How did she know you was back?"

"From peeking behind her lace curtain, I suspect," Catherine replied. "There's nothing Mrs. Talley likes better than to keep an eye on the comings and goings on Main Street. You go ahead and put the kettle on and I'll do my best to satisfy her need to pry."

Mary Lee headed for the back room and Catherine went to meet Lavinia at the front door.

"Hello, Mrs. Talley. I haven't seen you for a few days."

Lavinia was huffy, "Indeed you haven't, Catherine. Where have you been? There is no excuse for you to leave town without letting us know where you were. Even Reverend Smythe has been concerned."

"I will apologize to him. I certainly didn't mean to cause consternation with my neighbors." Catherine smiled at Lavinia.

"We are more than neighbors, Catherine. Your mother and I were good friends. I did promise her that I would keep an eye on you."

"Yes, Mrs. Talley. I am sorry that I had to leave so suddenly. Mr. Burke's family was in an automobile accident. I needed to go to Washington in haste."

The news sent Lavinia abuzz. "An auto accident? Oh, how dreadful! Were they badly hurt? I am so sorry." And then, after her condolences, "Where did you stay my dear? Do you have friends that put you up?"

Catherine couldn't resist, "Why I stayed in Mr. Burke's house."

Lavinia gasped, "Catherine, you didn't!"

"Well, yes I did. Along with his sister-in-law and the house servants." She placed her hand on Lavinia's arm, "Believe me, Mrs. Talley, it was all quite proper."

"I do hope so, Catherine, for your mother's sake. You have already been quite bold with this courtship. It is a courtship, isn't it?"

"It is indeed. Now, you will have to excuse me as I have much catching up to do."

"Of course you do. Mary Lee has done the best she knows, but…"

"Which means I left the shop in capable hands," Catherine interrupted.

"I suppose. Well, I must be on my way. I just wanted to make sure everything is all right with you."

"Rest assured that I am fine. It was nice of you to drop by."

Catherine watched as Lavinia toddled down the steps and waited for a passing buggy before she ventured to cross the street.

The big black horse pulling the buggy snorted when he passed by the stout little lady. Did he disapprove of the editor's wife? Catherine knew Lavinia would pass her news as she saw fit. Accuracy was not one of her virtues.

Catherine closed the door tightly and went to sit with Mary Lee in the back room. The boiling kettle gave a sharp whistle. Mary Lee lifted it from the flame. She had placed tea leaves in silver teaspoons, closed their lids and was pouring tea when Catherine entered and asked, "How has business been?"

"I took a few orders fer spring hats, but other than that not too much. Miz' Levi came by and bought that purty hat you had in the window. She said she's had her eye on it since after Christmas and her husband said if she wanted to buy it she oughta' 'afore its gone." Mary Lee pulled a chair out from under the table. "I guess that's why I had time to straighten up everythin'…in the shop, I mean."

"Did you stay in my quarters while I was away?" Catherine asked, as she pulled out another chair and took her place at the table.

"No ma'am. I didn't feel right about it so I went on home. O'ourse I did go up and check to make sure everythin' was okay."

"You know you were more than welcome to stay up there. I do thank you for all you did." Catherine took a sip of tea and gazed out the window into her familiar back yard. Today was one of the rare January days that seemed to indicate spring was on its way. In the back of her mind, she knew the snows of February and the bitter winds of March would follow.

Catherine turned her attention back to Mary Lee, who was busy fiddling with a piece of material she had in her hand.

"I cain't never seem to get this hatband to do what I want it to do."

Catherine was edgy. "Stop tinkering with that. It makes me nervous. I have something very important to discuss with you."

Her tone startled Mary Lee and caused her to look up in wide-eyed surprise. "Did I do somethin' wrong?"

"Not a bit. I want to talk to you about taking over this business."

"Oh, Miz' Catherine. I don't know 'bout that."

"Mary Lee, I married Mr. Burke while I was in Washington."

The news caused her to spill her tea. "You was married?"

"Yes. So, I need to make some changes. One of them is what to do with the hat shop. I thought, if you are interested, I could help finance you so you could buy it. Would you like that?"

"Oh, Miz' Catherine. I would love to own this hat shop. But you know I don't have any money. Besides, people 'spect you to be here. They might not come if it's just me."

Catherine was put out. "For heaven's sakes, Mary Lee, you know this shop and business as well as I do. Wouldn't you like to have a chance at something better?"

"Course I would. Do you really think I can do it?"

Catherine sighed. "I wouldn't even suggest it if I had any doubt. If you don't think you can I'll just put a For Sale sign in the window." Catherine got up from the table and stood looking out at the back yard. Her back yard was prettier than the one in Georgetown. Of course, Patrick had done nothing to improve the grounds, he had just seen to it to have a house built. Her yard held a beautiful large oak tree and the small town run that ran through the middle of the yard. Today it had a coating of ice but still it trickled on. And there was the gazebo that had been her haven from everyday cares.

She turned back to Mary Lee. "We all have to make changes in our lives and we always hope they are for the better."

"Well, I surely think ownin' this hat shop is a whole heap better than what I got now. If you can help me, Miz' Catherine, then I want to try it."

The milliner gave the young girl a hug. "I am overjoyed. I'll sit down with the lawyer and the banker and see what we can work out."

That evening Catherine found she had no appetite because she missed Patrick. She made a sandwich of peanut butter and strawberry jam before she retired, or tried to retire. The light from the kerosene lamp on her bedside table threw enough light that she attempted to read a story in a McCall's magazine. Reading always helped to lull her to sleep, but not tonight. She was unprepared for the oppressive feeling that gripped her. How could her feelings change so drastically? Her own bed in her own apartment had always been a comfort after long days in the millinery shop. But, this night without Patrick by her side was dispiriting. It solidified her determination to free herself of any obligations so that she could return to Washington with him on Sunday.

Nothing else mattered to her. Not the shop, not her apartment, not her mother's china or the treasured ornate silverware or the cherished mahogany dining room set. All of those things that had seemed so important to her, nothing mattered except Patrick.

When morning came, Catherine dressed in a hurry in the cold bedroom. In the kitchen she lit the kerosene stove and put the kettle on for a cup of hot tea. Glancing out the kitchen window she saw the trees swaying in a stiff breeze.It was time to pull from the chest the Persian lamb coat that her mother had passed down to her.

Her mother had said it would never go out of style. But it had. Catherine had cut it off to make a long jacket, then trimmed the collar and cuffs with rabbit fur. She fashioned a belt with the material she had salvaged after altering the coat and trimmed a hat to match.

Chapter 17

Catherine was sitting in the office of the vice president of the Bank. Mr. Williams had recently been appointed to the position after spending some years in banking in Fairfax, Virginia. Charles Williams was the son of a prominent local family and a nephew of the bank president. According to local gossip, he had spread his wings, after graduating from the University of Virginia, and had returned to the nest to finally settle down. Many people were under the opinion that he was aware of the fact that his uncle was nearing retirement. Wouldn't it be a plum to step into his shoes?

She watched as he perused information regarding her request to help Mary Lee obtain a mortgage for the hat shop. It was her first meeting with him. He was polite and aloof, characteristic of a banker.

"So, as I understand it, you are wanting to sell your millinery shop to Mrs. Thompson, but she is short of funds. Is that correct?"

"Yes, that's my intention. I would like to give her a fair price. I thought we could make arrangements for her to get a mortgage from the bank. I have every confidence she will do as well as I have."

He sat back in his big, leather chair. "Have you established a price?"

"No," she answered. "I hoped you could help me with that. The hat shop and the apartment above were bequeathed to me."

"They were bequeathed free of a mortgage?"

"Yes."

"You are fortunate." He leaned back on the desk and rolled a pencil with his fingers. "Why don't you rent the shop to Mrs. Thompson? In that way, you will receive income and, if by some circumstance she isn't successful, the shop will revert to you."

"I had hoped to be rid of any obligations regarding my holdings."

He gave her a friendly smile. "Miss Ramsburg, my advice is to hold onto your shop and your apartment. Real estate is always a sound investment. Are you planning on leaving Berryville?"

The chair became uncomfortable and she shifted her position. This was information she had not planned to divulge. She felt she had no choice so she answered in a clipped tone, " Mr. Williams, I am recently married to Patrick Burke. Yes, I will be leaving and living in the Washington, D.C. area with my husband. If I am living there, I can't very well keep an eye on what I own here."

Catherine had not wanted the news known in this way. Her intention was to tell Reverend Smythe so he could announce it in church on Sunday. That seemed the proper way to handle the situation. The damage was done.

He showed no change of emotion except for a slight smile. "I would say that congratulations are in order. I understand how difficult it must be to make these decisions about your property. What is your husband's opinion?"

"I haven't consulted him. This is my property."

"Once you are married your property becomes your husband's also. Therefore, he will have to sign any papers that we draw up unless he concedes his part of the ownership."

Catherine's ire was rising. "So, what you are telling me is that if I signed these papers a week ago, before I was married, I would be free to do as I pleased? And, even though all of the ownership is in my name, because I chose to be married my husband has to be included?"

"Yes, ma'am, that's the way the law works. I suggest you discuss this with your husband. Now, if he is willing to give up his rights, you can have that done at the lawyer's office."

He picked up another file. "To get back to your first request for a mortgage to Mrs. Thompson. I'm afraid the bank cannot allow that kind of borrowing without a substantial down payment. I took the liberty of examining Mrs. Thompson's account. Just looking at it, I'm sure the bank would not allow her to take on that kind of a debt."

Catherine hesitated before she stood. Mr. Williams had told her what she didn't want to hear, but he had been kind and she made an attempt to swallow her disappointment.

"Thank you. I will talk with my husband this weekend. I had hoped to have all of this behind me before he came."

"My best advice to you, Mrs. Burke, is to hold onto what you own. You may need it one day."

Catherine left the bank feeling disgruntled. She glanced over at her millinery shop and wanted to throw a stone through the window. Instead, she went to the general store and bought a Hershey candy bar.

Once she had opened for the day some of her frustration had abated. A customer had no sooner left from paying the last of the installment on a beautiful velvet hat Catherine had put away for her when she spied Lavinia coming across the street.

What can the busybody want now, she thought. Surely, she can't have gone to the bank and heard of my marriage this quickly. But, that was exactly what Lavinia had done.

She burst into the shop saying, "Catherine, what is this I've heard. You have been married!"

Catherine looked up from sewing. "News travels fast in this town. Did you hear it from Mr. Williams?"

Lavinia gave a condescending shake of her head, "No. I didn't hear it from Mr. Williams."

"I'm sure it wasn't Mary Lee."

Lavinia could hardly keep her body still. She blurted out, "Someone was passing by Mr.

William's office when you were leaving and heard him call you Mrs. Burke."

Catherine sat calmly sewing on a hat. "Someone has good ears," she said.

"Well, is it true?" Lavinia was point blank.

Catherine put her sewing down. "Yes it is. Patrick and I were married last week when I went to Washington."

"Catherine, without even a proper period of engagement? You know that should be six months at the least. People will talk."

"People will talk anyway, Mrs. Talley. I will tell you truthfully there is no need for Mr. Burke and I to hurry up a marriage as we have done nothing improper. I will be leaving to live with him in Georgetown."

"Oh my," said Lavinia, fanning her face as if the news were more than she could bear. "You haven't known him that long, Catherine, just a few short months. Are you sure you have done the right thing?"

"I have never been so sure of anything in my life." Catherine rose and went to Lavinia. "Patrick is a wonderful man and I want you to be happy for me."

"Of course I am, but you'll leave us and I've always had to look after you after your mother, my good friend, passed away."

"Just look at it as one more burden that has been lifted." Catherine was kind. Knowing Lavinia, as she did, she was sure her neighbor's bluster was only because she hadn't heard the news first. If people at the bank were talking, the news of her marriage would be all over town and Lavinia couldn't be the first one to peddle it.

The nosy neighbor left the shop with a bit of a slump to her shoulders. Catherine smiled to herself. No more secrets, she could relax.

It was three o'clock in the afternoon when she decided to close the shop and pay a visit to Reverend Smythe. It was only right that she apologize to him if he had had any concern about her welfare when she was gone for those few days. She wanted to tell him of her marriage. Perhaps he had already heard, but she knew she must meet with him face to face.

The January day had turned bitter cold and dark clouds were forming in the sky. From her vantage point on Main Street she could see few pedestrians. To bundle against the cold, she wore her navy cape with the fur wrap over it.

Reverend and Mrs. Smythe were at home when she arrived. Mrs. Smythe answered her knock and bid her inside the large, two-story, red brick rectory that sat behind the Grace Episcopal Church.

The big house was deathly quiet except for the footsteps that could be heard tapping across wooden floors. Catherine was seated in the pastor's study. The walls were lined with books and there was a hearty fire blazing in the fireplace. It was her first time in that room. It was small and cozy. She had expected the pastor would have a large desk similar to the one in the banker's office, but she was surprised to find a secretary's desk placed in a corner and a couple of small embroidered chairs facing each other in front of the fireplace. Catherine sat in a straight-backed chair nearest the door and held her fur over her arm. Mrs. Smythe had offered to take it, but Catherine was still chilled from the outdoor air when she arrived.

Reverend Smythe entered wearing a black suit with a white-banded collar. He was a slight man of average height and wore spectacles. Catherine rose from her chair.

"Catherine, how good to see you," he said as he held both her hands. "I am relieved. Come and sit nearer the fire. It has turned into a bone-chilling day. May I take your wrap?"

"No, thank you, Reverend Smythe. I'm still warming up from the walk. It is bitter out there."

He motioned to her to move to one of the comfortable embroidered chairs where he took a seat opposite her.

Leaning forward with crossed arms resting on his knees he looked directly at her. His look was part concern and part admonition, "I must say you had us a bit worried. What brings this unexpected but most welcome visit?"

Catherine sat straight as a board. "Have you talked with Mrs. Talley today?"

"No. I made a home visit and had just gotten in a short time before you came. Is there something wrong?"

Catherine relaxed a bit as she replied, "No, sir, nothing is wrong. According to Mrs. Talley I have caused quite a stir by leaving so abruptly so I came to apologize for any consternation I may have caused. And…to tell you that I was married on Saturday to Patrick Burke."

Reverend Smythe leaned back as if digesting the information. "Ah, yes. The young man I met earlier. He seems a good lad. Married, you say?"

Catherine laid her fur across her lap. The heat from the fireplace was beginning to make her uncomfortable or was it just the conversation she was having with the minister?

"Oh, he is, Reverend Smythe. It was rather a spur of the moment decision." At that admission he raised an eyebrow.

"What I mean is…" Then she told him the story. "I wanted you to hear the news from me. You are free to announce it at the Sunday service if you think that is in order. Patrick will be coming on Saturday and I know we would both appreciate receiving your blessing."

"That you will have," he said. "Is there anything more that I can do?"

"No, thank you. That will be more than enough. I believe I am as surprised with myself as everyone else seems to be."

The kind minister rose from his seat and offered her a hand up. "I am pleased you came to me in this way. It is a pity how stories can get twisted in their passage."

Catherine was relieved. This meeting she had dreaded turned out to give her a boost.

The minister's wife gave a knock on the door before she entered carrying a tray containing a polished silver tea service and ginger cookies.

"Catherine, won't you stay for tea? It's so cold outside."

The reverend was quick to step in, "Catherine is now Mrs. Burke, Jenny. They were married on Saturday."

He took the tray from his wife's hands lest she drop it.

"Oh, my!" was all she could say.

Her husband came to her rescue, "Isn't this good news, dear?"

The intercession had allowed the woman to collect her wits.

"Of course it is. Congratulations to you and Mr. Burke. I will have to say the news took me a bit by surprise."

"I believe it is having the same effect on everyone. Thank you, for the offer, Mrs. Smythe. I would love to stay for tea, but I must be on my way."

"Be sure and bundle up. There have been many people sick with the grippe. I think the best way to ward it off is to keep warm."

Catherine left the house feeling relieved one more obligation had been lifted. Mr. White was closing up the general store as she walked in. Her throat felt scratchy. She assumed it was due to the fireplace in the reverend's study causing dryness in the air. After she bought some Smith Brothers cough drops to soothe the irritation, she went back out into the cold and walked the half-block to her place.

Catherine unlocked her front door, removed her coat and hung it on the wooden coat tree in the foyer. Climbing the flight of stairs to her quarters, it felt as if the events of the day had taken their toll because her legs were weary as she mounted the stairs.

First, she placed her hat, gloves and scarf on a side table before she went into the kitchen and put the kettle on. With her wool shawl pulled tightly around her upper body, she went in to stoke the embers in the fireplace. Then she went into the bedroom and pulled on her flannel gown.

The fire began to blaze and the shrill sound of the teakettle told her that the water was boiling. It was only six o'clock but she was overly tired. The cough drops had helped and the hot tea added some comfort.

As Catherine sat in front of the fire she thought about her visit to the bank. The news that Patrick also had to be a part of it and that Mary Lee couldn't get a mortgage weighed on her mind. Well, if she couldn't do anything until Patrick arrived, then she would just have to wait.

The bank would be closed on Saturday. She and Patrick had planned to return to Georgetown together on Sunday. Perhaps she should phone him. That idea was put out of her thoughts because it might just upset him. She knew he wanted to have her back in Washington as soon as possible. He had enough to do with running the warehouse, taking care of the house on K Street and seeing to the folks in the hospital than to have her calling and sounding like a lost child. That was exactly how she felt.

By seven o'clock, she had banked the fire, taken two aspirin tablets and made a Vicks' poultice for her chest and neck. Her throat hurt, her legs and body ached and she knew these physical complaints had to be from the hectic pace she had been keeping. A night's sleep would do her good. She fell into her bed and cuddled under the down filled quilt.

Chapter 18

On Wednesday morning Catherine's bodily complaints woke her from sleep. Her throat was so sore it hurt to swallow. Any movement caused her whole body to ache. Her head felt as though someone was drumming inside. She struggled out of bed and threw her wool shawl around her shoulders. The fireplace was down to embers. Pulling a small log from the wood bucket caused her to stumble as she placed the log over the dying coals.

In the kitchen she put the kettle on and let it heat while she gargled with salt water. After brewing the tea, she mixed a teaspoon of honey with a spot of lemon juice and drizzled it into the teacup.

She sat at the kitchen table. The warm beverage was soothing to her throat and warmed her insides, but her head still drummed. She thought of taking a hot bath. It was too much work to put water into the ham boiler and wait for it to heat. No sooner had she finished the tea than she began to feel hot and feverish, followed by a bout of chills. Did she have the grippe that Mrs. Smythe had said was going around? How could she have developed it so quickly? This was only her third day home and she had felt fine when she arrived. There was nothing to do but to either crawl back into bed or sit before the fireplace. She poured a glass of water and took two aspirins before she carried the teakettle of hot water into the living room. She poured it into a basin and slid her feet into the warm water. There she sat with the woolen shawl pulled over her flannel nightdress, trying to warm her person from the feet up. She glanced out the upstairs window of the room and saw a heavy thickness of snow on the roof across the way. Snow was falling in earnest. There would be no need to open the shop in this kind of weather. She was not up to tending a shop and gave thanks for the intervention of snow. Was Providence at work?

Catherine spent the whole day sicker than she could ever remember. One minute she was hot and perspiring and the next she was a bundle of chills and shaking. The aching continued. The headache was relieved at times only to return with a vengeance. She was so alone. She missed Patrick desperately. He would be the one to keep the fire going, bring her hot tea, a cold cloth for her forehead or wrap his arms around her when the chills hit. She knew he would do all of those things if he were here. But, Patrick wasn't here so she would suffer through this by herself.

The next morning she was asleep on the sofa. The fire had gone out and the room was bleak in the cold. Apparently she had found the strength to pull the down quilt from her bed because it covered her, although she didn't remember doing it. Catherine was too spent to get up. If she just had to lie there and die, then she was resolved to that fact.

It was around two o'clock in the afternoon when a voice penetrated her foggy mind. She awoke in a groggy state with someone shaking her.

"Miz' Catherine?" Mary Lee Thompson stood over her with a concerned look.

Catherine struggled to focus her eyes. "Mary Lee?" she asked.

"Yes, ma'am. Are you all right?"

"No, Mary Lee. I'm not all right." Catherine's voice was hoarse.

"My goodness, Miz' Catherine, what's wrong?"

"I think I must have the grippe so don't come too close. It hit me all of a sudden. Maybe I picked it up in Washington or on the crowded train. All I know is that I am very ill." Catherine sat up with effort and wiped her watery eyes with a handkerchief, then hacked a dry cough.

"Lots of folks have got it," Mary Lee said. "Jake Fletcher got vomitin' and the runs so bad he had to go to the hospital up in Winchester, and ol' Granny Getz…I heard she died of pneumonia after she got it."

"Mary Lee, I don't need to hear that kind of news just at this time." Her own voice grated on her ears. "I am glad you came by. Would you mind fixing me some tea and maybe toast a piece of bread? I feel so bad I don't think I can move off this sofa. What day is this?"

"It's Thursday. Now, don't you worry none. I'll stay right here until you're better. I came by 'cause we had that bad snowstorm and I thought you might need some help shovelin' off the front stairs. It's a good thing I still had a key 'cause I let myself in the shop when I got scared that you hadn't swept any of the snow away." Her wide-eyed, worried expression confirmed that fact.

"Don't look so anxious. I hope I'll be better in a couple of days. Unless, of course, I get pneumonia like old Granny Getz and kick the bucket."

Catherine's attempt at humor was lost on Mary Lee. " Don't you be talkin' like that, Miz' Catherine. It makes me sad to think on it."

"The tea is in the right side of the cupboard. On the sideboard, you will find some honey. Put a spoonful of that in the tea. It's supposed to be good for a sore throat. It hasn't helped me much because my throat hurts so bad, I can't even swallow without pain."

"How about if I fix you a hot mustard plaster for your neck. My mama said that always works," Mary Lee offered.

"I'll try anything," Catherine replied.

"I hear a shot of whiskey's good too," Mary Lee continued, "but you prob'ly don't have none of that in the house."

Catherine waved the suggestion away, "Just bring me the mustard plaster and the tea." She flopped back down on the sofa. "I do believe I've forgotten my manners in all this misery. Thank you, Mary Lee."

The young rescuer gave a big smile and went off to the kitchen.

****

Mary Lee Thompson, dedicated friend that she was, stayed through to Saturday morning. Catherine, with her friend's help, had enough strength to take a sponge bath and wash her hair. Mary Lee pulled the long hair back into a braid, then helped her into a fresh nightdress. By the time Catherine was washed up she was washed out, so she resumed her reclining position on the sofa.

Patrick was to come in on the morning train so Mary Lee was comfortable leaving Catherine by herself for an hour until he arrived. But before she left, she informed Catherine that Patrick had called on Thursday.

"I went over to the hotel and took the phone call. I told him your throat was too sore to talk. I just couldn't tell him how sick you looked. It wasn't a real lie was it Miz' Catherine? Your voice sounded pretty bad and I didn't want Mr. Burke to have to worry none."

"You did fine, but why didn't you tell me earlier?"

"I maybe should have. I knew you would be worryin' that Mr. Patrick would be worryin' and…"

"I understand. I'm happy he's coming. I can't thank you enough for seeing me through these past couple of days. You had to leave your place unattended so I hope the cold hasn't caused any problems at your house. Why don't you take that fur stole down in the foyer for extra warmth? Help yourself to any food you need. There's a big sack of potatoes, some carrots, beets and a few cabbages in that cubby off my back room in the shop. It's cool enough to keep them good. Heaven knows I can't eat them all. Gertie Ellinger sends them over because she has so many. I can always find someone who can use the extras."

Mary Lee beamed. "That's mighty nice of you, Miz' Catherine. My brother has been stayin' with me 'til he can find a place of his own. He's hopin' to get a job out at the Audley farm and live in a tenant house out there."

"Well, I hope he does. Have you been having to feed him or has he helped with providing?" Catherine knew he hadn't. She knew Mary Lee's brother, Walter, to be a shiftless sort. He was not Catherine's problem, but it did cross her mind he was one more bad situation she hadn't considered when she thought of selling the hat shop. Mary Lee could never turn her brother down.

"Would you mind leaving the front door unlocked when you leave?" Catherine asked. "I want Mr. Burke to be able to get in. The hat shop is locked up, isn't it?"

"Yes, ma'am it is, and I'll be sure to leave the front door unlocked. I done left this hot pot of tea and a couple of aspirins on this side table. You gonna' be all right until Mr. Patrick comes?"

"I'll be fine."

"Bye, Miz' Catherine. I'll drop by on Monday."

"Good-bye Mary Lee and thanks again."

233

Catherine was better. The chills and fever had gone along with the sore throat. She still had a runny nose and hacking cough and her joints complained when she moved, but she could get up for a few minutes before she felt the need to collapse on the sofa.

Outdoors, the snow had not melted because of the cold temperatures. The winter sun was shining. From where she sat on the sofa she could see it glistening off the mounds covering the surrounding roofs. Catherine leaned back on the two bed pillows Mary Lee had propped behind her back on the sofa. The fire was casting its warmth and she felt an inner glow. Patrick would be coming. Just the thought of seeing him again lifted her spirits. When she closed her eyes, she could feel his gentle caress as she floated off into a restful doze.

Due to Herbert's late arrival with the twelve-passenger car at the Bluemont station, it was two o'clock in the afternoon before Patrick arrived. Catherine awoke to the sound of the irritating doorknocker. After there was no answer by the third attempt, she heard the front door opening.

"Catherine…Catherine?" Without hesitation she heard his footsteps running up the staircase.

"Catherine?"

"In the living room, Patrick." She was trying to get up off the sofa just as he came into the room.

"My God, Catherine, what's wrong?" He rushed to her side.

"Oh, Patrick. I have been so sick and I've missed you so."

He knelt down beside her. "I talked with Mary Lee on Thursday. From what she said, I thought it was just a bout of laryngitis. You look like you have been run over by a wagon."

"I feel like I have been run over by a wagon," she replied.

He was irritated. "Why didn't Mary Lee tell me? I would have come as soon as I could get a train out. It wasn't her place to keep that from me!"

"Patrick, don't blame Mary Lee. She didn't want to worry you. She stayed right here and took care of me until this morning."

"Still," his voice had mellowed, "I should have known."

Catherine took his hand in hers. "I'm much better and you're here and that's all that matters. I have so much to tell you but I am so tired. I don't want anything except to climb into bed with you and let you hold me all night."

He gave a tender kiss on her forehead and stood up. "I am going to fix us both a pot of soup, brew some tea and then, dear lady, I will hold you in the confines of your bed until you say we must leave it."

"Patrick, I'm not sure I have any soup."

"Aha, the medical man in me said there is nothing like soup when you're not feeling well. I picked up not one but two cans of Campbell's chicken noodle soup before I boarded the train. You just relax and Dr. Burke will have you feeling up to snuff in no time."

"You may never become a doctor. These past couple of weeks have been such a disappointment all the way around, I'm not sure anything is going to turn out the way we'd like."

"What do you mean disappointing? We're married, aren't we? And, we had two wonder filled days, didn't we?"

Catherine nodded her head.

He held her face in his hands, "Then, cheer up Mrs. Burke. There is nothing we can't do together if we set out to do it."

She couldn't help but smile. "The can opener is in the top drawer."

Chapter 19

Sunday brought Reverend Smythe to Catherine's door around one o'clock in the afternoon. Patrick was casually dressed for Sunday. He zipped down the stairs at the sound of the grating doorknocker.

"Good afternoon, Mr. Burke."

A surprised Patrick nodded and returned the man's greeting, "Good afternoon."

Reverend Smythe stood on the cold stoop patting his gloved hands. "I hope I didn't disturb you. Catherine had made a special request that I announce your marriage at this morning's service. I understand she has been ill, and when I didn't see her in church, I thought I should pay a call."

Both men held an uneasy countenance; Patrick, because neither he nor Catherine were dressed properly to receive a member of the clergy, and, the minister, because it was awkward calling unannounced on two newlyweds.

"Come in out of the cold, Reverend Smythe. Catherine is right upstairs. She's been down with the grippe but I do believe she's on the mend. She'll be delighted you stopped by," knowing full well how unwelcome his visit would be.

Patrick led the minister up the stairs calling to Catherine on the way up. "Reverend Smythe is here."

She was still in her nightclothes and lounging on the sofa. "Do come up," she called back, quickly covering herself with a crocheted shawl that had been draped over the back of the sofa.

The men entered the room and Patrick angled a straight-backed chair for the minister to sit.

"Catherine, I am so sorry to hear that you've been ill. Are you feeling better?"

"Oh, much. I do apologize for my appearance. I didn't know the news was out that I was ill, but I guess not having the shop open was a good indication."

The minister cleared his throat. "Well, to be honest, Mrs. Talley was the bearer of that news. I believe her words were that she had to shake it out of Mary Lee. I'm sure she didn't mean it literally." He smiled at Catherine and glanced over at Patrick, who had taken a seat in the chintz chair.

"This probably isn't the way you two planned to spend your time together."

"You're right about that," Patrick agreed. "I believe Catherine and I have had the most unconventional wedding and honeymoon period anyone has ever heard of."

"Yes, I suppose that's true. It will all smooth out, I would hope." The minister turned his full attention to Catherine. "I not only wanted to see how you were faring, but to tell you that I followed through with your request to have your marriage announced at services this morning. As it was, hearing of your illness allowed me to give a reason for your absence. I am happy to find you recuperating, and to see that Mr. Burke is able to be with you. I'll be sure and relay the good news to Mrs. Talley," the minister informed them. He rose to leave. "She said she was worried about you but knew she would catch whatever it is you have so she stayed away."

Catherine gave an impish smile. "God works in wondrous ways, does he not, Reverend Smythe?"

"He does at that," he chuckled. "Perhaps, Jenny could send over some soup."

"That's very kind, but that won't be necessary," Catherine replied, regaining her usual polite demeanor. "Patrick is taking wonderful care of me while he's here. I expect I will be out by tomorrow or the next day. I have much to do. It is kind of you to stop by, and please give Mrs. Smythe my good wishes."

"Indeed I will," the minister answered.

The men went down the stairs. Patrick bid the preacher good day and watched as he headed off in the direction of the Grace Episcopal Church.

When Patrick went back into the living room, Catherine had removed the shawl because the heat from the fireplace was too hot.

"I believe you put a bit too much wood on the fire. We may have to open a window. The poor minister must have been sweltering while he was here."

"He wouldn't hear of me taking his coat. Besides, it probably felt good to him. As I recall, there isn't an ounce of fat on his body."

"You should talk," she laughed. "I think you have lost weight since I left you on Monday. Are you running yourself ragged with the business and tending to the invalids in the hospital? I do worry about you, Patrick."

He came over and squeezed onto the sofa next to her. "I'm not the one who caught the grippe," he chided in a good-natured way.

"No, and I hope you don't." She snuggled next to him. "We have to talk about what I am going to do with the shop and this apartment. I went to the bank last Tuesday and talked with the vice president. Mary Lee is not going to be allowed a mortgage as she doesn't have the assets required."

He tightened his arm around her, "Truthfully, Catherine. Do you think Mary Lee is capable of running a shop by herself?"

"She does a fine job when I've had to leave."

"Yes, but you return. I would guess your regular customers will continue to buy in your shop because they know you will be coming back. Mary Lee is a good help and a good person, but she doesn't have the refinement I suspect your customers appreciate."

Catherine sat up and fanned herself. "Patrick, I do think you will have to raise that window."

He left the sofa and pushed the window up a couple of inches.

"There's a piece of wood in the corner you can prop it with," Catherine informed him before she continued with her story. "My visit to the bank wasn't what I expected. I found out that, because we married, you are the owner of my assets. That means you will have to sign any papers or make any decisions about my property that you see fit." She made an attempt to keep the cynicism out of her voice but failed.

"My, my, my," he headed back toward the sofa. "Not only snagged the most desirable woman in this part of the country, but I've become endowed with wealth in the process."

"I doubt that people in this area look on my holdings as a sign of wealth. Did you know about this archaic law?"

"I must confess that I did." He leaned over and kissed her on the cheek. "And, if I'd told you about it, you would have put off marriage. I was not going to let that happen. I want nothing to do with your holdings. All I have to do is to sign off my rights and you may dispose of your properties as you wish."

His kiss gave her a warm glow. "You would do that?"

"Do you think I married you for your money?" His devilish grin caused her to laugh.

"With the luxuries I've seen in Washington, I can honestly say that thought never crossed my mind."

****

On Monday morning Patrick inched out of bed so he didn't disturb Catherine's slumber. The room was cold with frost on the windows. He dressed quickly before going to the living room to stoke up a fire in the fireplace. There was not an ember alive. He chastised himself for allowing that to happen. He should have known better than to let a fire die out in the cold of January.

Patrick put on his gloves, hat and jacket to go in search of some kindling wood. He didn't have to go far because Catherine had kindling and logs stacked neatly on the back porch. It wasn't long before he had a nice fire going. Catherine would wake up to a warm room and never be the wiser that he had erred in his caretaking. Patrick thought of putting over a pot of coffee. Instead he went to the Berryville Hotel for breakfast. The smell of coffee might wake his ailing wife and he wanted her to get as much rest as possible. He was not going to return to Washington without her. She needed to be well enough to make the trip.

The hotel smelled of breakfast. Patrick seated himself near one of the large windows so he could observe the town waking up. There were only a few customers in the dining room. They nodded a friendly greeting as Patrick entered.

The owner's son, a young lad with a peach fuzz beard, came to take his order. "Good mornin', Mr. Burke."

"Good morning, Henry."

"What can I get for you to eat?"

Patrick never glanced at the menu that sat on the table. "I'll have a piece of ham with scrambled eggs, a couple of biscuits and fried apples. And Henry, I want a big cup of coffee."

"Yessir," he replied. The young teen hesitated and cleared his throat as if unsure of his next words. "We heard you and Miz' Catherine was married."

Patrick smiled at the embarrassed young man, "You heard right, Henry."

"Miz' Talley told us that Miz' Catherine is sick."

"That's true also," replied Patrick. "I'm happy to report she is doing much better."

"That's good. I'll tell my mom. We all like Miz' Catherine."

Henry brought the coffee right away. Patrick added some cream and savored the taste as he watched out the window. At six o'clock on that Monday morning the town was beginning to wake up.

Henry's mom had fixed a piece of ham that covered the plate and piled the scrambled eggs on top of it. The biscuits were warm allowing the butter to settle in. Patrick drizzled honey over the buttered biscuits emanating an aroma of fresh baked dough.

After he finished breakfast, Patrick called the warehouse from the hotel to tell them he wouldn't be in for at least a couple of days. Joseph, the accountant he had left in charge, would have to handle matters until he returned. Patrick was comforted with the thought that Miss McKay, his secretary, would be there to answer any questions Joseph had. Nothing got past Eva W. McKay, and the rest of the employees knew it.

Catherine was still asleep when Patrick returned. He put a kettle of water on the stove for tea.

He sat at the kitchen table and let his thoughts wander. He had been married for a little over a week. His wife is sick, his brother and mother in the hospital, his hopes for medical school put on the back burner and his house in Georgetown sitting idle. This obsession of Catherine's laboring over what to do with the hat shop only caused him to feel more aggravation. He had enough money that she could turn the key in the lock and leave. They could get on with their life and…

"Patrick?"

"I'll be right in," he called.

One look at her and his heart melted.

"You're awake early," he said.

"I think I slept well. You smell like bacon."

"Ham," he corrected her as he leaned over and kissed her cheek. "I went to the hotel for breakfast. The whole place smells like fried pig."

Catherine laughed.

"How do you feel?" he asked, "Are you ready for some breakfast?"

"I feel so much better since you're here. I guess I should eat something but my stomach is still queasy." She hacked a dry cough and laid back on the pillow.

"Your breakfast will be served shortly."

He went to the kitchen and returned with milk toast and tea. "This should rest easy on your unaccommodating stomach."

He propped her up with pillows, placed the tray across her lap. He sat on the edge of the bed while she ate.

"Aren't you supposed to be at the warehouse?"

"Yes, but I called and told them I wouldn't be in for a couple of days. I am not about to leave here without you."

"I don't know if I'm up to solving any problems today. I want to get up and when I do I want to fall right back in bed."

"It's going to take some time before you regain your strength, Catherine. Why don't you just close up the shop, come back to Washington and leave everything as it is until you have time to decide what to do?"

She looked at him wide-eyed, "How could I possibly do that? That shop has always been open."

"Then leave Mary Lee in charge; you've done that before."

"Yes, but not indefinitely. I couldn't."

"You could but you won't." he said. He left her side and walked to look out the window.

Catherine was calm and sipped her tea. "Are we having an argument?" she asked.

Patrick turned and cocked his head. He smiled. "No," he said. "We're having a difference of opinion."

He came back to the bed and took her face in his hands, "Damn it, Catherine. I just want to get on with life."

"And so do I," she replied. "As soon as we get me on my feet, your family out of the hospital, Liam back running the warehouse, and you and I snuggled into our house in Georgetown." She scrunched up her face. "That should only take about six months."

They burst out laughing and Patrick climbed onto the bed beside her. "Mrs. Burke, you were right. We are a pair!" he said.

****

It was Wednesday before Catherine felt the desire to get dressed in street clothes. Patrick had drawn a hot bath for her. The water was warm and soothing to her still aching joints. It was an effort to dress, but she managed. She was determined to settle her affairs.

Perhaps there was a positive side to her illness. In the days she could do nothing but lay around and think, she made her decision about her property. She would close up the hat shop until spring. If Mary Lee Thompson were willing, Catherine would leave designs and material for spring hats. Mary Lee could work on them during February and March for an April reopening. That would give her employment during the remaining cold of winter. The shop, although it would be closed to customers, wouldn't be left unattended. Mary Lee could use the upstairs quarters whenever she needed. If this idea worked, then Catherine

246

could return to Washington, with relief, knowing that her holdings were watched over. This idea was so appealing it smoothed the way for her to tell Mary Lee the bank wasn't going to allow a mortgage.

Catherine was flushed after she dressed. The nagging, hacking cough was an exertion that continued to drain her energy. Would she ever feel strong, and self-sufficient again?

Patrick had breakfast ready when she appeared in the kitchen. "Pancakes," he announced. "A specialty taught to me by my favorite kitchen maid, if you'll recall."

"Yes, I recall your story. Did you ever have to eat pancakes?"

"Why, yes I did. When I was going to the university, I had spent my allowance on other than what I was to use it for. My father was not one to dole out extra money. Eating pancakes for a week made me realize I'd better watch my funds." He pulled out a chair for her to be seated at the table. It was set with cups, utensils, and two glasses of apple juice.

"I'm not sure how much of an appetite I have," she apologized.

"Any nourishment is good." He poured her a cup of tea, poured coffee into his cup, and lifted two pancakes each onto warm plates.

"I always heat the plates because I don't like cold pancakes." Taking a seat opposite her, he smiled. " It's so good to see you up and dressed. Not that I mind seeing you in your nightgown," he added. "It makes me feel you are getting back to normal."

She sighed. "Patrick, I have decided what to do. Tell me if you agree."

He was excited about her plan. "Let me get Mary Lee over here and see if she will agree. I'll go to her place right after we eat."

"You do realize it will only be a two month respite before I have to make a permanent decision."

"We'll cross that bridge when we come to it." He gave a gratified smile.

Chapter 20

Thursday morning Patrick and Catherine prepared to depart for Washington. Mary Lee had accepted the milliner's offer and didn't seem disappointed she would not be allowed a mortgage for the hat shop. The look on Mary Lee's face was one of relief. It was agreed Catherine would mail the designs and materials for the spring hats. Mary Lee promised she would have them ready for an April opening.

With a feeling of weakness still lingering after her bout with the grippe, Catherine was surprised at her own relief when she hung a sign in the window of her beloved hat shop: Closed until April 1st. That was bound to cause a stir in the community. She was sure a few good yarns could be woven out of her avant-garde behavior. But, that morning, Catherine wasn't bothered about what people might say.

She was not looking forward to the long train ride into Washington, but she was not about to let Patrick know how she felt.

He had seen to her trunk, the one he'd packed for her. It had been taken to the train station on Monday and sent on ahead. What he had packed, she didn't know. They carried two small traveling bags.

"Patrick, are you sure you don't want me to bring a lunch for the train? We'll be famished by the time we arrive."

"Catherine, we'll buy something at one of the stops. It isn't necessary to pack a lunch." He was busy checking to see all was locked up and that there were not any live embers in the fireplace.

"It would be less expensive for me to take sandwiches," she continued.

"What would you make sandwiches with? We gave Mary Lee the bread and what was left in the icebox."

"You have a point. My mind isn't working well. I should have thought of that before I gave the bread away."

"I can afford lunches for us," he replied in a peevish manner.

"Of course you can. I didn't mean it in that way."

Patrick came and put his arm around her. "I'm sorry, Catherine, I think we're both a bit on edge. I know you don't feel well, and I didn't mean to sound harsh. I'm just ready to put this trip behind us."

"As am I," she said. "The car will be leaving in fifteen minutes."

"Good," he replied. "I believe I've checked everything. You're sure Mary Lee has the keys?"

"Yes, I wrote instructions along with the telephone numbers for the warehouse and the house in Georgetown. Mary Lee was aghast we had our own telephone."

He chuckled. "Let's leave. It's warm enough we can wait on the stoop."

"You know Mrs. Talley will be watching our every move. I don't want to give her time to scuttle across the street to ask a dozen questions."

Patrick glanced out the living room window. "The car is parked on the street. We can sit inside until Herbert's ready to leave."

"I like that much better. I'm not sure how long I would be able to stand on the stoop."

"I promise you once we're back in Washington you won't have to do a thing until you feel up to it." Patrick picked up both traveling bags. They went down the stairs side by side. He locked the door and they took their seats in the long automobile.

Herbert got into the driver's seat once they were seated. "Saw the note on your door, Miz' Catherine. It's not like you to close your shop."

"No, it isn't, but Mr. Burke and I are on our way back to Washington. I'm leaving it in Mrs. Thompson's hands until I can return."

Herbert was a tall, skinny man with a pointed nose. He reminded Catherine of a stork as he craned his head to look at her and she stifled a grin.

"Heard you was pretty sick."

"Yes, but I'm much better now." She wished he would start the car on its way to Bluemont.

As if he read her thoughts, he said, "I got one more passenger comin' out of the hotel. We'll be on our way soon's he comes."

Herbert set the throttle and turned the key. It took a few turns before the engine settled into a rough idle. The smell of gasoline was strong.

"I got to treat this thing like a baby because if it gets flooded I have to wait about ten minutes before I can get it goin'."

Patrick smiled at Catherine and took her hand, as if to say that all would be well. The move was enough to ease the tension building within.

Out of the hotel came a stubby little man carrying a shabby suitcase. He gave a nod to Patrick as he settled himself into a seat.

"Mornin' Patrick," the man said, and tipped his hat to Catherine.

She smiled and threw a questioning glance at Patrick.

"Catherine, this is Raymond Baker."

"Raymond, my wife, Catherine."

He tipped his hat once again. "I am pleased to meet you, Mrs. Burke. Your husband and I have shared a few meals while staying at the hotel. He has spoken highly of you."

"I am pleased to make your acquaintance, also." Catherine replied. "I don't recall seeing you in Berryville before. Do you come here often?"

"This is in my sales territory. I come once or twice a month, but usually I come in late and leave early. That's the life of a salesman on the road. It just so happens your husband and I stayed at the hotel at the same time." He winked at Patrick.

Catherine made a mental note to find out the reason behind the wink.

Herbert revved the engine before he started east out of Berryville. Catherine looked out the window as they pulled away and felt no pang of regret to leave her familiar surroundings. She even waved in the direction of Lavinia's as they passed, where she spied an ever so slight movement in the lace curtains.

****

The train ride took its toll. Catherine was exhausted by the time they reached the house in Georgetown.

"I thought we would be stopping by the house on K Street," she said.

"This is our home. Catherine. Why would you think I would go to my mother's house?"

"Oh, Patrick, I'm pleased that we're here. I just thought that Sarah has been by herself, and you might want to check in on her."

"Sarah has managed while I was gone. It's good for her to have to take on some responsibility. I'll check in with her and the invalids tomorrow. Right now, I want to see that you have your supper and get tucked into a nice warm bed. I can see how tired you are."

She put her fingers to her face. "Do I have dark circles under my eyes?" she asked with alarm.

"I love raccoons," he grinned.

"Careful Patrick, they have sharp teeth."

He chuckled and touched her cheek. "You look lovely."

When they reached the front door, Patrick said, "We'll see if Mattie and Jacob were good to their word."

"Mattie and Jacob?" she questioned.

Patrick turned the key in the lock. "They're a couple I've hired to help around the house. Mattie was going to leave dinner, while Jacob was going to get the place warmed up. They're good people, Catherine."

"They're not going to live here!" she said, incredulously.

"No, they have a place a couple blocks away."

"I'm glad, Patrick. I don't want anyone living here but you and me."

He tucked a strand of hair off her forehead. "And, neither do I. Just think of all the improper things we can do together."

Catherine blushed. "I'm afraid you will have to put those thoughts out of your mind, Mr. Burke. I'm not sure I can even make it up the stairs to fall into bed."

They had removed their outer wraps and Catherine was heading in the direction of the kitchen.

Patrick intercepted her. "You, my dear, are going straight upstairs. I will bring your supper up on a tray." Before she could protest, he swept her up in his arms and carried her up the stairs.

Catherine laid her head on his shoulder. "I have to admit I am very weary."

There was concern in his voice when he said, "Now that we are home, I want to see you getting stronger. Both of us have had much to deal with over the past two weeks. You get back on your feet and I'll get the business squared away. We'll haul Mother and Liam out of the hospital, if we have to, and I'll hire someone to come in and take care of them. Then, we will get down to the business of being husband and wife. Does that sound agreeable?"

"Most agreeable," she replied. "How are you or we going to do all that?"

"By not thinking about it tonight." He deposited her in the bedroom. "You change into your nightclothes. I'll bring on the supper," he ordered as he headed out the door.

"One more thing before you go, Patrick. Why did that Mr. Baker wink at you in the car?"

With a tilt of his head he gave her a cocky smile. "Because he knew my sole purpose in your fair town was to snag the lovely milliner. I do believe he appreciated my conquest."

"And, well he should," she said in a playful way. "Now, I'm crawling into bed."

Catherine's nightclothes were laid out on the turned down bed. She freshened up and climbed onto the soft mattress. A flood of comfort embraced her as she smiled to herself. "I feel like I'm home," she whispered.

In the meantime, Patrick had arrived in the kitchen to find a pot of vegetable soup still simmering on the stove and sandwiches wrapped in wax paper. He searched the cupboards for a tray. He took a quart of milk from the icebox and poured two glasses.

As he loaded the dinner onto the tray, he noticed an envelope on the table with his name on it. Inside was a note:

Dear Patrick,

The doctor said that Mother Burke was allowed to leave the hospital on Tuesday, but you were not here to take care of things. She was most upset.

I informed her that Catherine was ill and you needed to go to   Berryville to accompany her back to Washington. That didn't seem to matter to her.

Please call me as soon as you return.

Sarah

Patrick reread the note and tossed it back onto the table. He didn't need another problem. Tomorrow would be soon enough to deal with his mother.

Chapter 21

Patrick was up at five o'clock the next morning. He hadn't slept well. Catherine was in a deep easy sleep and never stirred when he left the bed. He hoped she would stay in a restful slumber.

He dressed quickly in the adjacent bedroom so as not to disturb her. The room was cold and bereft of furniture except for an oak four-drawer chest. Patrick's trousers laid across the top of the dresser. His suit coat was hung over a floor length oval mirror with an oak pedestal base. Once he was dressed, he peeked into their bedroom to assure himself that Catherine was still asleep. Then he went down the stairs to fix some breakfast.

The pace of the past two weeks had taken its toll on him also. He felt as tired as Catherine had looked. Oh, for the luxury of a couple more hours in bed, but he had too much to do.

First he would check into the warehouse to see that all was going well before he went to the hospital to see to his mother. From the tenor of Sarah's note he assumed his mother had recovered. Without a doubt she would be in a snit because he hadn't been available. He would have to make arrangements to take her home and find someone capable to stay with her. Polly was the only housemaid they had. It wasn't fair to shift the burden of his mother onto her unless he found someone to take over the house duties.

There's no sense in putting the cart before the horse, he thought. He would solve each problem as it presented.

Patrick made a meager breakfast of coffee and buttered bread. He was eating the bread on his way out the door and met Mattie coming in.

She was a tall, stocky woman with a broad face and firm mouth.

"Mrs. Burke is still asleep, Mattie. Be sure she has a good breakfast when she wakes up. Don't let her do anything that will tire her out. I have a feeling she will want to go and explore the little house. The key is hanging by the cellar door. If I can get all of my affairs in order, I'll try to get back for lunch."

"I'll be sure to have it ready. And, Mistah' Patrick, I don' know the Missus so I can jus' pass on what you tol' me 'bout her not doin' any work."

"Yes, that's right Mattie. I think you're really going to like Mrs. Burke. Now, I've got to be on my way."

Mattie nodded her acknowledgement as she tied a long white apron around her large frame.

Patrick walked to the warehouse in the early dawn. He opened the locked front door and was content to have an hour to himself before anyone arrived for work. It gave him time to go over the accounts for the past few days and check the shipping and receiving areas. Both Patrick and Liam had inherited their father's penchant for neatness and cleanliness in the warehouse. He would also check to be sure the inventory process was progressing according to his orders. There were those employees who would become lax if someone wasn't there to nudge them along.

Patrick was pleased when he finished. Everything was the way he hoped to find it. He was determined to reward the workers in some way, but that would have to come later.

He went to his office to fine-tune the account books. He was sitting with a ledger in front of him when there was a knock at his door.

"Come in."

The door opened and he saw his secretary, Eva W. McKay peek around the door.

"Well, come in, Miss McKay. You're here early."

She stood ramrod straight with her tall slim body, clad in a spotless, starched, white blouse and long black skirt. Each strand of hair was neatly tucked into place.

"Sir, I wanted to tell you welcome back. I trust you find all is in order. I was able to answer the few questions Joseph presented," she said in her confident manner.

"I am very pleased," he replied.

"We have been concerned about your wife. We trust she is better."

"Yes, thank you for inquiring. She is here in Georgetown and much improved."

Patrick noticed an immediate change in Miss McKay's stance. Her shoulders relaxed, the pinched expression on her face lessened, and her folded hands dropped to her sides. Was she pleased Catherine was on the mend or relieved Patrick wouldn't be leaving again?

"Mr. Burke, would you care for some coffee? I have just brewed a pot. I stopped at the bakery on my way for cinnamon buns. I suspected you might be here early and not have time for breakfast."

She looked so satisfied with her offering Patrick didn't have the heart to refuse.

"That was thoughtful of you. There is nothing like a cup of coffee and fresh baked cinnamon roll."

Miss McKay beamed with pride and swept out the door.

By ten o'clock, Patrick was at the Georgetown hospital. It was the time physicians usually made their rounds and he needed to talk with the doctor regarding both his mother and Liam. The doctor was just leaving Liam's room when Patrick appeared.

"Mr. Burke, good morning. Your mother tells me you've been out of town for a few days."

"Yes, good morning." He shook the physician's hand. "Sarah told me that my mother is ready to be discharged."

"I'm ready to release her, and she's ready to go. But, she'll need someone with her at home. She's still unsteady on her feet. It wouldn't do for her to take a fall."

"I'm sure the household help can fill in for a couple of days until I find someone. Do you expect the unsteadiness to clear up soon?"

The doctor rubbed his temple. "That's something I can't answer. I'm hoping there is still some swelling that's causing the problem. Once that's resolved, she should be fine. Head injuries are tricky, so I can't promise this won't be a lasting effect from the trauma she's suffered."

That wasn't news Patrick wanted to hear. "Have you told my mother about this possibility?"

The doctor shifted his medical chart to his other hand. "I've told her, but she'll have none of it. She says that once she gets home she's going to be back on her feet in a couple of days."

"Yes, that sounds like Mother." Patrick gave a weak smile. "What about Liam? Do you have any idea when he can come home?"

"I'm happy to report that Liam is healing well. Another couple of weeks in this cast and we'll be able to put him in a partial cast from the thigh down. He'll have more movement and use of his right leg. The bad news is he'll have to remain in the hospital until we can change into the shorter cast. I expect he can go home once that's done."

Patrick shook the physician's hand. "Thank you. I'm on my way in to see him and then, I'll tackle Mother."

The doctor laughed. "Good luck," he said. "I'll leave my orders with the nurse for her discharge."

Patrick entered Liam's room after tapping on the door.

His brother had a growth of dark beard. His black, wavy hair was in disarray. The cast allowed movement of the upper body. Liam's appearance matched his gruff tone. "Well, I see you're back. I assume you and your wife are together again."

Patrick took a quick assessment of the cast and saw it was chafing him around the waist. A bar inserted into the cast at the ankles separated his legs. He could pull himself up toward the head of the bed with a suspended trapeze bar, but was unable to turn himself.

"And to answer your sarcasm, good morning to you, Liam. My wife's name is Catherine. Would you like to know how she's doing or are you so swallowed in self-pity you think of no one but yourself?"

"If you were laying in this bed hour by hour, day by day, night by night, you might have the same kind of attitude."

"Perhaps so. But, I don't have time for your incivility. You're not the only one who's suffering. This accident has altered my life also. You know I intended to go back to medical school, but that's been put on hold. Sarah left me a note that mother is ready to go home. Now, I have to see she gets there and find a caretaker for her. It's up to me to make sure the business stays afloat. Instead of spending amorous hours as a newlywed, I end up playing nursemaid."

Patrick walked over to the window that overlooked the Potomac River in the distance. With his back to Liam, he said, "I'm on my way to get Mother. Do you have any words of good cheer you want me to pass on, or, better yet, do you know of anyone I can find to come in and take care of her?"

There was a heavy silence between them before Liam spoke, "I'm not the only one feeling sorry for himself."

The words hit home. "Look, Liam." Patrick came back to the bedside. "In a couple of weeks you're going to be getting a smaller cast, which will give you a little more mobility. I'm going to see what we can get set up at home for you. Once you get there, I don't see why you can't do paperwork for the warehouse. It'll keep your mind occupied and take some of the burden off me."

"I'd like it faster, but I should be able to handle two more weeks…if the staff can put up with me. I think I even managed to drive Sarah away. She's gone to visit her parents for a few days."

"Good for her," Patrick said. "She can use some time for herself."

"Don't be so damned understanding, Patrick," Liam held a playful smile. "How is Catherine? I didn't mean to sound so crass."

"She's on the mend. When I arrived in Berryville, I was shocked to see the condition she was in. I had to stay until she could make the trip back here."

"Don't apologize, big brother. I would have done the same."

At that moment Patrick felt as though a burden had been lifted. Putting his troubles into words had not only eased his mind, but his brother had understood. He gave a deep sigh. "Anyways, I'm back and now I need to tend to Mother."

"I don't envy you that job," Liam said as he hoisted himself up in the bed by the bar. "See, I've strengthened my arms so I can get home and be up to the job of lifting the pen for the paperwork."

Patrick shook his head. "Still a note of sarcasm, but I'm glad to see your mood's improved. I'll stop by in a couple of days."

Patrick was lighter of step as he approached his mother's room. She was fully dressed and sitting in a chair when he entered. Her floor length coat and fashionable hat were on the bed. There was an arrangement of flowers on the bedside table and a packed valise sat next to the chair.

"It's time you got here, Patrick. I could have left this place a few days ago."

"Good morning, Mother. I'm sorry I wasn't here, but as Sarah told you, I had to go to Berryville where I found Catherine ill."

"What was she doing in Berryville? She is a new bride, after all. Her place should be with you."

Patrick sat in a stiff wooden chair next to his mother. "Now, you know Catherine has her own business and she needed to attend to it."

"Sarah told me the woman was gone for a week! Whatever would she need to attend to that took that long? She merely locks up her shop and puts a For Sale sign in the window."

Patrick was not going to be drawn into a debate. "I'll call the nurse to bring a wheelchair for you. I'll meet her at the hospital entrance with a hack."

"Going home in a taxi? Surely, you could have found more suitable transportation."

"Mother, just be glad you're going home." He didn't wait for a response before he went directly to the nurse's station.

****

Once they were home, Patrick helped his mother settle into her suite which was on the main floor toward the back of the huge house. Polly met them at the door.

"It's good to have you back, Mrs. Burke," Polly said as she began taking care of her employer's belongings. "Miz' Sarah tells us about how you and Mister Liam are doin'."

"Polly, you don't know how happy I am to be home. The doctor says I need to have someone with me as I'm still unsteady on my feet. I plan on spending much of my time right here in these two rooms."

Patrick spoke up, "Polly is going to stay with you until I can find another helper."

"Patrick, that's not going to be necessary. I'll be back to my old self in a few days. When do you expect Sarah to return?"

"I'm not sure, Liam didn't say."

"I guess I can get along without her as long as you and Catherine are here. Polly, check and see if you need to add more water to those flowers. Patrick didn't want me to carry them home from the hospital but they would have just thrown them away."

Patrick cleared his throat. "Catherine and I aren't going to be here. We'll be in our home in Georgetown."

"Georgetown! This is your home, Patrick."

"No, Mother, this is your home. I love this big house, but Catherine and I want our own place. I'm sure you can understand that."

She squeezed a false tear from her eye. " No, I don't understand that. I have always depended on you, Patrick. Now, when I really need you, you're going to forsake me."

He wasn't in the mood for games. "I won't be that far away, and it won't be long before Liam and Sarah will be back. Meanwhile, you will be well taken care of. Now, I have to get over to see Catherine. You haven't even inquired about her health."

"How thoughtless of me," she said in a cool tone. "Yes, Catherine. I think you could have aimed a little higher, Patrick. How is she?"

"She's getting stronger," he answered in a clipped tone.

"That's nice. You'd better be on your way. Don't worry about me. I'll be fine."

Patrick motioned for Polly to follow him out of the room. "I will get someone here as soon

266

as I can. Forget any of your responsibilities with the house and stay nearby. She's going to need your assistance, although she may not want to admit it. The doctor was most concerned that she might take a fall. Miss Sarah will be back soon, and I'll check in every day."

"Yessir, I can handle it. Don't you worry."

"Good. Now, I do have to go and see how my wife is faring."

"You be sure and tell Miz' Catherine, Samuel and I hope she's doing better. I think your wife suits you fine."

"I do too." Patrick picked up his overcoat and hat. "I'll be sure and tell her, Polly. Thank you. Especially for helping me out with my mother."

"I would do anything to help you out, Mister Patrick."

He smiled at the tall, slender, black woman who had been a part of his life for almost twenty years.

Chapter 22

It was around nine o'clock when Catherine awoke. The January sun was streaming in the south window of their bedroom. She pulled a warm shawl across her shoulders and walked to the window that faced the back yard. There were a couple of tall oak trees, bereft of leaves, and a few smaller trees and bushes. Catherine was content to wait for spring to bring them forth in their glory. For now, there wasn't anything attractive about them.

Today she felt stronger. After she dressed for the day she would see to unpacking her trunk. Her hairbrush and mirror laid on the cherry dressing table. Had Patrick put them there for her? She remembered being so exhausted when they arrived she couldn't think of anything but sleep.

As Catherine absentmindedly ran the brush through her long hair, she spied the reflection of the four-poster cherry bed she had recently crawled out of. It would be lovely and quite romantic covered with an organdy, flounced canopy. Then she had to smile because Patrick would refuse to sleep in it; he was not one for showy decorations.

The bedroom was large. A cherry chest stood on one wall and a tall double-door chifforobe was next to it. Catherine left the dressing table to check her image in the oval mirror in the door of the wardrobe. Her reflection down to her toes revealed how her illness had altered her appearance. Her skin was sallow, her face drawn with large dark circles shadowing her eyes. The bout with the grippe had caused her to lose weight and it showed in the drape of her dress. It was no wonder Patrick was concerned. Feeling up to it or not, today she would start on a course to help her body gain back its appeal.

The smell of coffee and bacon were in the air as she went down the stairs. In the kitchen was a large colored woman. The size of the woman seemed to dwarf the kitchen.

"Good morning. You must be Mattie," Catherine used her most cheerful voice. "My husband told me we would have help."

The woman turned and eyed her with a wary look. "I done be Mattie," she answered.

"I am pleased to meet you. Mr. Burke said he was fortunate to find you and your husband. I hope you will like working here with us."

With her back to Catherine, Mattie said, "Mistah' Patrick say he want you to have a fine breakfast." Then in an almost inaudible voice, she added, "An' you ain't suppose' to tire yerself out."

"I plan on taking an easy course. I'm not going to do anything strenuous. The breakfast smells delicious. I believe I have my appetite back." She could see a loosening in the big woman's shoulders.

"Did Mister Burke say when he would return?"

"Yes, ma'am. He say he would be home for lunch, but he didn't give me no firm time."

The maid brought a big plate to the table loaded with bacon, scrambled eggs, grits and a warm biscuit.

Catherine offered a weak smile. "I'm not sure I can eat it all, but I'll certainly try."

Mattie gave no reply and went about her work in the kitchen. Catherine felt awkward. She had never had anyone around when she ate breakfast. She had her own routine of preparing her own food and cleaning up after herself. Patrick had done what he thought was best by hiring help, but Catherine was not keen on having another woman do work that rightfully belonged to her.

Mattie started to pour a cup of coffee. Catherine waved it away. "I'd like a cup of strong tea."

"Yes, ma'am," Mattie said. Without showing a sign of approval or disapproval, she went on to do Catherine's bidding.

There was something about the woman that made Catherine uncomfortable. Perhaps Mattie didn't like being there any more than Catherine wanted her to be there.

"Mattie, my Christian name is Catherine I'd prefer you address me with my given name."

Mattie looked neither right nor left, but continued fussing around the stove, "Yes, Miz' Catherine, ma'am."

Catherine rolled her eyes. She sipped her tea, while gazing out the kitchen window facing the side yard. There was a short colored man working around picking up branches and small limbs that were remnants of the wind of a few days before.

"Is that your husband, Jacob, in the yard?

"Yes, Miz' Catherine, ma'am."

"After I finish breakfast, I shall go out and meet him."

Mattie shrugged her shoulders and began sweeping the kitchen. Catherine piled her dishes together to take them to the sink. As she rose from her chair, Mattie whisked the dishes off the table before Catherine could reach to pick them up.

"That done be my job, Miz' Catherine, ma'am."

"Mattie, can't you just call me, Miss Catherine?"

Mattie shook her head, "No Miz' Catherine, ma'am. That wouldn't be right. My mama tol' me to always call the white ladies ma'am."

"Then we will stay with you calling me ma'am. Do you also call Mr. Burke, sir?

"No ma'am. I calls him Mistah' Patrick," Mattie replied and turned away.

Catherine was sure she caught the crinkle of a smile beginning on the maid's face. Had Mattie won the first round?

Determined to get some fresh air and explore the area around the house, Catherine bundled up in a wool coat and threw the fur stole over it. She tied a wool hat on with a scarf and picked up her muff before setting out to meet Jacob.

"Good morning," she called as she walked to where he was busy stacking up the limbs. "Mr. Burke told me you would be helping us. Your wife just fixed me a delicious breakfast. My given name is Catherine."

He looked up from his work and gave a bow of his head. He had a beautiful smile that spread from ear to ear. "I'm mighty proud to meet you, Miz' Catherine."

"I'm glad to hear you call me Miss Catherine. Mattie doesn't seem to think that's the right thing to do."

"Now, don't you pay Mattie too much mind. She's a good person, but it takes some doin' to know her."

These words spoken from Mattie's husband weren't reassuring to Catherine. She wanted to feel at ease in her own home. She wasn't sure she was going to reach a level of comfort when Mattie was around.

Catherine walked to the front of the house to view the place that was to become her hat shop. It was a short distance from the larger house connected by a brick walk. It faced the street and sat far to the right so it didn't obstruct the view of the bigger house. Just looking at it, Catherine could see why Patrick thought it would be a perfect size for a millinery shop. She walked down to peer in the windows.

As she got closer, she saw a heap of something that looked like a dirty pile of snow in front of the back door. There were small mounds of snow about, but this one was different. The closer she got the bigger it looked. She thought she saw some movement. Catherine hurried on and was earnestly brushing away at the heap when she heard Patrick call.

"Catherine, leave whatever you're doing and come to the house."

"Patrick, come here. I need your help," she called back.

He came on the run. "What is it? You're going to be right back in the bed the way you're…" Then he saw it.

"Look! It's a dog and he's half-frozen. We have to get him inside."

Patrick nudged the large animal with his foot. The only sign of life was a flicker of an eyelid. "You don't know anything about this dog, Catherine. He could be carrying a disease."

"No, Patrick, I think he's half-frozen and probably hasn't had any food. Providence has delivered him to our doorstep and we have to see he gets some help."

"I don't see where he is our responsibility. Besides, I'll be surprised if he lives another few hours. I'm sorry, love, but I think he's done for."

Catherine stood up placing her hands on her hips. "Patrick Burke, how can you say that? We have to give him a chance."

It was probably the look of determination on Catherine's face that caused Patrick to give in. "You may be right. You're not in any shape to haul him around. How do you propose we move him? Obviously, he's not going to get up and walk in."

"We'll drag him in. You must have an old quilt or something. Maybe there's a blanket inside this house."

"Did you bring the key?" Patrick asked.

"No, I didn't plan on going into the house. I was just going to peek in the windows."

"Stay sheltered from the breeze. I'll hurry up to the house for the key," he ordered.

Within minutes he returned with Jacob at his heels and Mattie following carrying a big quilt. The men set to work rolling the dog onto the quilt while Catherine opened the door. Mattie stood back hunched against the cold.

They left the dog wrapped. She had Jacob start a fire in the fireplace while she pumped water into a chipped enamel pan she found on the floor of the room that had served as a kitchen.

Patrick was concerned about the fire. "The fireplace hasn't been used for years. It might burn the place down."

Catherine was content to get the dog inside. "It's just enough to take off the chill. Jacob didn't make a hot fire."

On their way back to the big house, Catherine could hear Mattie grumbling to Jacob. "I don't take care of no dogs," she said just loud enough for Catherine to hear.

That was fine with Catherine. In her heart she knew this dog had been sent to her for a reason. She vowed to do her best to see that he survived.

Chapter 23

One week later, Catherine was feeling back to normal. Her appetite was good and much of her strength had returned. She and Patrick sat on a couch in the parlor.

"Mattie tells me you spend much of your time taking care of that animal. It may send you back to your sickbed," he warned.

"Patrick, walking to and from the little house three times a day in the crisp air has been good for me. It's not Mattie's business to tattle to you."

"She wasn't tattling. I told her to keep an eye on you because I don't want you overdoing. She was concerned."

"Hah. I'm sure she was. I don't think Mattie likes me. You'd think this house was hers the way she doesn't let me lift a finger. I think Rex was sent to give me purpose."

He laughed as he took her hand. "Rex? Rather a regal name for that mangy cur."

"You haven't even been down to see him. I've combed and clipped what wouldn't brush out of his coat. He's beautiful. He has silver hair and blue eyes and he stands as tall as my knees. You'd be surprised at the transformation."

"He has brought the sparkle back to your eyes so I owe him a debt of gratitude for that. Have I lost my wife to a dog?" He kissed her cheek.

"Patrick, you've been so busy I hardly see you."

"And for that I apologize. Liam should be coming home next week. I am planning on letting him do a lot of the paperwork that has to be done."

"Good. Now that I am well it's time I visited your mother. When Liam gets settled in I'll go with you to see both of them." She took his hand. We have some time before Mattie puts dinner on. Would you like to go down and let me introduce you to Rex?"

"I believe I would like to see this other man who has stolen your heart."

She threw her arms around his neck and kissed him heartily. "Nothing or anyone will steal my heart the way you have."

They put on their outerwear. Hand in hand they walked down to the little house to see the dog brought back from near death.

As soon as Catherine turned the key in the lock, Rex was waiting for her. He wagged his tail and pushed her with his nose until she scratched his head. "Rex, this is Patrick. He's my other love."

The dog let out a couple of happy barks enjoying the attention he was getting before he gave Patrick a thorough sniffing.

"He is a beauty," Patrick admitted. "I can see why you are so taken with him. I have to say that I never expected to see such a change."

Catherine let the dog out the door while Patrick toured the house.

"I didn't get a chance to wander through after we dragged the dog in. It brings back memories. You can fix it up any way you choose. It's your place. I'll come by once in a while to check it out."

Catherine caught the nostalgia in his voice. "Patrick, I don't want to do anything that will ruin it for you."

He put his arm around her. "You won't. I'm interested to see how you fix it up. If the dog is any indication, I'll be in for a treat."

She was pleased. "Let me call Rex in and we can be on our way for dinner. Mattie won't take kindly to our being late."

****

Catherine had become accustomed to having Mattie and Jacob around the house. Mattie took her responsibilities seriously when it came to her role in keeping the house. Catherine kept out of her way.

She asked Mattie to fix up some oat gruel with adding honey and ground chicken to the mix.

"Waste of good food on a dog," Mattie grumbled, just audible enough for Catherine to hear. Catherine pretended she didn't.

Mattie fixed the gruel and Catherine carried it down to the smaller house. Jacob had fenced in an area so Rex could come and go out of the back door.

She and Jacob stood outside the pen watching the dog shake and stretch in the morning sun. "He's

277

a mighty fine looking dog, Miz' Catherine," Jacob said. "What's Mistah' Patrick think of him?

"I don't think he thinks he's a noble dog but he's glad I have a companion and something to keep my interests until I get the hat shop set up. As for Mattie, she has no use for Rex. I know she thinks I spend too much time and money for food for him. I don't let her know I hear her grumbling."

Jacob slowly shook his head. "You done be right about that, Miz' Catherine. Mattie don't cotton to dogs."

****

It seemed Patrick and Mattie were both satisfied the dog was out of their sight. What they didn't know was that Catherine planned to bring the dog up to the big house. There was a nice sheltered spot on the back porch next to the pile of wood used for the stove and fireplaces. Jacob had built a small shelter and was going to put it in place.

Rex had become fond of the old quilt Mattie had brought when they dragged the dog into the little house. Catherine planned to put it in his place once it was ready. Rex would feel right at home. Because she had become fond of him, it gave her comfort to have Rex near. It didn't occur to her Patrick would object.

On Sunday morning, before they were scheduled to visit Patrick's family, Catherine, with a sense of pride, brought Rex up to the big house. He sniffed around until he found the familiar quilt and immediately climbed into the shelter where he laid down like he was reunited with an old friend.

278

Patrick was upstairs.

Catherine called to him, "Patrick, I'll be ready to go as soon as I wash my hands and put on my gloves."

"I'll be right down," he answered. "I'm sure Mother will be watching the clock."

He came down the stairs looking dapper in his suit and tie. "Where have you been? I called down a few minutes ago."

Catherine evaded his inquiring eyes. "I put Rex on the back porch," she replied as she pulled on her elbow length gloves.

The moment of hesitation before he spoke made the ticking of the grandfather clock in the hallway sound like a sledgehammer.

"I hope I didn't hear you right. You put that dog on our back porch?"

She still did not look at him. The thought rippled through her mind that she should have asked him. That thought along with the tone of his voice was enough to give her serious doubt, but only for the moment. She secured her hat on her head and turned to look at him.

"Yes, Patrick. I put him on the back porch. He's a beautiful dog and he deserves to be close to us after all he's been through."

"Close to us or close to you?" came his retort.

"Why Patrick Burke, I do believe you're jealous of a dog."

He just stood looking at her. Then he laughed. "If I take an honest look at myself, I do believe I am. You've spent a lot of time with him."

"As you have with your family and your business," came her quick reply.

"Touché, Mrs. Burke." He swept her into his arms and gave her a full-bodied kiss. "No more petty disagreements. Let's go greet your kingly dog. Then you can work your charms on my mother."

Catherine looped her arm through his. "I do believe greeting Rex will be the easier of the two."

****

Two o'clock in the afternoon found Patrick and Catherine sitting in the opulent parlor of the Burke house on K Street. They sat side by side on one of the uncomfortable crewel-embroidered settees, a prized possession of Mrs. Burke.

Patrick's mother entered, leaning on a cane, with Polly at her side. It was evident from her wavering footsteps she still required assistance.

They rose when she entered. Patrick went to her and kissed her cheek. "It's good to see you, Mother. Catherine is feeling good as new so we are both here, as you can see."

"Yes. How very nice to have you come, Catherine. Patrick told me you had been quite ill. I assumed he was being a good boy and telling me the truth." She smiled a condescending smile and patted his hand.

Catherine was not pleased but she kept her feeling in check. "Yes, I'm happy to say that I am recovered. I'm pleased you are improving."

280

Before they resumed their seats on the settee, Sarah came into the room. She rushed over and gave Catherine a hug. "I am delighted that you are so much better. Mother Burke has ordered dinner to be served at three. We can all be together once again. Liam will be along as soon as he has himself settled into the wheelchair. He insists he doesn't need any help."

"Thank you, Sarah. It must be a relief to you to not have to make that trip to and from the hospital every day."

Sarah took a seat next to the settee as Patrick and Catherine resumed their places. Catherine had to get used to the idea of having a sister-in-law. It was good to see Sarah looking less drawn than the last time Catherine had seen her. She appeared more settled and confident in her manner. It seemed the Burke family was on the mend.

"We had to convert the library to a bedroom," Sarah informed, "but it seems to be working out very well. Liam is eager to get back to doing his work."

"He will have good support from our capable staff of workers," Patrick said. "You know, Sarah, I fully intend to go back to medical school once Liam can take over. He won't be able to have the free time he's had in the past. It will be a change for you also."

"I realize that. If Liam is happy with what he is doing then I can adjust."

"You could help him with the business," Catherine chimed in.

The newly acquired mother-in-law let out a gasp. "Become a working girl? I think not!"

Catherine felt the heat rise in her face. "Yes, I guess those of us women who work for a living are not considered the plums of society."

Patrick's mother shot a hard glance at Catherine.

He cleared his throat. "Shall we adjoin to the dining room? I see they are about to ring the bell."

"By all means," agreed his mother. He helped her from the chair.

Sarah leaned and whispered into Catherine's ear, "We will have to talk of this again."

Might she find an alliance with Sarah?

Liam wheeled himself into the dining room, sitting a little cockeyed to accommodate the unwieldy cast covering his thigh to ankle. He took the place at the end of the table. "Catherine, how good to see you. You had quite a bout yourself from what Patrick tells me."

"Thank you, Liam. I'm happy to see you getting around so well."

"That stint in the hospital did me good. I've got muscles I didn't know I had. Amazing what the body can handle. Just ask mother, here. She's still giving orders like she never rattled her brain."

"Liam, I can still take you over my knee and give you a spank."

That brought a laugh and lightened the mood for everyone. When they were seated, Patrick said grace before carving the roast.

It had been many hours since breakfast and Catherine was hungry. She savored the sweet potatoes and green beans that accompanied the main course. Dessert was a piece of three-layer pineapple cake. She devoured every bite.

Once dinner was over, Mrs. Burke asked to be taken back to her room. "I do believe it's time for a nap. Liam, we are pleased to have you back home, and Catherine, it is good that you are well. Patrick needs a good woman at his side. Now, if you will excuse me, I must get some rest." She rang the bell for help. Within seconds, Polly was there to see her charge back to her suite. Catherine watched Mrs. Burke leave the room suspecting her encouraging words were masking the woman's true feelings.

The two couples lingered over cups of tea. "What do you think about Mother, Liam?" Patrick asked. "I don't think the doctor is as optimistic about her recovery as he was a week ago."

He replied, "Maybe she just needs more time."

"She's had me in tears a few times," Sarah said in a small voice.

"Well, so have I," agreed Liam. "I'm sorry for being such a bear."

This appeared to be a new revelation. Sarah left her chair and put her arms around him. "I'm pleased to hear you say it. There were times when you were insufferable in the hospital." She kissed him on the top of his head.

"If you two don't have to get back, why don't we all go to my room and play a game of canasta?" suggested Liam.

"What do you say, Catherine?" Patrick asked. "Are you ready to show these two what we're made of?"

"Like you, I am not one to shy away from competition. I do believe we can give them a run for their money."

"That's the woman I married," he said as he pulled her to her feet. With one arm around her waist and the other pretending to hold the Olympic torch, he saluted. "Let the games begin."

Chapter 24

In February, Catherine's life took on new meaning. Jacob was helping her transform the little house into a workable hat shop. Of course it wouldn't open until she settled her other shop in Berryville. She had sent designs and material to Mary Lee Thompson to create so they would have a varied selection of hats for the spring opening in April. Patrick had filled the list of items Catherine had given him and, for the most part, his choices had been satisfactory.

Mary Lee wasn't much at correspondence, but she had sent a note to Catherine:

February 15, 1916

Dear Miss Catherine,

Mr. Pierce brought the package you had sent to me. He asked how you was. He said it ain't the same around here you not being here. I told him you was fine. I hope that's true.

I am working hard on these hats and they are pretty. I will be glad when you come back here in April.

Your friend,
Mary Lee

Catherine sighed after she read the short note. She was sitting in the smaller house where she

285

had set up an area to work on millinery. The front of the house faced the south. There was a large front window that let the light in which was helpful for the fine work that needed to be done.

Her dog, Rex, had become her constant companion. He laid at her feet as she worked and she felt comfort in having him near. Catherine didn't want to admit she had a twinge of homesickness after reading Mary Lee's note. She knew in her heart that she missed seeing Lloyd Pierce bring the mail and Irene Butler opening her dress shop. Yes, she even missed watching Lavinia Talley waddle across the street with the latest news. How many times she had sat in her shop in Berryville and wished to be gone from the small town. The arrival of Mary Lee's letter had sparked a twinge of longing. Catherine reached down and patted Rex.

Catherine hadn't seen her friend, Carolyn, since the wedding. Daily life had moved too fast over the past weeks. The bout with the grippe, the move to Georgetown, the new house, the hat shop, the Burke family reunited all in a two-week span. She decided to call Carolyn and invite her to tea. The thought pleased her so much she put her work aside to make plans.

"What do you say, Rex? Shall we call it a day? Wait until you meet my friend, Carolyn. You'll love her just as much as I do." Rex got to his feet, stretched and wagged his tail.

She tidied up her workspace before she closed the door and pulled the key from her apron pocket. Outside she was turning the key in the lock when a flicker of quick movement at the side of the house caused her to look in that direction. She saw nothing. Rex raised his ears, turned his head toward the same spot but remained at her side. It must have been something caught in the breeze, she thought. Still, it gave her an unsettled feeling. She glanced in that direction once more before she went up the brick walk to the big house.

Jacob was trimming out some hedge as Catherine neared the back of the house.

She called to him, "Jacob, did you see any movement down near the little house while you've been out here?"

"No, Miz' Catherine," he answered, "There's been some old leaves flyin' around in the breeze."

Just some leaves caught in a whirl, she tried to convince herself.

****

Patrick arrived home around six o'clock. Mattie had already left but she had food warming on the stove. Catherine was happy to have the kitchen by herself. They still ate in the kitchen until her dining room suite could be brought from Berryville. Patrick had told her that she, no doubt, would bring her cherished mahogany dining room set so he had not bought any furniture for that room. Also, he had left one bedroom bare for her familiar bedroom suite. Transporting the furniture would be made when Catherine decided what she wanted to keep.

"Patrick, you're home early. I'm delighted." She threw her arms around him and gave him a welcoming kiss.

He didn't let her move out of his arms. "Let's just stand like this for the rest of our lives." He smiled down at her and playfully nuzzled her neck.

"We'd die of hunger. " She was practical.

"Yes, but what a way to go," he quipped.

Mattie had made a sumptuous beef stew that Catherine dished up into two pewter bowls. She sliced a few pieces of bread and scooped some applesauce into side dishes.

Patrick had uncorked a bottle of wine and poured them each a glass before Catherine was seated.

"Wine?" she questioned.

"Celebrating," he answered. "It was good to leave the warehouse at a respectable hour. I feel confident that Liam will be able to carry on from here." He generously buttered a piece of Mattie's fresh bread. "The accountant and I went over the books and they are up to date. No more burning the lamp until all hours."

"Does this mean we can count on spending our evenings together once again?"

"Unless we have some unforeseen obstacle thrown at us, I plan on being here every extra minute I can."

Catherine smiled at him across the table. "We certainly haven't had that luxury, have we?"

"Indeed we haven't," came his reply.

"Patrick, I called Carolyn this afternoon and asked her to tea."

"That's a wonderful idea. How is she feeling?"

"She says she's fine. I'm glad I called her. She sounded concerned about Asa. Something about the problems in Europe."

Patrick took a sip of wine. "I hope we don't get involved with what's going on over there. We don't need any more wars."

"I'm so happy I invited her to come and visit."

"And, so am I, love. What do you say we clean up this table, leave the dishes for Mattie, and you and I go right up and snuggle in bed?"

"I would never turn down such a fine offer," she teased him. "I must let Rex out for an evening run."

"That dog again. But, I do have to say I was pleased he didn't bark when I came in."

"He knows your footsteps and he knows you belong here."

Patrick came around the table. He pulled her to her feet. "Well, go ahead and let him out for his romp because I fully intend a good romp with his mistress when she returns."

"Patrick Burke, you are shameful with that kind of talk." She turned at the door. "Although, I think I shall look forward to it."

****

The next morning Catherine was up early. She and Patrick had breakfast together before he walked to the warehouse to begin the day's work.

"Have you got a busy day lined up?" he asked.

"I'll be working with the hats for much of the day. It's only about a month away before I go back to Berryville. I still haven't decided what to do with the shop up there. It nags at me."

Patrick rose to leave, "I can't make the decision for you, but I do think you should search your conscience as to why you don't want to let go of it. Discover that and it may give you the answer you're looking for."

He leaned over and kissed her cheek. "Time for me to be off."

Mattie was coming in the door with a big load of kindling cradled against her large frame.

Patrick spread a wide grin and held the door for her, "Good morning, Mattie. You're as welcome as the flowers in May."

Mattie came as close to a genuine smile as Catherine had ever witnessed. "Mornin' Mistah' Patrick."

Catherine raised her eyebrows. "Mister Patrick and a smile? That wasn't the Mattie Catherine knew, no siree it wasn't.

Mattie emptied the kindling into a metal bucket. "What time you say your fren' is comin' for tea?" she asked Catherine.

"Miss Carolyn will be coming at one o'clock in the afternoon on Friday."

Mattie grumbled to herself, loud enough for Catherine to hear. "Don' know how she 'spect's me to set a decent table with no decent furniture in the dinin' room."

Mattie was a star when it came to mumbling and grumbling. Catherine found it annoying. "Mattie, I've told you before, if you're going to complain, at least complain to me and don't go off grumbling to yourself. I heard what you said. To put your mind at ease, we will take our tea in the parlor using the tea table."

"Yes ma'am, Miz' Catherine."

"And, I wish you would drop the ma'am." Catherine was standing by the table gripping the back of a chair. "Mr. Burke is having my dining room furniture brought from my home as soon as he can arrange it. In the future, when we have dinner guests, we will have a proper place for you to serve."

Mattie kept fussing while putting kindling into the stove. "Yes ma'am, Miz' Catherine."

"You need serve only sandwiches, tea and sweets on Friday, which I'm sure will allow you to make do with the tea table. Do we understand each other?"

"Yes ma'am, Miz' Catherine."

Catherine was piqued and turned on her heel to leave when she heard Mattie mumble, "Dint' spect' she'd get so all fired mad."

"I heard that!" Catherine shot back.

That little spat with the maid was energizing. Catherine put on her coat and hat and called to Rex to come with her. They headed for the little hat shop. There was much to be done. Halfway down the brick walk she realized she had forgotten the key in her huff so she and Rex turned back.

Mattie was waiting at the back door with the key in hand.

"You don't miss anything, do you Mattie?" Catherine said as she snatched the large key out of the broad hand thrust toward her.

The little house felt damp and cool. The fireplace would warm it up to a comfortable temperature so she set about starting a fire. There was enough kindling but she had to go outdoors to the wood shed, at the side of the house, to get a few logs.

"Rex, I've got to get some more wood. You can stay here or follow me out." The dog got up from his rug on the floor to go with her. Catherine didn't bother to put her coat on because it would only take a couple of minutes. Jacob had seen to it that there was plenty of wood split for her to use.

She had an uneasy feeling for no reason. Looking around before she picked up three good-sized logs, she saw nothing. The dog sat and waited patiently while she retrieved the wood and followed her back into the house. Once inside, Rex's ears perked up and he let out a low growl.

The growl caused a prickly feeling on the back of her neck. "What is it, Rex?" She saw nothing unusual in the room. Her work sat on the table undisturbed. The dog sniffed around the table and the chairs. "You're making me nervous. Stop that and go lay on your rug." She dropped the logs by the fireplace and knelt to light the kindling.

Then it happened! Rex snarled and leapt up just as Catherine was pushed from behind. The side of her face struck one of the logs she'd carried in. Rex was in full turmoil snapping and flinging his body at a large hulk. Catherine struggled to get up. The defending dog let out a loud yelp of pain and the barking stopped. She was yanked to her feet by strong arms. Dazed from the fall, she couldn't see his face, but his clothes smelled of sweat and filth. She battled but her attacker was too strong. "I don't have any money here."

"It ain't yer money I'm after, Missy," he laughed, a deep, wicked laugh that struck fear in her heart. She was being pulled toward the back room of the house when the back door burst open. Wham! Wham! Wham! Mattie flew into the room, her massive body in full motion, wielding a hefty broom.

Catherine's adversary was no match for the fury of the incensed woman. "I done seen you hangin' aroun' this place and I knows you wuz' up to no good. Now, you git your stinkin' backside outta' here 'afore you find yerself either dead or rottin' in jail, an' I don' care which."

The big oaf became a sniveling coward protecting his head from the blows. "I'm goin', just don' hit me no more," he pleaded.

"An' you tell anymore of them jack rabbits you might know, that this here's a place to stay clear of!"

He limped off trying to stop his bloody nose with a battered arm.

"You done be okay?" Mattie asked, turning to Catherine.

She folded into the arms of this hulk of a woman who had saved her. "Oh, Mattie. Thank God you came. I have never been so frightened in all my life. What kind of a place have I come to?"

"It's gonna' be fine from now on, Miz' Catherine. We got to see to your dog."

Her dog! "Oh, my God. Where's Rex? What has he done to him?" Catherine ran and knelt down by her loyal dog.

"I'll carry him on up to the big house," Mattie said.

"No. He's too heavy for you. Get Jacob to help."

"Jacob ain't here, today. Mistah' Patrick say he need him to help at the warehouse," she answered. She scooped up the limp dog as easy as a sack of flour.

Catherine followed her rescuer, who carried her limp silver haired dog up the brick walk. "Mattie, he tried to help me. I just don't know what I'll do if he dies."

"I know, Miz' Catherine. It was his noises that got me there. I knew somethin' was bad 'cause he don' never make a fuss like that. An' don' you worry none, 'cause we done gonna' see he gits better."

This was a new Mattie. Or was this the real Mattie that emerged after a near tragedy? Whatever, it pleased Catherine. This might be a new start. She looked up at the colored woman carrying her precious dog. "I'm sorry about our disagreement this morning."

"That done be over with, Miz' Catherine." And, from the tone of Mattie's voice, Catherine knew it was.

When they reached the back porch, Mattie gently laid Rex on his quilt. The attacker had hit him with one of the logs Catherine had carried in for the fire. Blood had trickled out of his nose so the blow must have landed on his skull. Mattie's big hands felt around his body and his head. "I think he done be knocked out. I don' feel no swellin' or broken bones. If'n he comes to by tomorra', he be all right."

"How do you know that, Mattie? I thought you didn't like dogs."

"When I was young, my daddy had some dogs that he made fight. I hated it, Miz' Catherine. I never did go to see it, but I sure enuf' had to help take care of them poor torn and broken babies when my daddy brought them home. Some of them I held in my arms when they was pups." Tears came to her eyes and she quickly wiped them away with the sleeve of her sweater.

"I'm sorry, Mattie. That wasn't fair to you."

"No, Miz' Catherine, it sure wasn't."

When Patrick came home he was furious after hearing about what had happened.

"Mattie, you said you've seen him on the streets. You come right with me and point him out. I want him in jail!"

Catherine sported a swollen black eye and a large bruise. "Patrick, I'm sure he's never coming back here. Not after the way Mattie clubbed him with that broom."

"No one is going to come onto my property and attack my wife without paying for it!"

"Mistah' Patrick, I can go with you, but I don' think we goin' to see him aroun' these parts no more. I know his likes. They play tough 'til they get what's comin' to 'em and then they hides like scairdy cats. You and Miz' Catherine better eat 'afore your supper gets cold. I gotta' be on my way 'cause Jacob ain't here to walk home with me."

"Oh, that's right. I had him working at the warehouse all day. I'll be happy to get a hack for you."

"No. If I go now, I be home in ten minutes."

"You leave right now, Mattie. I can see that we get our supper. You have certainly put in an exciting day," Catherine said.

Mattie put on her coat and hat.

Catherine smiled. "Would you like to take the broom? It might come in handy."

Mattie gave a shy smile, "I done 'enuf whoppin' for one day. I be back in the mornin'."

Patrick pulled Catherine into his arms. "Are you sure you're all right? I don't even want to think about what could have happened. You are never to go back down to that house by yourself again."

"Patrick, I have a lump on my head and a black eye, but otherwise I'm fine. I will have to go back to the house or I will always be afraid of it. I don't think this will ever happen again, but it has taught me to be on my guard. I had an uneasy feeling when I went to the woodshed. He must have slipped in the door while I was getting the logs. Intuition is an innate part of the being. I will be sure to heed it from now on." She gave him a gentle kiss. "Now, we must eat because I'm starved."

"What about Rex?" he asked.

"He whimpered when I last went out. Mattie thinks he's going to be fine and I trust her judgment."

"Mattie?" he asked with surprise. "Since when does Mattie know anything about dogs?"

"It's a long story, Patrick and our supper awaits."

Chapter 25

Carolyn Thomas was lost in thought as the taxi made its way through the streets of Washington on the way to Georgetown. She was elated at the prospect of seeing her good friend, Catherine.

"Here's your place, ma'am," announced the driver as he pulled the car to the side of the street.

She paid the fare and asked him to return at four. That would allow three hours to visit and still return home before Asa arrived for dinner.

Carolyn walked up the brick walk and mounted the four steps leading up to the small covered porch. She used the wrought iron railing as a guide. She felt clumsy these days. If the doctor were correct, her baby would be born earlier than she had expected.

Before lifting the doorknocker, she smoothed her skirt, tucked her long, dark hair into the sides of her teal blue felt hat and pulled a warm shawl tighter around her wool jacket.

The door opened.

"Yes ma'am?" was all that Mattie could say before Catherine rushed from the parlor and embraced her good friend.

"Carolyn, I'm so happy to see you. Come right in here this minute."

Catherine removed Carolyn's shawl and handed it to the maid.

"You don't know how happy I am to be here," said Carolyn.

"Mattie, take care of Miss Carolyn's shawl and then we will take tea in the parlor."

Mattie did as she was bid and headed for the kitchen as the two young ladies went into wait for tea.

"A maid?" Carolyn asked in a hushed voice. "That's unlike you Catherine."

They sat opposite each other at a small tea table. "Patrick's decision," she replied. "I wasn't keen on the idea at first, but he said she could use the money and I could use the help. He is right now that I'm involved with hat making once again. Her husband, Jacob, takes care of the yard. They live a few blocks away."

Carolyn looked across the table and was startled by what she saw. "Your eye, Catherine! My heavens, what happened to your eye? It's black and blue."

Catherine laughed and pulled her hair back from her forehead for a better look. "Yes, isn't it colorful? And, I have this lump to go with it."

Carolyn gasped. In a confidential voice she said, "Catherine. Please tell me that it was an accident. I don't want to think that it was…"

"Caused by Patrick?" Catherine finished her sentence.

Carolyn blushed. "You can never be too sure. They say you don't know a man until you're married to him."

Catherine reached over and took Carolyn's hand. "No, Patrick is not that type and we are very happy. Let me tell you what happened."

At that moment Mattie came in with the tea tray. It gave Catherine a flush of pride the way Mattie had adorned the tray with the flowered china teapot, an attractive array of sandwiches and cookies and a yellow daffodil peeking out of a silver vase.

"Mattie, this is lovely," Catherine praised the maid. "This is my friend, Miss Carolyn. I hope she's going to be visiting us often."

"Yes, Miz' Catherine," was all Mattie said before she left the room.

"She seems a bit sullen," Carolyn whispered.

Catherine poured tea. "No, cautious. Mattie is just as strong willed as I am. I owe her much."

"Tell me everything. How you like married life, how you got that black eye, what you did with the hat shop in Berryville, whether…"

"My goodness, Carolyn, slow down."

"Oh, I know. Asa says, if I'm not careful, I'm going to mark the baby and it will come out asking questions. You know me well enough to know that I find life full of wonder."

Catherine poured the tea. "Of that I'm sure," she said. "Do you believe that adage about marking babies?"

Carolyn waved her hand, "It's an old wives tale, I do believe. Besides, if I had a baby that came out asking questions, wouldn't we have the bright one?" She sipped her tea and took a sandwich onto her plate. "Doesn't this feel like old times, having tea with your mother's cherished china? We sat so many times in your kitchen apartment, having our tea and gabbing about the doings around town."

"Don't make me homesick, Carolyn. I am doing my best to put that little town out of my thoughts. We can't turn the clock back."

"Not that I want to. By the way, what did you do with the hat shop?"

Catherine sat her cup on the saucer she held. "That's a nettle under my skin. I haven't had the heart to sell it. Mary Lee Thompson is helping me and we're going to open it in April. The shop has been closed since I left in January."

"So that means you will be traveling back up soon."

"Patrick is going to make the arrangements for me."

Carolyn took a sip of tea, hesitating before she asked, "Could I go back with you when you go?"

Catherine was caught off-guard. "Is that wise? I mean, to travel in your condition, is that prudent?"

"I am so bored. I must do something to break the monotony. Since I had to give up nursing at the infirmary, I have had to sit home and twiddle my thumbs."

Catherine laughed. "Aren't you supposed to be twiddling knitting needles or a crochet hook? The baby will need some clothes."

Carolyn reached over and held her friend's arm, "And those he will have. Oh, Catherine, please let me go with you. Asa will understand. Besides, I would like to ask Dr. Hawthorne some questions. He is an excellent baby doctor."

"I would love to have you as company. I'm not sure how long we will be there. Talk with Asa, and, if he is in agreement, call me so I can ask Patrick to make the plans for both of us."

Carolyn clapped her hands. "This is exciting."

Her friend offered a wan smile, "Taking the train to Berryville? You must be desperate. Once we finish our tea we can walk to the little house and I'll show you the hats I have ready for the April opening up there."

"I would love to see them. It's time for me to change positions anyway. Bear with me while I raise this top-heavy frame off the chair." As she rose, she took another sandwich from the plate. "This will give me sustenance."

Catherine chuckled. "Here, wrap some cookies in this napkin and drop them in your pocket. You may need them for the ride home."

"What a grand idea," Carolyn answered as she followed Catherine's suggestion. "Now, let's go see your handiwork. And, if you've forgotten, you're supposed to explain how you acquired the black eye."

Catherine found Carolyn's shawl and threw it around her friend's shoulders before she put on her own. "I'll tell you all about it as we walk."

"Good, because I'm dying to know. I hoped you noticed that I was polite enough not to beg it out of you. You also need to tell me about your bout with the grippe. You have lost weight."

Catherine shook her head, "You haven't changed a bit."

****

On the way home Carolyn felt renewed. She opened the small black hatbox with a scene of Washington D.C. painted on top. Catherine had given her a lovely spring hat intended for the April opening. She wanted to tell her to keep it for the shop opening but Catherine's beaming smile, when she handed it to her, was so genuine that Carolyn had graciously accepted. She felt a pang of guilt because she had not presented Catherine with any gift. Then, she had almost pleaded with her friend to let her go to Berryville with her. Shameful behavior.

How was she going to tell Asa? He talked about the war in Europe so much she wondered if he knew more than he was telling her. Austria and Hungary were at war with Serbia and other countries were now joining in. Could America be next?

Asa was a top horse trainer of war horses. Would he be sent to train others? Before she met him, he had been to England for that very reason. The thought was unpleasant. Carolyn pulled Catherine's gift from the hatbox and admired the straw hat with a bunch of dried flowers laced with peach ribbon on either side of it. They lightened the bleak, early March day.

Tonight she would tell Asa of her plans to go to Berryville. She could tell him that Catherine had asked for her help with the spring reopening. No, Asa would see right through that because he knew Catherine well enough to know she had run the hat shop by herself for years.

Carolyn did want to see Dr. Hawthorne to be sure all was going well with the baby. That was it. If it involved the baby, she would use that excuse and Asa would agree. She hoped he wouldn't ask how long she would be gone because even Catherine didn't know. Ah, well. He would either be for or against it and she didn't want to think about it. Her attention was turned back to the hat before she placed it in its rightful place in the hatbox.

Asa was at their home when she arrived. He welcomed her with a kiss.

Carolyn was apologetic. "I didn't expect you to be here until five. I haven't started supper."

"I'm home early," he replied. "You have a special glow. I can only guess that it's because of your afternoon at Catherine's."

He pulled a kitchen chair for Carolyn to sit. "Is Catherine doing well…recovered from her bout with the grippe?" He took a seat next to her.

"She's recovered from that but I was stunned to see her with a black eye and a lump as big as a piece of coal on her forehead."

Carolyn related the story of the attack and Asa shook his head.

He left the chair to look out the kitchen window. "Carolyn, there's another reason I'm home early. I don't know quite how to tell you."

This was unlike him. She rose from her chair, put her arms around his waist and rested her head against his back. "Just tell me, Asa, because I think I know."

He turned around to face her with the unborn baby sandwiched between. Carolyn had never seen his dark eyes so intense. "I have to go to England and I'm not sure when I will return."

The news wasn't unexpected. "I knew it! It's that awful war in Europe. I have been concerned about it for quite some time."

He kissed her forehead. "What am I going to do about you? I can't leave you here without anyone and a baby coming on top of it. I tried my best to have them send someone else."

"That's what you get for being the best." She tried to smile. "You read the Post while I get us something to eat. We'll talk it all over during supper."

He gave her a weak smile and a playful pat on her bottom as she turned to ready the pots and pans. Tears fell while she peeled potatoes. With her back to Asa, she had made sure that he couldn't see. It would just upset him and she wanted him to see a brave face, although bravery was far from what she felt.

Carolyn fried up the potatoes and mixed in some leftover roast beef, along with brown gravy. There were cooked carrots in the icebox, which she heated up. It wasn't a grand supper but it was quick and food always seemed to settle trying concerns.

They sat at the dining room table. "You know, Asa, Catherine always says Providence intervenes when we least expect. This may be one of those times. She is going to Berryville to reopen her shop in a few weeks. I would like to go with her."

He poured some milk into his tea. "Did you discuss that this afternoon?"

"Yes." She took a bite of food.

"And this was before you knew that I would have to go away?" He looked directly at her.

She kept her eyes on her plate. "Yes, I wanted to talk with Dr. Hawthorne about the baby."

"I suppose sitting here all day without anything interesting to do didn't play a part in it?"

When she looked up, he had a wide smile and a sparkle in his coal black eyes. She reached over and twisted a piece of black hair that had tumbled across his forehead. "You know me too well, my observant husband."

He reached for her hand and kissed it. "I think a change will do you good. How long will you be gone?"

Carolyn went back to eating with gusto. "Catherine doesn't know for sure. I can't imagine that Patrick would want her to be gone for a lengthy stay."

"If I'm going to be out of the country, do you think you should stay up there so Dr. Hawthorne can deliver the baby? Perhaps there is an extra room you could rent in that large Hawthorne house. We can afford it, and I'd feel more comfortable knowing you will be well taken care of."

Her look was pensive. "The last time I lived there you came back from a trip out West and got stabbed outside of Union Station. I wouldn't want that house to be an omen for bad news with you going away again."

A look of surprise came upon his face, "Carolyn, you're not the superstitious one. Are you concerned that something is going to happen to me?"

She looked directly at him. "You are my life, Asa."

He left his chair to come and offer comfort. "I am just going to be training men and horses. I'm not going to be in their war. Our country is an ally of Britain and I am in the army."

She sighed, "How well I know. I have never been pleased with your choice of a career, but I did choose you and you came wrapped in that package."

He patted her shoulder. "We'll get through this. You keep a good outlook and I promise that I will stay out of harm's way. Agreed?"

She held his hand. "Agreed."

Chapter 26

Two weeks later Catherine and Carolyn were on the train heading for the Bluemont station.

"Do you think Herbert Marks is still driving that twelve-passenger car into Berryville?" asked Carolyn.

"I'm sure he is. Will he be on time is the question," answered her friend. "I'm not all that fond of sitting in the cramped station waiting for the car to arrive. The last time I waited close to an hour." Catherine pulled some handwork out of her traveling bag.

Carolyn fingered the yarn. "That's very nice quality, Catherine, what are you making?"

"It's something for your little one. If I don't start now, he'll be walking before I finish."

They both chuckled.

The train had stopped at the Aldie station before continuing on its way. "Does this jerking and rumbling bother you, Carolyn? I'm still not sure that it was the best idea for you to make this trip."

Her friend shifted her weight. "This pillow I'm sitting on helps. I wouldn't have come if I thought I would be a problem for you."

Catherine raised an eyebrow as she peered up from her crocheting. "Do I detect an edge to your voice? That's unlike you."

"I'm sorry. It's just that Asa's off to England and most likely won't return until this baby comes." She turned and looked at Catherine. "If we get into their ridiculous war in Europe, he may never come home."

"Don't think like that. He's going over to offer his knowledge of horses."

"War horses," Carolyn corrected.

The train pulled into the Leesburg station. "We have fifteen minutes. Let's get off and stretch our legs," Catherine suggested. "I'll buy you a drink of something. I packed some peanut butter sandwiches for us to eat."

Carolyn stood with difficulty. "I had better pass on getting a drink or I'll have to go to the bathroom before we get to Bluemont. That's a chore in itself."

"Do you just want to stay here on the train? Fifteen minutes will pass quickly."

"No. You go in and get a drink and I'll walk around on the platform. It will do me good." She put her hand on Catherine's arm, "I'm sorry I was so short with you. I didn't mean to be. I had to get my frustration out, I guess, and, anyway, I feel much better."

Catherine patted her friend's hand that lingered on her arm. "Good. I'm glad you have that out of your system. We are wasting precious minutes. I'm all for getting a cup of hot tea."

The short, round-faced conductor helped Carolyn negotiate the three steps from the train car. "You've got about ten minutes, ladies," he said.

Catherine hurried into the station where she stood in a line of people. When the person ahead of her got to the counter he said nothing and pointed to the sodas.

"What'll you have?" asked the clerk.

"The man's face flushed and all Catherine heard was, "S-s-s-s..."

"What'll you have?"

The man again pointed to the sodas, "I'll h-h-h-have a s-s-s-s..."

"There's people waiting, mister," admonished the frustrated clerk.

"Hurry up. We've only got a few minutes," came a voice from the line formed behind Catherine.

She tapped the man on the shoulder. "Do you want a soda?" she asked in a low voice.

He shook his head yes.

"Do you care what kind it is?"

He shook his head no.

"Good." She stepped up to the counter. "The man will have a birch beer, please."

The clerk grabbed the cold soda and popped off the cap while the man placed his money on the counter.

He whispered to Catherine, "Th-th-thank you. I st-st-stutter."

Catherine smiled. "You're welcome."

To the clerk, she said, "I'll have a birch beer also." It was too late for hot tea. She could take the bottle of soda onto the train to wash down the peanut butter sandwiches, and perhaps Carolyn would like to share it.

Carolyn was waiting by the door when Catherine came out of the station. "It was good to do some walking. I see you have a soda. Did you change your mind?"

"Ran out of time," Catherine responded.

They boarded the train for the ride up the mountain. When they were seated, Catherine handed Carolyn a flowered cloth napkin and a sandwich wrapped in wax paper.

"I knew we'd be hungry. Mattie packed this for me so she'll have some goodies in there along with the sandwiches."

"She is a good help, isn't she?" Carolyn said.

"She is that. According to her, I shouldn't go off and leave Mistah' Patrick, but she would see that he was taken care of 'right fine' while I was gone. She is going to take care of Rex for me, also. You know, neither she nor Patrick were keen on saving that dog, but I suspect Patrick is going to find him good company while I'm away."

They shared a laugh. "Dig out those cookies, Catherine. There's nothing better than Mattie's cookies."

By the time they reached the Bluemont station they had devoured their lunch and finished the bottle of birch beer. Neither the twelve-passenger car nor Herbert Marks were in sight when they left the train.

****

It was close to four in the afternoon when Herbert pulled the long car to the north side of Main Street in front of the bank. Catherine and Carolyn stood on the sidewalk while the driver retrieved their traveling bags.

Catherine felt irritable. Perhaps it was because of Carolyn's incessant chatting about the Women's Suffrage Movement. No. She couldn't blame it on her friend. She knew it was because she had left Patrick behind and silently chastised herself. She kept her feelings hidden.

As Catherine stood there and looked over at her hat shop, it looked different. She glanced up and down the street. Nothing had changed: the hotel, the bank, the printing office. No. The change wasn't in the town, she realized. The change was within her.

"I'll tote your bags across the street," came Herbert's voice, interrupting her thoughts. The young ladies followed.

He sat the bags down on the stoop. "You want I should carry them up?"

For another dime thought Catherine. "No thank you. I can manage from here." She took the large key and fit it into the mortise lock. The heavy wooden door stuck, swelled from the damp weather. Putting her shoulder to the door and giving a hefty thrust, the door flew wide open. The physical energy she expended also took some of the irritable feeling away.

"You go ahead on up, Carolyn, and I'll bring the bags."

312

"Both bags are too heavy for you to haul up the stairs. We should have let Mr. Marks carry them up."

"No, Carolyn. I may have to make two trips, but I think it is exactly what I need at this moment."

Carolyn shot her a quizzical look before starting up the stairs. "I'll put the kettle over for tea," she said, over her shoulder.

"A grand idea. I can use a cup." Catherine bent to pick up a large satchel.

Carolyn stopped in mid-stair. She leaned over the banister, and in a cheerful, taunting voice asked, "Are we in a fretting mood, Mrs. Burke?"

Catherine lugged the bag off the floor. "Does it show?" was her sarcastic reply.

Carolyn remained on the step. "Probably it's because you know you will not be snuggling up with Patrick. Believe me, Catherine, the honeymoon wears off."

"I can't say as I've had much of one, and, if you weren't seven months with child, I'd chase you up those stairs."

"Oh, come on, Catherine. Struggle up the stairs with those and we'll discuss it over a nice cup of hot tea."

Catherine had to smile to herself. There was no hiding her feelings from Carolyn. She admitted that she felt much better just knowing her friend understood.

****

The next morning found Catherine in the hat shop at five o'clock. It had been a wakeful night with jumbled thoughts swirling in her head, keeping her from sleep. She had made a plan. She would go into the hat shop with her eyes closed and whatever feeling hit her when she opened them would tell her what to do about the shop. Perhaps it wasn't based on strategic planning, but that's what she was going to do.

When she opened her eyes, she found the shop neat and tidy, not much different from when she had left. Mary Lee's hats were displayed on the work counter and shelves. What a lovely job she had done. Spring colors trimmed with dried flowers, ribbons, sequins, feathers and lace. She had followed Catherine's design instructions and created hats that would most likely be bought within the first week of opening. That was fine with Catherine because she was going to sell the shop, or close it up if a buyer didn't surface. Her place was with Patrick. If that meant Georgetown, then she would be there also.

Catherine sat in her familiar chair behind the work counter letting her mind wander. There would be no more of Lavinia waddling over for the recent news, no more collaborating with Irene Butler on hats for her dresses, no more of the amiable Lloyd Pierce bringing the mail, no more Sunday church services at the Grace Episcopal Church. Was there not a pang of guilt?

Then Catherine remembered her loyal, Mary Lee Thompson. What would become of Mary

Lee? She would offer Mary Lee to come to work in the hat shop she was going to open in Georgetown. Surely there would be enough sales to keep them both employed. Most likely it would be too much change for Mary Lee, but Catherine would make the offer.

What a fool she had been to hold onto what she felt was security. When she returned to Georgetown, she would get busy with getting the new hat shop up and going. Hadn't Patrick told her it was an easy decision? He was so wise, she thought, not only wise to see how easy it would simplify her life, but he had stepped back and allowed her to solve the problem. How had she been so blessed as to have this wonderful man walk into her life?

Catherine rose from her chair and watched as the morning sun began to wake up the main street of town. It was going to be a beautiful day.

****

Patrick Burke took a break from the paperwork and stood looking out the grimy window of the warehouse that overlooked the Potomac River. Georgetown University sat high on a hill and he had a good view of the place. The thought of medical school pulled like a magnet. He belonged up on that hill until he became Dr. Patrick Burke.

His life was beginning to smooth out. Liam was coming along. His attitude could use some improvement, but he was taking care of the work Patrick brought to the house on K Street. He was learning the part of the business that he had had no taste for before his accident. Liam accepted the paperwork and was making suggestions of how the business could be improved.

Mother Burke, on the other hand, was not progressing as the doctor had hoped. She was still unsteady on her feet. Polly had been assigned to her care full time. His mother was adamantly opposed to anyone caring for her but Polly. That meant Patrick had to find someone to run the house to his mother's satisfaction. At this time, they were on the fourth maid.

And then there was Catherine. How he missed her! He wanted to call the hotel just to hear her voice but he knew she did not want the whole town to know her personal business. He had to be content with the few letters he'd received.

The short break from the work on his desk gave him pause to consider. Taking his hat and coat from the wooden coat rack, he decided to walk to K Street and have a talk with Liam. Then he was going to take the first train out to the Bluemont station.

"Miss McKay, take care of the place. I'm on my way to see my brother. Then I'm going to see my wife. I'll be back in a couple of days," he called over his shoulder as he went out the door. He didn't wait to catch her reaction.

Chapter 27

Catherine knew that the reopening of her hat shop next week was going to be a success. It would be in time for Easter. She and Mary Lee had made lovely hats with prices to suit any customer that came through the door.

Mary Lee was supposed to come at nine. Catherine planned on talking to Mr. Williams at the bank about putting the shop up for sale. He seemed to be knowledgeable and she trusted his advice. Things were looking up.

She was in the back room of the shop having her morning tea because Carolyn was still asleep and she wanted her to have her rest. Mary Lee came in the front door. She walked straight back to where Catherine sat at the small wooden table.

"Miz' Catherine, the place looks like a wonderland of hats. And the way you've draped them scarves and showed off them gloves makes me want to buy every one."

"Those scarves and gloves, Mary Lee."

"Yeah, all the ones you got out there."

"Pour yourself a cup of tea because I have something to discuss with you."

"Oh, that sounds important."

"It is."

Mary Lee fixed her cup of tea and added hot water to Catherine's before she took a seat.

Catherine was to the point. "I'm going to sell the hat shop."

The news caused Mary Lee to slop her tea. "Miz' Catherine, why would you want to go and do that now that it's all fixed up so purty?"

"Because I need to be with my husband. I've been to the bank and Mr. Williams will not grant a mortgage. I'm going to open a shop in Georgetown. Would you like to come and work for me? You could stay in the shop, there's plenty of room."

The young woman looked dazed but Catherine could tell she was mulling over the possibility.

"You don't have to give me an answer right now. I'm going over to the bank in a few minutes to make the arrangements."

"I don't have to think on it. And, ownin' this shop would be too much for me. I'm right pleased that you asked but I can tell you right now, I'm not about to leave here."

"But I worry about you. Wouldn't you like a change? What will you do for an income?"

"I'll find a way to get along. Maybe whoever buys your shop will need a helper, and I can clean houses and take care of kids and people. Don't you worry 'bout me, Miz' Catherine. I can take care of myself."

Catherine wanted to cry. She swallowed her tears and took a sip of tea that had now turned cold. It was an emotional tug she hadn't considered. She pulled a hankie from under the cuff of her sleeve and blew her nose. "I'll be back as soon as I can."

"You go right ahead. I'll straighten up around here."

Catherine slipped a shawl over her shoulders. "Miss Carolyn is still asleep. She hasn't been feeling well. You might want to see if she can eat some breakfast if you hear her moving around upstairs."

"She has looked a bit peaked."

"Today she sees Dr. Hawthorne. I hope all is well with this baby that's coming."

"You go on to the bank. You've got enough to worry about. I'll see to Miz' Carolyn."

****

Mr. Williams had just bid goodbye to a customer when Catherine came to the door of his office. He rose from behind his desk. "Mrs. Burke, it's good to see you."

"I would like to discuss some business."

He came to greet her. "Come in and have a seat. I have time."

Catherine took a seat in the chair facing his desk while he closed the door.

"How can I be of service this morning?"

"I want to sell the hat shop."

He leaned back in his leather chair. "Real estate is still a good investment. What does Mr. Burke think about your decision?"

"I haven't told him, but he has said that he wants no part of it."

His calm, confident manner continued. "He still has to sign off his ownership. Sometimes people change their minds when it comes to signing on the dotted line. What about your apartment? Will you be selling that also? I haven't looked at the deed, but it seems logical they are tied together."

The apartment had completely slipped her mind. Frustration was seeping into every pore. "Can't I just stick a For Sale sign in the window and iron out those complications later?"

"Of course you can do that," he agreed. "When do you expect Mr. Burke to be in town?"

She rose from her chair, "I don't know, but I am going to put that sign in the window right after I have the reopening on Friday."

His smile was jovial. "Perhaps you can hunt up the deed in the meantime. I'll be happy to help anyway I can."

"Thank you. I don't want to seem ungrateful. You have been a help."

"This is a big decision for you, Mrs. Burke. I know it is one you have given much thought."

"It wasn't an easy decision to make, but I'm satisfied that I am doing the right thing. Good bye, Mr. Williams."

Catherine left the bank feeling at low ebb. Her cheery outlook at the beginning of the day was falling apart. Before she returned to the shop, she went into Mr. White's general store and bought two Hershey candy bars, one for her and one for Mary Lee. Carolyn didn't need one because she was already disgruntled about her weight.

When she walked into the hat shop, Mary Lee met her at the door with a worried look. "Miz'

Carolyn don't look good. I think she needs to see Doc Hawthorne as soon as you can git her there."

Catherine rushed up the back stairs where she found Carolyn sitting on a kitchen chair; her face an ashen color.

"Carolyn, what's wrong?"

"I don't know. I feel like I'm going to throw up. Look at my ankles, they're swollen three times their size."

"We're getting up to see Dr. Hawthorne. Can you walk?"

"I'm not sure."

"Maybe I should send Mary Lee up and have him come here."

"I think that's a good idea. I hope he isn't on a house call."

Catherine put her arm around her friend. "Let me get you back to bed."

"No. I don't want to move."

Catherine fled down the back stairs. "Mary Lee, run up and get Dr. Hawthorne down here as quick as you can. Miz' Carolyn is very sick."

Mary Lee was out the door and running up the street toward the Hawthorne House.

The doctor arrived about fifteen minutes later with his medicine bag in hand. He took one look at Carolyn and said, "Help me get her to bed."

He tipped back the chair she was sitting in and ordered Catherine and Mary Lee to grab onto the front legs. They carried Carolyn back into the bedroom and rolled her onto the bed.

"How long has she been like this?" he asked as he pulled a stethoscope out of his bag.

"She said she didn't feel well last night. She was sleeping when I got up this morning."

Carolyn was awake but groggy.

"Carolyn." It was the first time the physician had addressed her by her first name. "The baby's heartbeat is still strong but your body is retaining too much fluid. I'm going to put you in a bed at the Hawthorne House. I'll give you some medicine to try to relieve the edema. You'll be on a strict diet with no salt and you will have to be on bed rest until this baby comes. We've got to get this under control or we may have to take the baby."

Catherine gasped.

"I'll get the car ready; it's parked out front. You will both have to help me get her into the back seat." He went out of the room and down the stairs.

Mary Lee stood bug-eyed.

Carolyn, who had seemed in another world, spoke, although in a weak voice. "Catherine, I trust Dr. Hawthorne. I know how serious this is for both me and the baby, we may not make it. See Catherine? It's your Provident intervention bringing me here so Dr. Hawthorne can take care of us."

Mary Lee left the room in a flood of tears.

Catherine ran and put her arms around her good friend. "Carolyn, don't talk like that. You have to fight back and do everything the doctor tells you to do. Asa will be coming home and, when he does, he wants to be greeted by a wife and baby."

The good doctor returned with one of the boys who helped at the hotel. With her arms around their necks, they were able to carry Carolyn down the stairs and into the car.

Catherine was worried. "Shall I come on up?"

"No need right now. Grace and my nurse will help me get her settled in. It's good you sent for me. She'll be looking for company later today. In the meantime, you can put items together that she will need. We're in for a long haul."

Catherine and Mary Lee, who had recovered from her outburst, turned back to go into the hat shop when Lavinia came hustling across the street. Catherine had never seen her waddle so fast.

"I saw Dr. Hawthorne's car. Is anything wrong?"

"Carolyn has had a bit of a setback. She will be at the Hawthorne House until the baby comes."

"Oh dear, oh dear," exclaimed Lavinia. And off she went up the street to peddle the latest news.

Catherine smiled at Mary Lee. "You know, I don't think I'm going to miss that little lady at all."

"Ain't she the one," remarked Mary Lee.

"Isn't, Mary Lee. "Isn't she the one."

"She sure is."

****

Later that afternoon Catherine was making a list of what she thought Carolyn would need when she heard the irritating grating of her doorknocker. Before she could get to the landing it had sounded

323

three times. "I'm coming," she called, perturbed at the impatience of whoever was there. She hurried down the stairs and threw open the door.

"Hello, Mrs. Burke."

"Patrick!"

She yanked him into the foyer, fell into his arms, and burst into tears.

"Is that how I affect you? It's not flattering."

She quieted herself to a respectable sniffing. "You don't know how happy I am to see you."

"You have an interesting way of showing it," he said.

She stepped back and wiped her face with her apron. "You can kiss me one hundred times." She wound her arms around his neck and welcomed him with a long, enduring kiss. "Come upstairs. I have so much to tell you. Do you want a cup of tea?"

"That would not be my first choice," he replied. Once upstairs, he guided her into the bedroom.

****

Catherine fixed sandwiches and soup for a late afternoon snack. They sat at the kitchen table.

"I have to gather a few things for Carolyn and take them up to the Hawthorne House. When I get back, we will have to talk about my decision to sell the hat shop."

That was news! "Sell it?" he questioned.

"Yes. My place is with you, Patrick. I'll open the new shop in Georgetown and we can get on with our lives."

"No regrets?"

"None. I have to find the deed because the apartment is probably tied in with the shop. If you are still willing to sign over your rights, then I can sell all of it and be rid of the burden."

"You'll be reopening the shop on Friday."

"Yes, and I'm putting a For Sale sign in the window."

"You'll probably have to keep it open until it sells."

"If it doesn't sell by the end of May, I'll ask Mary Lee to work it, or maybe I will just have to close it up. I'm ready to leave."

He came to her side and kissed her cheek. "And, you made the decision all by yourself."

"Fancy that," she chuckled. "I'll clean up these dishes and then pay a visit to Carolyn. I am worried about her."

"I'll give you a hand," he offered.

Chapter 28

In the middle of May, Catherine was sitting in the hat shop, putting little energy into making a hat. She missed Patrick. He had been accepted back into medical school and would start the first of June. Her plans were to close up the shop as there had not been a buyer. She wanted to spend time with her husband before he started school.

The door opened and she was surprised to see Mr. Williams come into the shop with a middle-aged couple and a girl who looked to be in her late teens or early twenties. The banker explained that the couple was looking for an investment for their daughter.

The daughter was a pretty, petite young woman with clear blue eyes and blond hair that curled around her face. She appeared to be a coddled product from a finishing school not a proprietor of a hat shop. Fairchilds was their name.

Catherine greeted them and explained the workings of the shop before she took them up the back stairs to her apartment.

"My husband is arranging for the big fur-niture to be moved to our house in Georgetown. I will leave everything in the kitchen and odds and ends, if you want them."

"Will that change the price?" asked the stout mother.

"No. I just don't have room for them. If you are not interested, I will give those items away."

The daughter seemed detached and disinterested. There was a sad look about her and Catherine tried but failed to elicit a smile.

"Come over here and look out this window, Elizabeth," ordered the mother. "You will have a nice high porch and you can view the whole street."

The young woman gave a wry look before she did as she was bid.

The father had remained quiet but inspected both the shop and the apartment by opening doors, examining window sills, checking ceilings, while Mr. Williams behaved like a true banker, extolling the benefits of investing in real estate.

"I would be glad to stay for a week or so to help with the transition," Catherine offered. If these people were interested, she didn't want them to get away.

They took one more tour through the shop before leaving for the bank.

Catherine sat back at the workstation and let her mind contemplate. Her friend, Carolyn, was close to delivery. She was still at the Hawthorne House in her old apartment. Dr. Hawthorne allowed her to get up for the bathroom and to brew pipsissewa tea. It had worked to alleviate the dropsy in her ankles. Catherine ran errands for her, and made sure that she had plenty of reading material and handwork to keep her busy. Sometimes they played cards and checkers on a flat board that rested on the bed. Dr.

Hawthorne expected the baby would be arriving within the week. Catherine knew it couldn't be too soon for Carolyn. She had tired of her confinement after the first week.

"I think it is going to be a girl and I think she is going to be stubborn like me," she had said to Catherine. "God knows, I have had to learn patience!"

Catherine's concerns about Mary Lee were alleviated because she had a job of caring for the children of the nurse at Dr. Hawthorne's office. 'I don't like it as well as makin' hats but the pay's good enough.'

The thought of her friends and that they were settled brought a smile to the milliner's face.

She got up from her chair and puttered around the storage room for about an hour before she heard the tinkle of the front bell. She put a hat back into its box and went to the front. There was the bank vice president waving a paper in his hands.

"They want it! Seeing your husband signed off his rights the last time he was here means I just need your signature to seal the deal."

Catherine felt a rush of excitement. They sat at her worktable to discuss the terms of the contract. It would mean that she would have to stay one week to help with the transition, which meant one less week with Patrick but that was the way it had to be.

Mr. Williams left the hat shop with Carolyn's signature on the contract.

As soon as he left, she pulled the key from her pocket, locked the door and hurried to the Berryville hotel.

"I need to use the telephone," she told the desk clerk.

Putting the ear piece to her ear and raising the speaker to her mouth, she said, "This is Catherine Ramsburg Burke. I'd like to make a long distance call to Washington, D.C. to Mister Patrick Burke. The number is: 8372-J."

The operator repeated the name and the number. Catherine heard muffled sounds in the background for what seemed an eternity until she heard, "Go ahead, Mrs. Burke, your party is on the line."

She was so excited she blurted out, "Patrick?"

"Catherine! What's wrong?"

"Nothing is wrong, everything is right. I love you, Patrick! Tell Mattie, Jacob and Rex…I'm coming home!"

CPSIA information can be obtained at www.ICGtesting.com
Printed in the USA
BVOW070105031212

307116BV00001B/1/P